Praise

"*Haven* not onl[y] ... unflinchingly examines how much of our humanity we're willing to sacrifice for comfort. Absorbing and uncanny."
—Tracy Sierra, author of *Nightwatching*

"Hands down the trippiest book I've read all year, Ani Katz's *Haven* marries the feverish anxiety of new motherhood with a level of techno-paranoia worthy of *Black Mirror*. Plotted on shifting sands, and with a cast of inscrutable locals, mystical card games, a teenage coven, and a missing baby, *Haven* operates as both a futuristic fable as well as a truly unhinged thriller." —Ellie Eaton, author of *The Divines*

Praise for *A Good Man*

"[An] ingenious slow burn." —*Entertainment Weekly*

"Powerful and unsettling . . . Produces in the reader a sense of foreboding that builds with ever-increasing intensity to the inevitable and brutal climax . . . [A] masterly first novel."
—*Publishers Weekly* (starred review)

"As she expertly builds a growing sense of dread, Katz creates an unsettling atmosphere of paranoia, fear, and rage, hinting at the catastrophe to come through ominous comparisons to the tragic operas Thomas loves. This is the sort of relentless novel you can't put down even when you're afraid to read what happens next. An unnerving and absorbing exploration of modern masculinity and how the seeds of violence are sown." —*Kirkus Reviews*

"Chillingly good . . . Katz has delivered a whip-smart, beautifully written meditation on marriage, masculinity, and the thin line between happiness and disaster." —*BookPage*

"A mature and wicked debut . . . Evokes Highsmith's Ripley, or Denise Mina's *The Long Drop*, and heralds the entry of a fantastic new voice to the genre." —*CrimeReads*

"Simultaneously nightmarish and utterly compelling . . . A masterful, suspenseful tale told by an ultimate unreliable narrator."
—*Booklist* (starred review)

"Sordidly gripping." —*The Guardian*

"*A Good Man*'s exploration of masculinity in a world of instability makes it a timely read." —*Vanity Fair*

"Highly impressive . . . A striking modern tale of violence, sexual abuse, and vindictiveness." —*The Independent*

"Ani Katz is a brilliant writer. I sat down to read *A Good Man* and didn't move until I'd finished it. This is a spellbinding work of psychologically potent art. I can't wait to read what she does next. I loved this book." —Caroline Kepnes, author of *You*

"Katz draws a life in its most delicate lines, then destroys it. And this is a story you won't forget."
—Nico Walker, *New York Times* bestselling author of *Cherry*

"*A Good Man* slinks into the dark heart of a ripped-from-the-headlines crime fueled by toxic masculinity. As in Leïla Slimani's *The Perfect Nanny*, the slow unpeeling—layer by layer—of the conventions of sanity left me breathless, saddened, and spooked."
—Miranda Beverly-Whittemore, *New York Times* bestselling author of *Bittersweet*

"A profoundly disturbing and deeply unsettling story of a man struggling to reconcile himself with the horrifying act he has committed. Katz deftly embodies her narrator, giving voice to his self-serving re-creation of the past and presenting him as he sees himself: a provider, a protector, a patriarch. Richly drawn and laced through with dread, this bold novel is an unflinching examination of what it means to be a man, and how easily a man can become a monster."
—Kathleen Barber, author of *Are You Sleeping*

"Surprising, daring, and thrilling to read."
—Flynn Berry, *New York Times* bestselling author of *Northern Spy*

"Gripping, sly, and ferociously intelligent. I couldn't put it down."
—Jennifer duBois, author of *Cartwheel*

"*A Good Man* will hold you in its creeping spell from the first lyrical line to the bitter, bitter end. As the narrator's tale of selfless, industrious striving on his family's behalf unravels, you'll be too caught up to look away from the ugly business of a 'good man' bringing himself and the others around him down. Ani Katz's debut is a gorgeously written, profound examination of contemporary masculinity and its potentially lethal side effects."
—Laura Sims, author of *How Can I Help You*

PENGUIN BOOKS

HAVEN

Ani Katz is a writer, photographer, and teacher. She was born and raised on the South Shore of Long Island, New York, and lives in Brooklyn.

ALSO BY ANI KATZ

A Good Man

HAVEN

Ani Katz

PENGUIN BOOKS

An imprint of Penguin Random House LLC
1745 Broadway, New York, NY 10019
penguinrandomhouse.com

Copyright © 2026 by Ani Katz

Penguin Random House values and supports copyright. Copyright fuels creativity, encourages diverse voices, promotes free speech, and creates a vibrant culture. Thank you for buying an authorized edition of this book and for complying with copyright laws by not reproducing, scanning, or distributing any part of it in any form without permission. You are supporting writers and allowing Penguin Random House to continue to publish books for every reader. Please note that no part of this book may be used or reproduced in any manner for the purpose of training artificial intelligence technologies or systems.

Set in Stempel Garamond, Amondi, and TEXTA
Designed by Sabrina Bowers

LIBRARY OF CONGRESS CONTROL NUMBER: 2025033982
ISBN 9780143138679 (paperback)
ISBN 9780593512814 (ebook)

Printed in the United States of America
1st Printing

The authorized representative in the EU for product safety and compliance is Penguin Random House Ireland, Morrison Chambers, 32 Nassau Street, Dublin D02 YH68, Ireland, https://eu-contact.penguin.ie.

For Edwin and Ramona

HAVEN

She would never understand why, when she knew her baby was gone, she had whispered his name into the dark.

She knew that her son didn't know his name yet. On a beach towel that morning, she'd babbled at him, sprinkling his name here and there on the foam of language burbling from her lips, and he had stared up at her with an expression of forbearance, refusing to offer any sign of recognition. His name was still just sound to him, an unknown word like any other.

She had taken a photograph of the moment—his slack mouth, his blank dark eyes, his face the color and shape of her husband's. She knew immediately that it was a boring picture, that, though she didn't want to admit it, she was getting bored with her baby as a subject.

She whispered his name now in the darkness, as if he could respond and tell her where he had gone so late in the night, how she might find him. He would recognize her voice, at least. He would cry out to her if he were close by.

If he were close by. He had to be close by. But it was so dark in the unfamiliar room. Her panic was a heavy blanket thrown over her head. She pawed and pounded at the wall, feeling for a light switch that she remembered being there but that was not there anymore.

At first, she whispered. Soon she was screaming.

CHAPTER 1

It was Caroline's fault that they missed their boat.

She knew that was what Adam was thinking when they emerged from the meat locker of the car and set foot on the roasted dirt of the parking lot. What he said was *moments*.

"Moments! Mere moments!"

Adam shook his head and laughed with his teeth bared. He didn't say that it was her fault, but he didn't have to; Caroline knew her husband. She knew the tense jollity of his speech and gestures when he thought she had made a mistake, when his engineer's mind saw the better way of doing something, and she knew that he was thinking that if she hadn't made them stop at the Gulf wedged between the east- and westbound lanes of the Grand Central so she could piss out her ill-advised yet desperately needed late-morning iced Americano, they might have made their boat.

That had been her first mistake. Her fault.

"Don't be mad, babe," she said.

"I'm not mad!"

Adam's eyes were hidden, confidential behind black lenses. It was her fault. He hid his face in the car seat, sputtered a flatulent kiss onto the soft dark head hiding in there.

"Mere moments!" he groused to Gabriel. "Can you believe it?"

Not mere moments, Caroline thought. Adam should have known it was impossible to miss anything by mere moments when you were traveling with a baby. Because it hadn't just been the stop at the Gulf. It had been a chain of delays—the long line at the coffee shop to acquire the Americano, the last-minute packing, the puzzle of loading the car, the frantic and ultimately fruitless search for the package with the swim diapers that had arrived in the mail the day before, the discovery of damp and stinking laundry untransferred to the dryer, and the kitchen still a mess from the night before, when Caroline had passed out immediately once Gabriel finally fell asleep after two bedtime books, three bedtime songs, six minutes of nursing on each side, and an unknown number of minutes of bouncing on the yoga ball in total darkness. It was a chain of delays that stretched all the way back to the five a.m. wake-up when, dazed and nauseated with fatigue, Caroline had failed to do anything but fall asleep again as Gabriel nursed, which she was not supposed to do.

They were still learning things about this new life, or at least Caroline was—how the hours could be at once harried and interminable, and how many more of them were needed for all the tasks you'd never thought about before.

"Not mere moments," Caroline said. Adam ignored her and slobbered on the baby some more. She felt the damp heat of the day suction onto her skin.

Caroline squinted into the glare of other people's windshields—new-model sedans, coupes, and hatchbacks packed together in tight rows in the dirt, too many trinkets in a sandbox. She hadn't seen a parking lot like this since high school, the last time she'd gone to the state fairgrounds. These weren't the battered Fords and Rams of her adolescence—they were the same cars that lined the curbs of their neighborhood in the city, luxury toys scooped up and carried east. Caroline raised a hand to shield her eyes. Adam had pulled his head out of the car seat and was looking at his phone, sending or receiving data, communication.

"When's the next boat?"

Adam went through the motions of pulling up the schedule

on the island's concierge app, but Caroline could tell he already knew the answer. He turned away from her.

"Five thirty."

"You're kidding." She knew that he was not kidding. "Five thirty?"

It was eight minutes past three. Caroline parted her lips, the complaint ready in her mouth—*Why couldn't he have gotten his shit together for five minutes and reserved them a water taxi before they were all booked up?* But she knew that saying as much would only invite criticism of her own disorganization, so she said nothing. Adam shrugged and turned to face her again.

"So what? It's perfect, actually."

"It's perfect?"

"Yes. Everyone else can get the house ready before we get there. They'll meet us at the ferry dock with drinks. I'll tell them to chill the Sancerre for you."

"And what will we do?"

"Strap him in. Or on, whatever. We'll walk around the town."

"Walk?"

"Yes."

"What town?"

"The town we just drove through—"

"I repeat, what town."

Adam laughed, reached out with his middle and index finger to scratch Caroline under her chin.

"I love when you're a little bitchy. It suits you."

"That's not nice."

"I mean it! It's sexy."

Caroline gave him a look that she hoped could be interpreted as withering, even as a smile tugged at the corner of her mouth. Adam raised his hands and bared his teeth again.

"Don't be mad, babe."

CAROLINE WAS RIGHT ABOUT THE TOWN—ANOTHER MISTAKE. After trudging up a block lined with flood-damaged Victorian houses, dead trees in standing water in dead yards, front porches black with mold or shorn away entirely, they reached a depressed main drag marked by other kinds of decay—dueling delis with nothing on their shelves, a shuttered combination spa and specialty food store beside a combination methadone clinic and HEOL (Humane End of Life) office, a sign in the window promising LIFE ON YOUR TERMS. The coffee place promised by Adam's phone was sealed behind a fortress of plywood boards.

"Oop," Adam said. "RIP the Beanery, we hardly knew ye."

A small multiracial squadron of teenage boys in basketball shorts and sweatbands brushed past them on a corner as they waited for the light to change. Caroline couldn't stop herself from envisioning hidden weapons, quick darting hands. The boys burst into raucous laughter as Caroline flinched and grabbed at Gabriel. The baby woke up and began to scream.

"He's hungry," she said, an exhausted, frightened quaver of tears coming into her voice as the little body bucked against her.

She had no idea if Gabriel was actually hungry. The cries were supposed to sound a certain way, but they all sounded the same to her. He wasn't a newborn anymore, and they were theoretically supposed to know each other better by now, but Caroline still didn't believe that you could have instincts and intuitions about your child, that you could know things about them like when they were hungry, when they had a fever, or when they were just unhappy.

"So?" Adam said. "Feed him."

"Here?"

"There's a bench right there. I'll get us a ride back now."

The boys had stopped a few yards away and were watching them, whispering and grinning. Gabriel continued to scream, kicking at Caroline with surprising strength. Adam held the black glossy shield of his phone up to the twin black glossy shields of his lenses, the app phrenologizing his features to summon them a ride.

"Sixteen minutes," he said, shaking his head again. "Manned, too."

"It's fine," Caroline said. "I don't care."

"Everyone told me the self-drivers hadn't made it out to the boondocks yet, but I didn't believe them, because what did they know? As it turns out, what do I know? Why are you crying, babe?"

Caroline sat down heavily on the bench, shoved a hand into the neck of her dress, and yanked out one flopping, naked breast, which she pushed into Gabriel's face before remembering she was supposed to bring him to the breast.

"Babe, come on. Don't cry."

Their son latched and began to suck. The boys on the corner cheered.

"I WAS RIGHT," SHE SAID. "WASN'T I?"

"You were right."

They were in the car now, sitting on gray velour, their silent driver sealed in his plexiglass pod. Adam was looking out the window, enjoying the poverty safari. Caroline kept her arms wrapped around Gabriel, tensing whenever another vehicle drew close. She couldn't believe they were driving without a car seat.

"Doesn't some part of you like it, though?" Adam asked.

"Like what? Being right?"

"No. Seeing places like this. Seeing they still exist."

"I know they exist. I don't need to walk around them with my baby or take my boob out on a street corner to know they exist. Those guys—"

"Those *kids*. Once upon a time you would have been desperate to take their photo. You would have followed them down the block, telling them how amazing they looked."

Caroline rolled her eyes.

"And if some woman with a baby had her boob out on the street corner, you would've wanted to take a picture of that, too. You would've told her she looked like a Madonna and Child."

"You think you're funny."

"I am funny."

They were quiet.

"It won't stay like this," Adam said finally, still looking out the window.

"What?"

"The town. Not with the ferry terminal. It'll be bought."

"By Corridor?"

He shrugged.

"Real estate isn't part of the plan this year. Not essential to any current research and development projects. Someone else will swoop in and get the town before we would get around to making an offer."

"Mosaic?"

"Maybe."

It had become more and more common in the last ten years, tech companies buying up whole towns. The town where Caroline had grown up had been taken in the first wave, when now-defunct Erestor purchased all the land in North Dakota above I-94, including the acreage that had belonged to Caroline's family for three generations. She didn't know who owned the land now that Erestor had been liquidated.

"You don't mind," Caroline said.

"About Mosaic? Not really."

"You have more important things to worry about, of course."

"Always," Adam said, either not catching or ignoring the sarcasm in her voice. He turned from the window to look at her. He probably winked, but she couldn't say for sure with his sunglasses on.

BACK AT THE FERRY TERMINAL, CAROLINE HAD A LOBSTER roll, and Adam ate shrimp cocktail out of a large fountain-drink cup with his fingers. Glutted, Gabriel slept again, wrapped against Caroline's body.

The terminal was crowded with travelers. There were bird-faced women with small, angry dogs. There were teenage boys in neon visors and bucket hats exchanging soft bricks of dollar bills. There were children everywhere, and they were either buttoned into blue-and-white Peter Pan–collared rompers or dressed like little Lolitas. There were senior citizens covered up like burn victims, their faces hidden by floppy hats, sunglasses, and surgical masks, their windbreakers billowing on their shoulders. These disparate types of people were grouped together in surprising alliances—a woman linked her pretzel-stick arm around a chubby girl wearing a bandanna for a shirt, a teenage boy with eggplant-purple nails nodded soberly as an elderly man dressed in an ivory caftan signed to him, hands chopping the air with each emphatic word. Caroline could just make out the delicate chain of the titanium bioharness under the man's caftan—it was the new lightweight, full-body kind with improved infusion capabilities, the one that wasn't supposed to be on the market until the following spring.

Caroline's mother could use one of those. Maybe they could send her one next year—the DNA recognition technology would prevent the staff at the Golden Sunset Homes from "accidentally" giving the bioharness to someone else, which was what had happened when they tried to have one delivered to the facility the month before.

Many of the ferry passengers were towing wagons towering with goods, as if stockpiling for a snowstorm or pandemic. It all had the feeling of a carnival, or a refugee camp—people straining, yearning, their eagerness tipping over into impatience. They were all watching the teenager in the cargo shorts and ferry company T-shirt, waiting for the moment he would part the wooden picket gates to the dock and call out *Haven*, the name of the town across the bay.

Caroline knew she was lucky. Aside from the diaper bag, the lightweight portable bassinet, and the super-compact fold-up stroller, they had only a single carry-on, one hard-shelled suitcase, and her camera equipment bag. The rest would be sent over as freight. If she were anyone else at the terminal, any of these overburdened, exasperated mothers, she would hate the ash blonde with the baby and husband, a family with the minimal, business-class luggage and glowing skin of money and ease. She would stare, too.

Why had that thought occurred to her? Were people looking at them? Watching her?

No. Caroline always had that feeling. When you stare at everyone, odds are someone will stare back.

And yet, she couldn't shake a feeling of angst. After Gabriel was born, her psychiatrist had increased the dosage of Caroline's anti-anxiety medication. Two small white pills, two times a day. She couldn't remember if she had taken her morning dose.

She reminded herself she was lucky. What a treat to enjoy a lobster roll as her baby slept. What a treat to have a husband who'd arranged an entire month at a beach house for them to get away.

And not just any beach house—a house in Haven. The island was a playground for the ultra-rich, and Haven was its most exclusive community, frequented by elites from the worlds of politics, business, and entertainment. According to Adam, the Corridor CEO had a house just outside the town, on the ocean but really mostly underground, a compound with state-of-the-art everything that had to be seen to be believed, though almost no one had ever seen it.

If they were lucky and played their cards right, Adam intimated, they *might* get invited over for drinks.

Caroline, Adam, and Gabriel would not be staying in a compound—just a shared house. The group rental had come through Corridor connections, though Adam had been vague about the details. He had been especially vague about the cost, which Caroline understood was at once significant yet also well within what Adam had taken to calling their "fun budget."

That was another thing she was learning about this new life—that money, even very large sums of it, could be meaningless.

Even if it was a shared house, at least no one's parents would be there. Caroline remembered a trip to the family summer home of her college roommate. At the cottage overlooking a rocky beach, Caroline had learned about rigging a sailboat and dressing for dinner, shelling lobster and stirring a perfect martini. One night, after drinking most of a pitcher of perfect martinis on the deck, her roommate's father had leaned in close to Caroline and whispered that he'd always wanted to fuck a farm girl like her.

She had tried and failed to imagine her own father doing something like that. He'd been so gentle, so mild, that people used to think he was slow. Touched. He'd kept it to himself when he started pissing blood, didn't mention anything to anyone until it was much too late.

They were good at keeping secrets in her family.

Caroline followed the line of Adam's gaze. He was looking at a dark-haired woman who was talking into her cell phone, and he was eyeing the dangle of her pendant breasts in copper crochet nets. Caught, Adam turned to Caroline and gave her another grin.

Did it bother her? Not really. Not this woman. Why would Caroline object when she was always looking, too?

These things weren't serious. She leaned into Adam and squeezed his shrimp-moistened hand. It was almost time to board.

CAROLINE WOULD HARDLY REMEMBER THE FERRY ride over, even though it took almost an hour and at the time seemed so much more memorable than missing the three o'clock boat, the abortive walk through the depressed town, and the crowd at the terminal. Eventually, to remember the ride at all, she would have to watch the video, which Adam recorded on her phone for her.

The video begins with a sweep of the vast blue bay and the island strung across the horizon for miles in each direction.

The camera takes it all in, tracing the length of the land, moving too quickly to linger on the tidy teak-and-white cluster of each town, the wild green of a national park, and the blackened ruins of a few collapsed buildings at the far east end of the island. The vista goes by in a blink, and the camera switches focus from the far to the near, landing on Caroline.

Caroline doesn't notice the ruins. She's standing at the railing with Gabriel and looking the other way, toward the prosperous village of Haven, where their boat will dock. She holds the baby while trying to hold her straw hat to her head. Adam, behind the camera, is trying to make her laugh.

"Look at me! Look at me!"

She turns to look at him and smiles.

"You look like one of those—tell me what I'm thinking."

"Movie star?"

"No. It's the hat, the baby."

"A saint. Madonna and Child."

"Not that. No Saint Caroline on this trip. Nothing but ayahuasca, meditation, and naked tantric crystal yoga—it's the new thing. Clears out the sinuses."

"I thought it cleared out the colon."

"No, not the colon! Where's the chakra—your gallbladder, right? Anyway, everyone's doing it. The crystals prevent kidney stones. You do some special breathing while you stick them up your—"

He goes on and on, trying to be funny, which he does when he is trying to please her, when he wants her to be pleased—chattering as they're seated in business class, as they're led to restaurant tables, as they're whispered to in private tours of galleries in upper Manhattan and northern Italy. Eager to show off, eager to impress, forever afraid that he was missing the mark somehow, that she would find him and his toys lacking.

How could she find him lacking? He made her feel safe, and he made her laugh. It all stretched before them—the promise of a life of ferry rides, of beach houses, of children building sandcastles as the backdrop to a New Year's card. A summer house with his friends. *Their* friends. Caroline had lost touch with her own friends over the years—first it was her work, then it was her marriage, and now it was her baby—but Adam's friends are her friends now, and they love her. Adam is always saying that they love her, even though she can count on one hand the number of times they've been in each other's presence, and she isn't sure if she's really spoken to any of them for more than a few minutes, or what they talked about. She tries to convince herself of their fondness, assuring herself that they're her friends, too, that they love her, that they will love Gabriel, that she will love them.

She's still standing at the railing as the boat begins to slow, baby bandaged to her body, bay and sky unfurling beside them in twin bands of blue. One hand is still holding her hat to her head, the other the small black compact of her camera, but she's not photographing anything. Another mistake. She's too distracted, too charmed by her husband, too caught up in the moment. She did not capture the ruffled bridal train of the boat's wake; her husband's face as he grinned into the wind, sun, and spray; the shaded crown of her sleeping son's head.

Now the camera swoops away from Caroline and Gabriel to the scene below. The dock is crowded with half-naked people holding up cocktails and squinting into the light. The camera finds the three men waiting for them and zooms in. The men shield their eyes and hold up arms bent at the elbows, as if fending off blows. They are waving.

Caroline waves back, takes her hand off her hat for just a moment—a mere moment—but a moment is all it takes for the breeze to lift the hat and carry it off her head and out of her grasp. The hat flies briefly, hovers on the breath of the air, then silently falls. The video ends with a zoom in on the hat, a pale circle on the dark water, Adam whinnying with helpless laughter.

Much later, Caroline would rub her index finger rightward and leftward along the slivered panorama on the bottom of the screen to see it all again, controlling the passage of each cross section of a second, time turning forward and backward at her will—her touch making the wind lift her hair and drop it again, making her neck bend and straighten, head dip and rise, to gaze at the baby and then at the blue of the bay, her touch making her turn to face the camera and away, making her lost hat rise and fall on her head, up and down, up and down, turning to face the camera and away again, forward and back, forward and back, forward and back, forward and back, until she could pretend there were no mistakes, that nothing was anyone's fault, that forward and back were one and the same, that she didn't know the difference.

CHAPTER 2

On the Haven ferry dock it was a carnival all over again, but less frenetic, everyone pacified by the relief of arrival. The same people who had been at the mainland terminal loaded their belongings onto yet more wagons, forming a caravan that dispersed as they made their way out of the town promenade. One by one they disappeared down pine-shaded raised boardwalks, up ramps and into hidden houses, their voices becoming distant murmurs on the breeze before falling away.

As promised, Blaise and Perry had brought their drinks—wineglass stems threaded through their fingers, bright bowls of rosé cupped in their palms. Wynn had brought the wagon. The lowering sun shot gold through the wine, streaked faces and bare biceps, yellowed white teeth and highlighted grease on black lenses. There was a suspended, tentative moment as they all stood facing each other on the dock, grins held just a beat too long as everyone seemed to wait for someone else to make the first move.

Then, all at once, the men were on Adam with happy shouts of welcome. They passed the pink wine from hand to hand and took turns slapping each other's backs with a hard, percussive sound, as if trying to save each other from choking.

No one hugged Caroline. She was still wearing the baby.

"At last!"

"He finally decides to join us!"

Adam withdrew himself from Wynn's damp embrace. In the choreography of four men's armpits opening and closing around broad shoulders there was a smell of bergamot and grass, something fetid underneath.

"Hey man, I already *told* you—"

"Oh, come on," said Perry. "You're not going to blame your beautiful, faultless wife for your fuckup again, are you?"

Again? Perry winked at Caroline. He was a bit taller than Adam, and willowy. There was something delicate, almost girlish about him. His dark hair was longer, his eyes were larger, and his skin was a deeper shade of tan.

"Of course not!" Adam said. "I'm not blaming her. The fucking traffic—"

"Oh *sure*, sure."

"Tell us, Caroline," said Wynn, brushing sandy hair out of his face. "Did he tell you it was time to go, and then 'hopped' in the shower for forty-five minutes?"

"Fuck off," said Adam. Wynn clapped him on the back again.

"Better late than never."

"We're hardly late."

"Exactly," Blaise said, hoisting their bags onto the wagon one at a time, one-handed. His long, curly brown hair was restrained by one of his signature man-buns, and his Olympic swimmer's physique made the luggage hauling look easy. "The party's just getting started."

The glasses of wine found their way into Adam's and Caroline's hands, and the group began their own trek east along the boardwalk bayfront, heading toward the private cove half a mile away, where the house was. Their walk took them past a gray-shingled Victorian mansion that had been converted into a grocery store, and, a bit farther on, a teak gazebo and wraparound deck suspended over the bay, apparently a yacht club. Tables spaced careful yards apart were arranged around a central turquoise kidney pool. Graying couples dressed in flowing, gauzy whites picked idly at nests of crab legs, unbothered by the screams and splish-splashes of the topless twentysomethings swimming not far from their sandaled feet. Seagulls circled, screaming—to Caroline they seemed unusually large, their bills heavy and deep red at the tips, as if they'd been dipped in blood.

"Where are the girls?" Adam asked.

"Jane stayed back to finish the ceviche," said Perry. "She wanted everything to be ready when you guys got to the house."

"Noa and Taryn went for a swim in the ocean, but I think Noa is in the shower by now," said Wynn. He was smirking. "I can't speak for Taryn, though. Blaise?"

"She stripped off everything as soon as we got to the house," said Blaise. "She's been working on her tan."

"Bard girls." Wynn sighed. "They teach them well. Remember the intern who—"

"Fellas, please," said Perry. "We have a lady and child present."

"Come on, I don't believe that's a real baby," said Blaise. "Haven't heard a peep."

Caroline tried to smile. Gabriel was awake again but quiet, his lips puckering weakly against her sternum, leaving flowers of drool on her skin.

"He must take after you," Perry said to Caroline. "We all know his dad never shuts up."

"We'll see how you feel at four in the morning," said Adam. "When Little Man wants to rage."

"What?" Caroline countered. "As if you ever get up with him and do the night feeding?"

The others oohed. Adam put his arm around Caroline.

"My beautiful, faultless wife." He sighed. "She neglects to mention I'm usually up already. Or still up."

"Trawling the Lonely MILF message boards for tasteful nudes," said Blaise.

"*Working.*"

"At four in the morning?" said Wynn. "Please."

"As you may recall, I pulled, like, ten all-nighters last month getting ready for *you-know-what*."

"Well, no wonder *you-know-what* is still *you-know-what* and not *everyone-knows-what*."

"No, it's because their offers have all been shit, that's why."

They were talking about the acquisition. This was Caroline's signal to tune out. She'd been hearing about the forever-promised acquisition since fetal viability, and months later it was still coming any day now.

Caroline tried to maintain an interest in the world of Adam's work. It *had* been interesting once, especially when he'd been a disrupter, working at his own boutique virtual reality start-up, Pantheon. Back then, he would tell her about such-and-such company developing such-and-such world-dominating technology, the links between such-and-such repressive government and such-and-such angel investor.

According to Adam, Pantheon were the good guys, of course—they refused to sell out to shady funders, and they were offering a truly human-focused product that touched—no, not touched, *healed*—real people's lives. Even if he was being a bit self-aggrandizing, at least it was all pretty stimulating.

But now Adam worked at Corridor, and everything was about *infrastructure*, a word that became ubiquitous in Adam's lexicon even while its specific meaning remained almost totally opaque to Caroline. Her husband's self-aggrandizement was still there, but it was mostly about the minutiae of system upgrades and code reviews, not changing the world for the better.

Mostly Caroline told herself that, when it came to his career, Adam had enough enthusiasm for both of them. As long as she was appreciative of the lifestyle that his work afforded them—which she *was*, no question—then did it really matter if she understood what was so compelling, so all-consuming?

Maybe Gabriel would have an engineer's mind like his dad. It wasn't as if Adam was all that interested in what *she* did, at least not these days. That was partly Caroline's own fault. Early on in their relationship, Adam had been invested in her art and career—helping her choose between images and showing up to every opening, no matter how tiny and poorly attended—but after he got the Corridor job, Caroline had essentially abandoned her own artistic practice. She made almost no work that entire year, aside from a daily self-portrait in bed, a series that purported to be about the body in space, the reclamation of the gaze, the catalog, the diary, the depredations of being a woman under late capitalism, but in fact was so vacuous and self-indulgent that later she would pretend she had never made the pictures at all.

She shifted Gabriel in his wrap to get him to stop wriggling so much.

Beyond the yacht club, they passed a sprawling leisure complex: a wide green field, a jungle gym in the shape of a pirate ship run aground in a sandpit, a cluster of cabins with painted signs that read CAMP HAVEN. The cabins surrounded a wooden amphitheater with a broad stage. A half dozen children in those blue-and-white Peter Pan–collared rompers appeared to be rehearsing some kind of protracted death scene. Another cohort in the same uniforms were on the field—at the sound of a digital whistle, six sets of skinny legs began pumping back and forth between distant cones, their pace growing increasingly staggered with each lap, until you could no longer tell they'd once been running shoulder to shoulder.

She would have expected to hear shouts and laughter. Aside from their hard breathing, the child sprinters were silent.

The men didn't seem to notice anything around them. They were talking ruefully about Mosaic, as usual. Caroline had heard a lot about Mosaic over half-eaten dinners and cast-aside blankets over the last year or so, but she still didn't really know what the company did. Something to do with infrastructure, she assumed, like Corridor. Whatever infrastructure was. She tuned out again, lifted her wineglass to take a sip, and saw that it was already empty. She looked behind her to catch a glimpse of the sprinting children once more, but now they were lying on their backs in the field, their narrow white chests rising and falling.

"And after all that wining and dining, after I give myself a goddamn pinched nerve eating her out for like, twenty minutes, you know what she tells me?"

"What?"

"It has something to do with storage optimization, and that's all I know."

"You're kidding."

"Nope."

"You said she was engaged to the CFO!"

"Total waste. Even Taryn was annoyed."

Around a bend in the boardwalk, right as the trees began to thicken, there was a pair of small white bungalows perched on their own wooden platform, signs above their doorways designating them as the offices of Public Safety and Public Health. Just beyond, Caroline and the others stumbled upon a group of broad-hipped men in Bermuda shorts, their sunburned necks strung with leis of camera straps weighed down by phallic lenses. Blocking the path, the photographers formed a semicircle around their subject: twin fawns on spindly legs, suckling at the teats of their mother. One of the fawns turned toward Caroline and she saw that it was half blind, the skin crumpled where its left eye should have been.

Blaise cleared his throat, let his forward foot fall on the boardwalk with a thunk. The family of deer froze, then snapped, shattering into the woods. Their quarry departed, the photographers hissed as they stepped aside to let the intruders pass. The path wound deeper into the trees.

"I'm sure Adam told you," Perry murmured.

Caroline turned.

"Told me what?"

"About the artist residency."

He was grinning, teasing. She tried to fit the components of the joke together, but the puzzle was sodden, the cardboard pieces furry and disintegrating. That was how her mind was when speaking to other adults, ever since the baby.

"Didn't you recognize them?" Perry nudged.

"Who?"

"Ansel and his buddies back there?"

"Ansel?"

"Adams."

"Adam?"

"No, *Adams*."

There it was. He was trying to help her, give her an opening. She knew she should say something about Ansel Adams photographing landscapes, not wildlife. She opened her mouth, closed it. Perry tried again.

"Your husband thought you'd feel at home among your colleagues, but I think you'll be disappointed."

"Oh?"

She could do better than this.

"See, they're a cutthroat bunch."

"I bet."

Couldn't she do better than this?

"All card-carrying Magnum members."

"They have cards now? That's new."

Better.

"Most of them have Guggenheims, too."

"Sounds like I have a lot to learn," Caroline said. Now that he'd given her enough to work with, the banter began to come a little more easily. "Maybe they'll take pity on me and let me sit in on their crit group."

"I wouldn't get my hopes up if I were you. I hear their crit groups are built around human sacrifice. Blood rituals, spirit cooking, that kind of thing."

"That's how you know they're serious."

"And they hate all women," Perry said, his voice low. "Especially ones with talent."

"Come on." She laughed. "Now you're just trying to win me over."

He touched her arm lightly, just above her elbow.

"How am I doing?"

Just then the trees fell away, and they could finally see the white spaceship of the house. A towering pair of ivory parentheses with no discernible structural function stretched in a sun salutation, reaching up and out of a ziggurat of decks and glassed-in rooms, which included two outdoor showers; whoever was inside would be clearly visible to anyone passing by.

Although Caroline guessed that would be no one, this being a private cove.

"Holy shit," said Adam, taking it all in. "You weren't kidding."

"Right?" said Wynn. "I told you EX would hook us up."

"Thank god for EX."

"EX?" asked Caroline.

"Employee Experience," Perry explained. "There's a whole department at work that just wants us to be happy."

As they approached the ramp, a naked woman lying on the deck came into view. She lay on her back, her knees spread into a diamond, one hand on her lower belly. A pile of black hair shrouded her face, revealing a close-shaved undercut; she must have arranged her hair like that, to block the sun. Caroline tried not to look at the red shard between her legs, even as she felt the men stare—Blaise, Wynn, Perry, her husband—all of them, mouths open. The naked woman breathed out with a sigh and brought her knees together, lifted her hips into a bridge. She raised her right foot, then extended her leg, dark blue toenails stretching to the sky. She did the same with the other leg, then lay supine and still.

Caroline felt the heat coming off the men beside her, smelled the bergamot and grass, but this time an even stronger fecal undertone. She knew if she looked at them she would see their faces deformed by their appetites.

The naked woman rolled to her left side, briefly tucking her body into a fetal position, then sat up, settling herself on crossed legs, hands pressed together in prayer. She opened her eyes and looked straight at Caroline.

"Oh my god, you're here!"

Before Caroline could respond, she was up and clinging to her, bare breasts smushed against the baby's head. He woke up and started to spit and mewl. The woman released Caroline from her embrace and gasped.

"And this must be—"

"Gabriel."

"*Gabriel!* I love that. What a little nugget!"

This was Taryn, Blaise's girlfriend. Caroline couldn't remember if she had actually met Taryn before, or how long she and Blaise had been together. She was pretty sure that Taryn was twenty-three. Adam had promised Caroline they had indeed met before and had named some event that Caroline didn't remember going to, but now that Caroline saw this woman naked in front of her, she had no memory of her face at all. The face was what she fixed her gaze upon now—the eyes too wide and sparkly, the grin a rictus of pleasure. Caroline tried to picture them hanging out, making small talk over a spread of plant-based sushi at the Corridor Christmas party, or waiting in line for the ladies' room together in some narrow, amber-lit hallway, but she came up empty. Then she tried to picture herself joining Taryn in a naked reclined butterfly, the two of them spread to the sun, breathing, open to whoever might be watching, the crest of their knees just barely touching.

No, it was too ridiculous—Caroline would look grotesque with her postpartum body, her marred and drooping flesh, her third-degree perineal tear that had taken weeks to heal after an infection. But she felt warm then, imagining the summer sun on her own vulva, stretched labia, scar tissue, and all.

"Babe," Blaise said softly. "Are you going to put something on?"

Taryn frowned for a moment, then threw back her head and laughed.

"I swear, I completely forgot what I was doing—no wonder y'all were looking at me that way!"

She winked at Caroline, touched her arm just above the elbow.

"Come on," she said. "You've got to see this house, it's so sick."

They entered the house through a sliding door. Two women wearing long white tent dresses stood at the long white marble kitchen counter, frowning in concentration as they sliced bright baubles of citrus fruit. EDM echoed from unseen speakers. A sleek black dog undulated into the room, an enormous eel swiftly swimming for the newcomers' knees with paws and teeth. All at once everyone seemed to be shouting the name Nora over the androgynous, Auto-Tune-strangled vocals of the deep house music. The big dog leaped and danced. Gabriel jerked, sensing danger.

"Nora! *Nora!*"

"Nora, *no!*"

"Nora! Nora! Come here, girl, here! Here!"

"Nora, I think she's—"

"Oh shit, I'm so sorry, *Nori—*"

"Come on, Noa, I thought we agreed—"

"Okay, *okay!*"

Noa, that was it. Noa and her dog, Nori. And Jane was the other woman. Caroline was sure she had met them before. Almost sure. A too-late dinner at a long table in someone's loft, hands carving a bloody log of beef tenderloin, a black dog looking on. A corner booth in a too-dark cocktail lounge, two faces lit by phone screens while Caroline tried to make conversation.

"You know what I hate? All those videos that say they're 'POV.'"

Noa and Jane had looked up briefly, then looked down again.

"They're not actually POV at all," Caroline had continued. "Because they're showing the person themselves instead of their point of view. And like, 'core memory,' when it's just, I don't know, a family eating spaghetti off a tabletop. Like what even is that? Or the whole 'altered my brain chemistry' thing—like, seriously? Is that even a thing?"

No response.

"Your skin looks amazing," Caroline had tried. "You have to tell me your secrets. Your routine."

Now Noa the woman had Nori the dog in a headlock. She patted Nori's flank and smiled at Caroline. Noa also worked at Corridor. She had a Disney Bambi face, dark gold hair with dark roots that showed in a purposeful way, like plumage. Her social media accounts had two channels: records of ramen and negroni consumption rated on a scale of one to ten to the first decimal point, and volunteer work at waterfront refugee camps.

Still standing at the counter, Jane did not put down her knife. Jane did not work at Corridor. Was she a psychiatrist? A therapist? No, a social worker. Sharp features, sleepy eyes. Something chilly and withholding about her. After a moment Jane remembered to smile at Caroline, too. She was still holding the knife.

Caroline's throat felt taut. She smiled back.

"I'm so sorry," Noa said. "Stupid dog. She's just excited to see you."

"She remembers us?"

"She remembers *everyone*. But also, she's been desperately in love with Adam ever since he made a fire for us in the cabin upstate. She wanted us all to sleep in the living room together, kept herding us back to the hearth when we were trying to go to bed, remember?"

"And that baby probably looks pretty tasty," said Wynn.

"Stop!" shrieked Noa. "You're the worst!"

"Nori's a Pisces," said Taryn. She'd put on a loose batik robe but had left it open so that one brown nipple tested the air. "She would never hurt a baby."

"She's so intuitive," said Noa. "When I had my third round

of nano to fix my primordium implant, she literally did not leave my side for a week."

"I believe it!"

Perry had gone around to the other side of the counter and was whispering to Jane, who kept her eyes on the quartered lemons and limes. Caroline watched them together until she felt Adam's hand on the back of her neck.

"Let's see our room," he said. "Settle in."

The house was a warren of white walls and blond wood floors, halls, and stairs, rooms spiraling jaggedly around the central triple-height atrium. That seemed like the layout, anyway. In truth it was hard to get a sense of the house when you were inside it. The maze of the interior seemed to have no relation to what the structure looked like from the outside, the spacecraft shipwrecked into the leafy overstory.

Their suite was up a half flight of curving stairs, through a sliding white wooden pocket door. Caroline had to give Adam credit: it was private, as he had promised. There was a bedroom and attached bath, and another sliding door—this one glass—that led out to a deck shielded from view by cedar planks and potted palms. Two cushioned chaises, a small table between them, open sky overhead. The dying-smoke-detector-battery of crickets chirping.

"Nice," said Adam. They went back inside.

The walls were bare, except for a single framed poster at the foot of the vast white platform bed. A beautiful woman who appeared to be part android, her skull scaled in silver, her lower back a tangle of mesh and glowing wires. Adam lay down, holding his phone to his face; Caroline undid the wrap and laid Gabriel on the bed next to him.

"Watch him, please?"

Adam kept his eyes on his phone and hovered a hand over the baby's face as if feeling for his breath.

"I got him."

Caroline went into the bathroom and saw that it was open to the living space, their privacy breached by an interior window cut into the wall. Voices wafted up to her from below; she peered down at the men lying on white couches that rimmed the room, watched the women loop around each other as they carried bottles and glasses and charcuterie boards from the kitchen to the deck, the black dog swirling along with them. Even though they'd turned the music back up, she was sure they'd be able to hear her flush.

So much for privacy.

The tautness in Caroline's throat spread to her stomach and bloomed hot and gurgling in her gut. Maybe it was the lobster roll. She clenched her butt and felt a sharp sting.

Fuck.

She went back into the bedroom and scooped up Gabriel from the bed. Adam kept his eyes on his phone.

"You've got him now?" Adam asked.

"Yes."

"I'll be down in a little bit," he said. "Just have to respond to a few messages."

"Okay."

"Have another drink!"

"Right."

"I love you."

"Love you, too."

Caroline didn't bother putting the wrap back on. She thought she'd have to make small talk, stand around and wait for the right moment to get away, maybe even explain herself, but no one seemed to notice her coming downstairs, and no one said anything at all as she slipped out one of the side doors, Gabriel wriggling in her arms.

The cove was a perfect circle, the bay a perfect blue. Caroline's feet moved from the planks of the deck to the pale sand, which cooled and moistened as she headed toward the water's edge, as far from the house as she could go. She sat down in a divot, Gabriel face up in her lap, his head balanced on her knees, eyes and mouth and hands opening and closing, opening and closing. She breathed and tried to calm her stomach, rested her eyes on the distant horizon. She couldn't see the mainland anymore. The sun wouldn't set for another hour or so. The light was heavy and golden, filtered through brown glass.

Along the grass-furred edge of the cove she could see other private beaches, patches of sand in front of other grand houses that were half hidden by tall reeds. On one of these beaches, not far to the east, she could see a family—a man, a woman, and three small children. The children were scaling the edifice of an empty lifeguard stand, leaping down into a pile of sand below, then running to the water and back. Caroline watched them climb, jump, and run, climb, jump, and run, climb, jump, and run. The man and woman were clapping and shouting, urging them on. When one of the children tripped and fell on their knees in the water the woman threw up her hands and screamed, loud enough for Caroline to hear her words.

"Come on!"

Caroline turned the other way. Farther to the west she could see another beach, another couple at the water's edge, no children this time, locked in an embrace. A Black couple, Caroline thought at first—the first Black people she'd seen on the island—but when she looked closer, she saw that they were in fact white, just backlit and dressed in black wet suits and scuba gear, but only from the waist up. Below the belt they were completely naked. When they parted, she saw the vague dangling shape of the man's penis. She looked away and down at her son, made faces into his face as she jostled him on her knees. She sang to him half-heartedly, self-consciously, sticking to the standard lullabies. She never gave herself permission to sing him the real songs she preferred—Johnny Cash or Townes Van Zandt, the kinds of songs her father had once sung to her. Gabriel frowned, then began to fret and fuss, slapping at her ineffectively. She shifted him sideways, then took out a breast and stuck it in his mouth.

She could make a lot of work on this trip. She should make a lot of work on this trip. She had even brought her compact portable printer. But sitting there on the shore, the possibilities for pictures overwhelmed her. Over the years she had walked down many beaches—city beaches, mostly—searching for subjects. She closed her eyes and saw them again now, the ones that had never made it into her photographs: the children piled on a unicorn float toy in the rushing surf; the woman in a soaked hijab with a tiny dog cupped in her hands; the men kissing against the jetty. She frowned. It was that light, oversaturating everything—the colors tremulous, unabsorbed ink on a page. The light made you think something was worth photographing, even when it wasn't.

Her gut knotted up again, tighter and lower this time. A hot puff of fart escaped her. She had to do something. She looked back at the glass box of the house, imagined the others looking out at her. Maybe there was a hidden corner somewhere, out of sight. She pulled her nipple from Gabriel's mouth and stood up, holding him in her arms. She walked west along the shore, around a blind bend, and had almost reached the end of the sand and the fence of sharp green reeds that cut off their beach from the rest of the cove when she came upon the heads.

There were three of them. Girls' heads—young teens, maybe thirteen or fourteen—decapitated, pasty white and crusted all over in sand. Their eyes were open, sightless, their mouths distended in silent howls. Caroline froze.

Then one of them snorted, and their dead faces broke apart into laughter.

"Did we get you?"

"Oh my god, look at her face, we *totally* got her."

"We definitely got her."

"Guys, *stop*. Look at her."

"Aw."

"Now I feel bad."

"It was just a prank!"

"Please don't be mad at us!"

"We don't know any better!"

Buried to their necks, they giggled up at Caroline. There

was a banging in her throat and her chest. She caught her breath.

"You scared the shit out of me."

Caroline examined the heads more closely. Their faces were white with zinc oxide and soft with fat, rinds of black eyeliner on their lower lids drawn in heavy crayon strokes. The blonde had dyed her hair red; the brunette had bleached her hair blond; the redhead had dyed her hair black. Their eyebrows gave them away.

Who had buried them so thoroughly? There was no one else around. The heads tittered at her.

"Your baby is *so cute*."

"The literal cutest."

"How old is he?"

"Three months," said Caroline. "Three and a half."

"Can we say hi?"

"Please?"

"He needs to know that we're not dead! He shouldn't be scared!"

Caroline's stomach roiled. She wanted to leave, but she couldn't go back to the house.

She didn't want to go back to the house, not just yet.

She sat down in the sand and laid Gabriel across her lap. The heads gasped with delight and sprouted a bit out of the ground, necks straining, faces moving closer together as they tried to get closer to the baby.

"What's his name?"

"Gabriel."

"*Gabriel!* Hi, Gabriel!"

"Do you ever call him Gabey?"

"Or Gabey Baby?"

"We call him Gabe, sometimes."

"Gabey is better."

"Much better."

"What's *your* name, Mama?"

Caroline blinked.

"Me?"

The heads laughed.

"Who else?"

"No other mamas here!"

"Not that we know of, anyway."

"Caroline," said Caroline.

"Caro."

"And you're staying in the spaceship house."

"Of course she is."

Caroline frowned, suspicious.

"How did you know that?"

The heads stared at her for a moment, then spluttered into a racket of laughter.

"How would we *not* know that?"

"Aren't we right in front of it?"

"Where else would you have come from?"

"Then where did *you* come from?" Caroline pressed. "I thought this was a private beach."

The heads fluttered their eyes innocently, mockingly.

"It *is*?"

"I don't even see how you could get out here," Caroline went on. "Without going through my house."

"Oh, don't you worry about *that*, Caro."

"You don't need to worry about that."

"But you should know—"

"What?" said Caroline. "What should I know?"

"That we babysit!"

"Yes!"

"You should let us babysit Gabey."

"We're the best on the island. Ask any of our references."

"Well, not *any* of them. Just the right ones."

"We can give you their names."

"They'll tell you everything you need to know."

"We're a hand-to-mouth operation."

"*Word*-to-mouth. Not hand-to-mouth."

"Ask around, but only ask the right ones."

Caroline felt drunk, suddenly. Or sleepy. It was her meds, probably. The meds and the glass of wine.

"But I don't know *your* names," she said to the heads. They laughed.

"You don't need to!"

"You'll find us. Or we'll find you!"

"Or you'll find the right ones."

Caroline sensed there was something they wanted her to know. A message just for her, a ball tossed before she was ready that she'd fumbled between her palms. Slowly, slowly, the sun slipped lower, and the warm air grew silkier. In the haze, the question formed on her lips.

"Is there something else I need to know?"

She almost said it aloud. Maybe she did.

No one answered. The heads were looking at Gabriel now, pouting with worry. Too late, Caroline saw what they had already seen, the black filigree of the horsefly landing on the baby's skin. Too late, she lifted her hand. Too late. The fly was gone. Gabriel screamed as a red-and-white bull's-eye swelled on his cheek. The heads gasped again, in horror this time.

"No!"

"Poor Gabey baby!"

"Is he okay?"

Gabriel sucked in a silent breath, then screamed louder. For a moment Caroline did nothing. Then she pressed the screaming red face to her chest, trying to muffle the sound the open mouth was making, her hands trembling.

"We need to go," she said to the heads. "I'm sorry."

She stood up. The contents of her large intestines churned, then compacted to a perilously low mass. She knew she would never make it to the house.

"Caro?"

"Are you okay, Mama?"

Gabriel was still shrieking in her arms when she walked out

into the bay. She held him as high as she could, but still his heels skimmed the water as she waded in far enough to submerge herself above the waist. The water was as warm and thick as the air, bloodlike. She unclenched and felt the shit bloom around her. The heads watched her from the shore.

CHAPTER 3

"Well, you wouldn't believe what we've seen."
"Try me."
"A woman shitting."
"So?"
"In broad daylight."
"Yawn," said Wynn. "Everyone's seen that."
"No, she was special," said Blaise. "She was squatting between two antique Bentleys. Gave me and Taryn the finger as we passed."
Taryn nodded vigorously. She and Blaise had put up their hair in matching top knots.
"We can beat that," Wynn scoffed, nodding at Noa. "Easy."
"Oh yeah?"
"Carousel by the bridge," said Noa. "Morning of Christmas Eve, kids and tourists everywhere. Spinning round and round. This woman strips down, squats in the middle before anyone can stop her. Smacked her own ass like bongo drums when she finished."
"I hear that's a powerful fertility ritual in some cultures."
"Oh, come on," said Jane. "Now you're overdoing it."
"When you first told us this story she wasn't shitting," Perry pointed out. "She was pissing."
"Different woman," said Wynn.
"The pissing woman was on Derby Day," said Noa. "She was wearing a little hat with feathers and everything. Pearls.

Piss absolutely gushing out of her, like a waterfall. The way it shone in the sunlight—it was obscene."

"Thanks for that image," said Jane.

"Why do you guys spend so much time at that carousel, anyway?" Blaise asked.

"The same reason they love going to Disney World," said Adam. "Because they're perverts."

On the long table there were platters of baked clams with savory guanciale granola and lemon-lovage gremolata, raw tuna and bresaola rosettes with dewdrops of aioli budding on a thatch of pickled shallots and watercress, cups of pink shrimp and lobster ceviche dotted with balls of dragon fruit and lychee, and grilled lab-grown baby lamb chops splayed around a central mound of chocolate hummus. Quick hands kept reaching for parcels of food, squirreling them onto glass plates. Mouths gabbed and gobbled. Nori circled the table, whining. Caroline kept hesitating, unsure what she wanted to eat. She glanced at the black-and-white surveillance footage on her phone, saw the fluttering of two tiny feet and looked away. The lights were low, the sliding doors open to the deck. She was sure the plan had been to eat outside, but the Wi-Fi signal out there wasn't strong enough for the baby monitor.

"I just never thought it would be so bad around the office," said Wynn. "That used to be the most photographed spot in Brooklyn."

"I try to avoid that area at night entirely," said Noa. "Since the machete attacks I don't even walk to the train anymore—I just get right into a car."

"It's so bad in our neighborhood now," said Taryn, her open mouth layered with raw tuna. "Like so bad."

"It's bad everywhere," said Noa. "Disgusting. You wouldn't believe the way people are living. Sit! Good girl."

She placed a lamb chop in Nori's waiting jaws. The dog ran off, hopped onto one of the couches, and began to chew. No one besides Caroline seemed to notice.

"Bad everywhere indeed," said Blaise. "Boom times for Jane."

"I'm a social worker," said Jane. "I don't charge my clients by the hour. And anyway, the vast, *vast* majority of homeless and disabled people are nonviolent."

"Here we go."

"In fact," Jane continued, "the homeless and disabled are the ones who are most vulnerable to assault."

Perry put his hand on Jane's bare shoulder blade. Caroline blinked.

"Come on, babe," Perry said. "Who are they going to believe? An actual expert, or their own misinformed, preconceived notions?"

Jane shrugged off his hand.

"She's right, actually," said Taryn. "When you actually stop and talk to them, most of them are just people."

On Caroline's phone, Gabriel was turning himself in a circle, his head the central axis of a demented human clock. His open eyes were white holes; Caroline thought of curious foxes caught on camera in the nighttime woods, malevolent ghosts captured by camcorders in haunted McMansions. Paranormal activity. Soon Gabriel would sit up and his head would begin to spin, his mouth a distended void. Caroline laid her phone face down to avoid looking at the demonic possession in progress.

"Here." Taryn nudged Caroline's wrist. "Have some water."

Caroline peered at the pitcher. Silvery flecks swirled before settling at the bottom in a clump of black.

"Activated charcoal," said Taryn. "Clears out your toxins."

"Ah."

"And lithium! It's mostly lithium. I almost forgot."

A cry came from upstairs. Caroline winced. Taryn and Noa made sad faces.

"Poor Gabe."

"He can tell all the fun is down here."

Adam was slurping a clam. He raised his eyebrows at Caroline, as if she had just said something interesting.

"I'm sorry," Caroline said, feeling around for the napkin that had already fallen from her lap. "Excuse me."

The baby's squalling was a physical presence at the open bedroom door. Gabriel lay on his back in his bassinet. He was an open mouth, an emotionless emission device. He seemed not to register his mother's presence.

She picked him up. He was wet. She changed his diaper and onesie, then swayed him in her arms until he grew heavy and limp. Loud laughter rose up through the floorboards. She put him down in the bassinet and he opened his eyes, looking right into hers.

"Please sleep," she said through her teeth. More laughter from below.

She padded back downstairs. As she rejoined the table Adam raised his eyebrows again. He had moved on to another clam.

"All good?"

"Oh, he's fine," Caroline said.

"Asleep?"

"Any moment now."

The platters of food had migrated from Caroline's end of the table. Perry whisked away the dead soldiers and came back from the kitchen with two fresh bottles of wine. A brown glass medicine dropper was being passed around. Taryn dribbled some into her glass of lithium water. Blaise did the same, then held out the dropper to Noa.

"Oh, none for me, thanks," said Noa. "I really shouldn't."

"Why not?"

"I already took my K dose before dinner."

"Why did you take your K so early?" asked Blaise. "We always take ours before bed."

"My prescription is three times a day."

"Seems like a lot."

"It helps me drink less. It's so good for my ADHD and anxiety, I don't need the social juice as much, you know?"

"But you're on vacation!"

"You work too hard. You have to play hard, too."

"Fuck it," said Noa. "Give it to me."

"That's my girl."

Noa opened her mouth, and Blaise squeezed two bulbous wet pearls onto her tongue. Jane watched. She looked dazed, dead-eyed. She must have already had her dose, while Caroline was upstairs.

Then the dropper was in front of Caroline's nose.

"Want some?"

She hesitated.

"What—what is it?"

Everyone laughed, including Adam. The muscles in their faces shimmied in the candlelight, gold flesh and black shadows like reflections on water.

"Molly."

"No, crystal."

"No, acid."

"No, heroin."

"No, DMT."

"Shut up, everybody. Caroline, it's just Q."

She'd heard of K. Everyone had. They even prescribed it at the Golden Sunset Homes, although not to Caroline's mother, even though Caroline had asked for it several times.

She'd never heard of Q.

"Q?"

"Just a microdose."

"I'm okay," Caroline said, thinking of her small white pills. "I'm nursing."

Taryn and Noa made their sad faces again. Jane, on the other hand, looked genuinely sad. Or angry, maybe. The dropper vanished.

"Another time."

"Actually," tried Caroline. "Could someone pass me the—"

Another cry from upstairs. Caroline looked at Adam. He was chewing a lamb chop, grimacing with the effort. His teeth were black with char. She shoved her chair back from the table, almost knocking it over.

"Excuse me," she said.

By the time she reached him, Gabriel had stopped screaming to suck on his fists. She nursed him. Left side first, then right when he demanded more.

"Hungry?" she muttered. "Tell me about it."

She put him down again, hoping he was milk drunk, that he would close his eyes. His eyes stayed open.

"Please," she whispered, backing toward the door and easing it shut.

Downstairs, the conversation had moved on.

"I still just can't get over what an unforced error it was," said Wynn. "Whoever said all press is good press is completely delusional."

"No one expected it to be such a hatchet job."

"That bitch?" said Noa. "I totally expected it."

"It was a calculated risk."

"Couldn't have helped with the *you-know-what*."

"Who knows."

"You know what I do know? I know you never see Mosaic in the press."

"That's not true."

"It's because they're cowards! Absolute cowards!"

"You're shouting."

"It's what people already think of us, anyway," said Adam. "That we're the ones standing between the masses and universal *you-name-it*."

"God."

"It's a total distortion of what we do."

"And it's because no one knows what infrastructure *actually means*!"

"Nope," said Taryn, holding up her hands. "Stop right there. I refuse to let y'all turn this into a work trip. Play hard, remember?"

"Hey," said Blaise. "I don't want this to be a work trip, either. But some of us still have to work while we're out here."

"You have to take pity on us, Taryn," said Wynn. "Engineers are retards. We don't know how to talk about anything else, so we make everyone around us suffer."

"Don't say that."

"Say what?"

"The *r* word."

"I thought it had been reclaimed," said Wynn. "Or rehabilitated, whatever."

"Only if you're an actual—you know."

"Retard?"

"Don't say it!"

"How do you know I'm not?"

"Wynn!"

"What, you want to see my papers?"

"You know," mused Adam. "I heard they're banning the DSM entirely."

"I heard that, too."

"In the future everyone will be treated, or no one will be treated."

"That's right. Everyone will be on their own journey."

"No addicts, no mentally ill. No such thing as aberrant."

"Or everyone is an addict, and everyone is mentally ill."

"Well, with HEOL, everyone can make their own decision."

"Heal?"

"H-E-O-L. Humane End of Life."

"I thought it was MAS—Medically Assisted Suicide."

"They rebranded for congressional approval."

"Boom times for Jane?"

"Boom or bust, who knows."

"Where did she go?"

"Who?"

"Jane."

"Bathroom?"

Jane returned to the table. She'd changed out of her dress into jeans and an oversize long-sleeve black T-shirt, *No Future to Believe In* printed in white letters across the chest. Her gray eyes were heavy, her mouth soft. She blinked at everyone slowly, smiled shyly.

"Hi Jane," said Noa.

"Hi," Jane whispered, her voice smoky.

"Jane feels good now," said Taryn.

"I love when Jane is high," said Noa. "She just acts like a normal person."

Jane tried to look very serious. Perry was looking at her, but he wasn't smiling. He opened his mouth and a baby's cry came out.

Caroline looked for Adam across the table, but he wasn't there. She heard a toilet flush.

"Bathroom," Jane said.

Caroline waited for Adam to return. The cries sharpened to shrieks. Everyone pretended not to look at her. Adam didn't return.

"Excuse me," she said.

Gabriel had rolled himself onto his stomach. Caroline would have been proud of him if she hadn't been so annoyed. Now that he could roll, she'd never sleep again. She checked everything she was supposed to check. Her son didn't need his diaper changed, and he wasn't hungry. He was just unhappy for no discernible reason.

"Same." Caroline sighed. "Same."

She laid him down on his back on the bed and dangled his floppy bunny over his face. He kept crying until she lay down beside him, her left middle finger clutched in the pocket of his closed hand. Their breathing slowed, lengthened and softened to the sound of ocean surf. *Shush. Shush. Shush.* They lay like that for a long time, until she was sure he was asleep, until she was almost asleep herself. Maybe she did sleep.

Then she was awake. She felt a rush of dizziness as she sat up. Gabriel was asleep on the bed. It was a terrible idea to leave him there, like that. Every parenting expert on social media said to never leave a baby like that.

But maybe she could do it just for a few minutes. Just so she could have something to eat.

She arranged the pillows around the edges of the bed, just in case he tried rolling again. Without pausing to steady herself Caroline floated headlong out of the room, down the stairs.

"So what you're saying is I should never approach anyone I don't know, ever."

"That's not what I'm saying at all."

"That's *exactly* what you're saying."

Adam was gone again, or maybe he still hadn't come back. More bottles had appeared on the table, crystalline, spindly-necked things that looked too fragile to touch. The crushed remains of a blackberry buckle looked like afterbirth. The other platters of food were picked over, almost empty. Caroline sat down.

"I refuse to have this debate with you again."

"But why? Aren't we having fun?"

Gabriel wailed.

"No!"

Caroline clapped her hand over her mouth. The others went silent. They watched her, waiting. She wondered what they would do if she just let the baby cry, if she pretended not to hear as he roared himself sick—if anyone would do anything besides stare and then shrug and look away and go back to talking, talking, talking, and where the fuck was her husband, anyway?

"Excuse me."

When she descended the stairs holding the crying baby Caroline wouldn't meet anyone's eye. She sat down again and lunged across the table for the last lamb chop.

"I'm sorry," she said, gripping the charred bone in her fist. "I need to eat."

Gabriel kept screaming, red-faced. Caroline gnawed at the chop, tasting the expertly engineered blood and fat, trying to rip the meat from the joint. She didn't care anymore. They were all looking at her. She didn't care. *She didn't care.*

Then Perry was beside her. In one smooth motion he had lifted the baby out of Caroline's lap and into an effortless belly hold—the way she always suggested that Adam hold him when he fussed.

"It's good for bonding," she'd say. "You need to get closer to him."

"I am close to him."

"Not like I am."

"You're his mother."

"You're his father."

"I feel like I'm going to drop him."

"You won't drop him."

"I feel like I will."

"You won't."

"I'm scared."

Gabriel stopped crying.

"Mama needs to eat," Perry cooed. "Can Mama eat? Can you let Mama eat?"

Caroline let the naked lamb bone drop to her plate, then snatched up two raw tuna rosettes with her bare hands, watercress under her fingernails. She ate and ate, her stomach finally settled. Who cared what she looked like.

None of them knew what it was like, having a baby.

Adam came back, finally. He looked at Caroline eating, then looked at his son in Perry's arms and frowned.

"What's that?" he asked Caroline.

"What?"

"That thing on his face."

Adam gestured at the red splotch on Gabriel's cheek before sitting down again. It was the first time he had said anything about the fly bite. Caroline had forgotten about it hours ago.

"He got bitten by something earlier," she said. "It's nothing."

"Doesn't look like nothing."

"It's fine."

"No wonder he's so upset."

"He's not upset," said Caroline. "It's just the four-month sleep regression."

"But he's not four months yet."

"I don't know! He's advanced!"

"What bit him?"

"Some kind of fly," said Caroline. "I don't know. A horsefly?"

"Haven't seen one of those in ages."

"They used to spray every bug to death out here," said Wynn. "Total annihilation, nasty stuff. All of it spearheaded by the Haven community association. They got them to spray the entire island. The summer I was five or six they didn't tell anyone when the trucks were coming, and I was out playing and got some right in the face."

"Holy shit."

"Explains a lot, when you think about it," said Blaise. "Based on how you turned out."

Wynn ignored him.

"My dad was so enraged, he tracked down the Haven association president at the ferry terminal and sprayed bleach in her face."

Silence. Wynn chuckled.

"You're kidding," said Blaise.

Wynn shook his head, ran a hand through his hair.

"He—ah. Yeah. He went to prison for a year."

They all looked at him, except for Noa, who looked away.

"He sprayed *bleach* in her *face*?"

"When you're super-rich, you have to freak out over minor shit like that," said Jane. She was leaning back in her chair with her eyes closed. "That's the only way other people know you're human."

"But we weren't super-rich."

"Come on."

"We *weren't*," Wynn shouted, bringing his fist down onto the table. "We weren't like these people, in this town."

No one spoke or moved. Even Gabriel was quiet.

"And it wasn't minor," Wynn continued. "It was poison. When you really think about it, my dad was a visionary. Before his time. He knew it was poison."

Caroline felt almost sorry for Wynn. She saw the photograph

of him that she would have taken at that moment—it would be like one of the pictures she'd made in college at the fraternity house, the way she'd found the beats of vulnerability behind the bravado of those golden-boy slobs, the bloat of alcohol on their faces and physiques. There was something interesting about it. She cast about for something to break the silence.

"I didn't know you grew up out here," she said finally. Wynn nodded.

"I didn't grow up in Haven," he said. "We stayed in another town nearby. Nice, but not as nice as Haven.

"Haven was always different. Really private, snooty. Fences and barbed wire around the whole perimeter."

"You're kidding."

"I'm serious. All the houses looked the same, and everyone knew everyone, because everyone had lived here forever. My friends and I would try to sneak in sometimes, just to walk around, maybe bother some girls, but it was impossible. No outsiders allowed. They had all these covenants set up so that people couldn't sell their houses to anyone who wasn't a member of one of the original families. I don't even think anyone actually owned their house or land. It was all long-term leases, like a giant co-op.

"But when the old generation finally started to die off, their descendants hadn't done well enough to keep the homes in the family. The inherited wealth wasn't enough—maybe for the children, but not for the grandchildren. It had all trickled away, bit by bit, every time some idiot let their soft, spoiled failson follow their dreams. The association fell apart, and people like us came in, got around the covenants."

"How?"

"Money, duh. After everything those snobs did to try to keep the new money out, all their nightmares came true. Because their own children were too weak."

Wynn leaned back in his chair and threaded his hands behind his head, grinning.

"It's irresistible, you know?" he said. "A multimillion-dollar home on an eroding beach. The perfect middle finger to nature. And to all those fucking snobs."

He sat forward, serious again.

"My family went through some really hard times," he said. "Like, we lost everything. *Everything.* My dad going to jail—I mean, him going to jail for the bleach, not the other stuff he went to jail for, later—that was just the beginning.

"There was a long while, coming out to the island in my teens and twenties, I couldn't even find a place to crash. Because of my family, I was persona non grata. Worse than nobody."

He looked at his hands. When he looked up again he was beaming.

"Now, I could buy a place just to torch it."

"WHY DON'T WE TAKE A WALK?" NOA SUGGESTED, CLEARLY trying to change the subject. "Maybe that will put Gabriel to sleep. Nori could stand to go out, too."

The proposition rippled around the table, infecting everyone with a light and jittery feeling of possibility that even Caroline had to admit felt pleasant.

They abandoned the table as it was and left their shoes behind (Wynn insisted on bare feet, the way of the island). Noa clipped a leash onto Nori's collar. Perry handed Gabriel to Adam; Adam fastened Gabriel into the stroller.

Outside the air was bathwater. They went two by two on the narrow boardwalk that threaded through the dark walls of trees, whispering as they looked up into the black dome of the sky, each taking their turn to exclaim at the number and brightness of the stars. When they passed the Public Safety and Public Health bungalows, each doorway illuminated by a single red bulb, Caroline knew they were getting closer to town.

They continued on past the ball field, pirate ship, and amphitheater, all the way to the yacht club overlooking the bay.

The elegant couples with their nests of crab legs were gone. The topless twentysomethings now wore baggy, sexless clothes and had colonized the gazebo, patio, and pool with their shouts and laughter. Silverback men in white linen pants rolled at the ankles and clingy at the crotch stalked among them.

With a start Caroline recognized the heads from the cove. They were attached to bodies now, bodies wearing nothing but T-shirts that fell to their knees, their arms linked as they danced. Surveying the crowd of revelers, Caroline realized that many of them were teenagers. They mixed with the twentysomethings and older men alike, chewing on plastic straws, cheesing for selfies, filming each other on their phones as they broke into choreographed dances.

"Wow," said Jane.

"Those girls are what," said Noa. "Twelve?"

Caroline watched one of the older men approach the heads. In each hand he held a plastic cup of what looked like Coke crowned with a bobbing maraschino cherry; a third identical drink dangled from his grinning teeth. Behind her, she heard a child's high, breathy giggle. She turned, expecting to see a face, or a rustle in the hedges, but there was nothing but darkness. Blaise cleared his throat.

"Should we—"

Everyone looked at him.

"Should we get a drink?"

No one answered. They had the dog and the baby. Everyone waited for someone else to make a decision. Caroline watched Perry watching Jane, who gave a small shake of her head.

"Nah," said Perry. "We're tired."

They all turned to go. Adam pushed the stroller with one hand. He grinned at Caroline, seeking her approbation. Perry caught Jane in an embrace from behind and thrust the tip of his tongue into her ear. Caroline looked away and didn't look at them again for the rest of the walk back to the house.

GABRIEL WAS FINALLY ASLEEP IN HIS BASSINET. They had turned out all the lights in the room except for a single dim sconce on Adam's side of the bed, farthest from the baby. Adam lay belly-up with his laptop propped on his chest, murmurs of music coming from his earbuds. The screen kept shifting between a map of medieval Europe and a rendering of a gloomy throne room populated with stiff humanoid figures: a decrepit king wearing a crown of thorns, a dwarf with a flaming turban, a courtesan with the face of a dog. Caroline swallowed her two small white pills without water and climbed into bed, resting her cheek against Adam's shoulder. She watched her husband play his game for a while, her eyes glazing over as his fingers stroked, tapped, and clicked, performing diplomacy, moving troops to a border. He hit save and shifted to face her.

"Listen," he whispered. "You might not like this."

Caroline sat up.

"Sounds like I definitely won't like it."

Adam sighed.

"I have to go back to the city during the week."

Caroline stiffened.

"Just this week?"

He hesitated. Caroline watched him run the mental math and figure out how to respond, which she knew was a response in itself. She decided not to answer the question for him. Finally he sighed again.

"I don't know, exactly."

Caroline blinked at him.

"Why do you have to go back?"

She already knew the answer to this question as well.

"It's work," he whispered. "Work stuff. I'm sorry."

It was not the first time. She remembered morning flights home after weddings attended alone, afternoons wandering unfamiliar cities solo while he stayed holed up in hotel rooms, late nights of waking with a start on their couch, every light in the apartment blazing, Adam still not there. Not the first time, not the last time. She didn't know why she had imagined that this time would be any different.

"Why did we—" she began.

She stopped, took a breath, tried again.

"Why didn't you—"

"Because I didn't know at the time," Adam said. "This thing—it just came up. This thing I have to do."

Caroline was silent. Adam kept whispering.

"It might not be the whole summer," he said. "It most likely won't be."

. . .

"Just a couple weeks, probably."

. . .

"I'll come out every weekend. Friday to Sunday, I'm one hundred percent yours."

. . .

"No work on the weekends, I swear."

. . .

"You'll have everyone else to keep you company."

. . .

"It will be fun!"

Caroline sighed, finally.

"Will it be fun?" she said. "Really?"

"Yes!"

"Adam, I don't even *know* these people."

"Come on, babe. Not that again."

She could feel her throat tightening, the pressure building behind her eyes. She tried to control her voice, to keep her volume low.

"After the fucking night I've had—"

"What do you mean? I thought we had a nice time."

He was looking at her in the puzzled way he often did when she was angry, frowning as if she were a line of bad code that someone had left for him to fix.

"You left me completely on my own at dinner!"

"Shhh. Don't wake him."

"Oh, *now* you care," she snarled. "First you were useless, and then you disappeared, and I was the one who had to keep getting up to deal with the fucking baby. *Our* baby."

"You can't get mad at me for not helping when you take it upon yourself to do something unilaterally."

"*Adam!*"

"Okay, okay, I'm sorry," he said. "I'm an asshole."

"You are. You're an asshole, and you're drinking too much."

They both knew it wasn't what she meant to say. Adam sighed.

"I'm not seeing her anymore, Caroline. It's been more than a year."

She lay down again and rolled onto her side, turning her back to him.

"I'm not," he said. "I promise."

She squeezed her eyes shut.

"Do you believe me?"

"I don't know."

"Look—look at my phone," he said, nudging the nub of her spine with its rounded corner. "No secrets. You can look at anything you want, go back as far as you want, I promise."

"Just stop it," she said. "Stop."

Neither spoke or moved for a long time. When Adam heard her crying, he curled himself around her, fitting his bent knees behind hers. He was a few inches shorter than she was.

"I promise, Caro," he murmured. "I promise. Do you believe me?"

She turned to study his face. He held eye contact—they had worked on this in therapy. After a long moment she nodded.

Adam smiled and rubbed her cheek with his thumb, pressing the dribbles of salt water into her skin. Caroline frowned.

"I don't understand," she said. "If it's for work, why do you have to go, and no one else?"

"They can all work remotely."

"And why can't you?"

"It's too sensitive."

"Sensitive?"

He was still trying to look serious, but now he couldn't keep himself from grinning.

"I really can't give you much in terms of detail. But it's big."

"This doesn't sound like an affair *at all*."

"If it were, wouldn't I be doing a better job at lying?"

"That's exactly what a liar would say."

They were grinning at each other now.

"I'm telling you the truth, I swear," he said. "It's a really important project, and only a few people know about it. It has to be that way."

Caroline sighed.

"But why?" she asked. "Why the secrecy?"

"Because not everyone can be trusted. Can you imagine this group keeping a secret? Taryn, with her lithium water? Jane, with whatever she's on? You think discretion is their strong suit?"

"I'm your wife."

"I know. And that's another reason I can't go into detail. You're a civilian."

Caroline rolled her eyes.

"But—"

"But what?"

"There's nothing preventing you from asking me questions."

She looked at him. Neither broke eye contact.

"Is it the acquisition?"

Adam shook his head.

"It's something else."

He nodded.

"It's something bigger," she said. "More important."

He nodded again.

Caroline had no idea what it could be. According to Adam, nothing was as critical as the acquisition. Nothing. Unless that had been a smokescreen for another venture. Although really, what on earth could be so important?

"Well, I wish you could tell me."

"I wish I could, too. Really. You'll just have to trust me. Once this comes through, our life is going to change."

"Sure."

"I mean it! Come on, babe."

"Okay, okay." She sighed, pretending to believe him. "I trust you."

There was something else Caroline wanted to ask. It was true that she had never paid close attention to the specifics of Adam's work, and she knew to take the more dramatically described elements with more than a few grains of salt, but she was observant enough to know certain things about how powerful companies operated.

"Just tell me one thing. If you can, of course."

"Okay."

"Is it—"

She didn't know how to say it. He waited for her to speak, and in his eyes and smile she saw that his engineer's brain had already anticipated her question.

"Is it—legal?"

He was still grinning when he took her by the chin and kissed her. She allowed herself to melt into him. She had felt this kind of relief before—that sensation of lying down in cool water, of letting her body go, of gratitude that she wouldn't have to do the hard thing.

The meds were in her blood now, calming her. Adam reached a hand up her nightgown and put his lips to her ear.

"If I tell you," he said, "I'll have to kill you."

WHEN CAROLINE WOKE UP SHE DIDN'T KNOW where she was. The room was still dark, but there were sharp seams of light running along the edges of the shades. Morning, a bright day seeping in.

She closed her eyes again. Tired as she was, she could not go back to sleep.

Sleep had been a challenge from the beginning. Like most babies, Gabriel had been born wanting to be held. The first few days after bringing him home, Caroline had stayed up all night, blinking hard at the algorithm's endless offerings of expensive nursing-friendly dresses and alarmist parenting advice, trying to keep herself awake while Gabriel dozed on her chest between feeds.

She didn't trust Adam to take a shift. He didn't trust himself, either, so he didn't insist.

Even after Gabriel began to tolerate his bassinet overnight, Caroline would fall asleep only to dream that in her exhaustion she had accidentally fallen asleep while holding him—that he was lost in the bed under the layers of linens and pillows, that she had crushed or suffocated him. The dream felt so real that Caroline would still be in its grip as she woke, palming around in disoriented panic for several seconds until she remembered Gabriel was safe in his bassinet beside her.

Caroline opened her eyes again. It came back to her. The island. Haven.

Caroline got out of bed, took out her camera, and inserted a new blank memory card. These would be the first photographs she'd take of their trip. She started wide, fitting as much of the room as she could: the disordered bed, the leak of light against the wall, the mesh bulk of the portable bassinet that seemed so out of place in its posh surroundings. Then she went for the pieces of her family sleeping in parallel, standing on the bed, an angled overheard view to get both baby and husband's bare legs in the frame, echoes of their bent knees. She moved in to get the bluish underside of Adam's arm thrown over his eyes, got as close as she dared to capture the angry bull's-eye on Gabriel's soft cheek.

Still asleep, both of them. She crept downstairs, giddy, her solitude a gift that she clutched to her chest.

The kitchen was a disaster, the dinner table just as they'd left it. In the morning light the remnants of their meal looked rotten. The smears of chocolate hummus looked like dog shit on a sidewalk, the raw tuna and rare lamb had turned shiny brown and gray. The watercress was wilted, and the clam shells reeked.

Caroline began to clean. She told herself it was because she wanted an uncluttered space to have her coffee, but she easily could have had her coffee on the deck. She remembered an early morning in the college roommate's family cottage up north, the hard, headache light on the water, rocks, and white shipboard walls of the house. It didn't occur to Caroline to take a walk on her own. Instead, she had kept herself busy, useful, washing the dishes and martini detritus, making the coffee and wiping the counters before her friend's family woke up. Before putting away the bottle of Beefeater, she had squeezed a single teardrop of dish soap into its open throat. It landed with a satisfying plop, and instantly dissolved, as if she'd only imagined doing it, as if she'd never done it at all.

Fuck a farm girl. Fuck a farm girl, indeed.

She had finished clearing the table and was waiting for the water to get hot when she felt the warmth of another body at her shoulder. Startled, she dropped the plate she was holding into the sink, where it cracked in two.

"Shit."

"Sorry," said Perry. "I didn't mean to scare you."

"You didn't scare me," she said. "You surprised me."

"I seem to do that a lot."

She looked up, but he was hidden behind the open door of the refrigerator, and she saw only her own blurred reflection. He closed the refrigerator, opened the glass bottle of mineral water in his hand, and drank with his head tipped back. He was shirtless, wearing little shorts the color of yellow buttercream. His chest and throat were flowered with dark marks—hickeys and fingerprint bruises.

"Hangovers in your thirties." He sighed. "I never seem to learn that trying to keep up with the kids is just going to hurt me later. How was the rest of your night?"

Caroline shrugged.

"We just went to bed," she said. "It was a long day for us."

She paused.

"What about you?"

"Jane passed out as soon as we got back," he said. "The rest of us stayed up for a while."

He touched one of the darker bruises on his throat and winked at her.

"Don't worry," he said. "Jane doesn't mind, as long as I tell her everything. And she knows she gets whatever she wants next time. That's our deal."

"Your deal?"

"Our situation. No, *arrangement*. That's the better word."

Caroline looked away, her face hot. Perry laughed.

"Sorry," he said. "I shouldn't have—"

"It's fine."

"Jane says I always make assumptions about what other people are ready for, and that I'm usually wrong."

"You're not wrong."

"No?"

"I don't mind."

"I wish you could see your face right now."

She made herself look at Perry.

"Why?" she said. "What does my face look like?"

"Close your eyes."

She did as she was told. She felt the air move as he took a step toward her, stopped her breath as she readied her body for his touch.

"Open."

She opened her eyes. He stood before her, grinning, one jagged half of the broken plate held up in each hand, the shards rising from his temples like horns.

THE MEMBERS OF THE HOUSEHOLD SPENT THE REST of the weekend recumbent—on deck chairs, on towels, on their backs on the still surface of the bay. Chastened by their hangovers, they fervently agreed to Taryn's suggested pact of clean living and sobriety for the rest of the week—no drinking, no drugs, and no red meat, lab-grown or otherwise.

As far as Caroline could tell, there was no more fooling around, either. She didn't hear any whispers or heavy breathing on Saturday night, and no one appeared on Sunday morning with any new bruises. She watched Jane carefully, looking for signs of resentment or impatience, but she couldn't detect anything other than languor in her hooded gaze.

Adam broke the news of his obligatory return to the city over cucumber-and-star-fruit smoothies on Saturday afternoon, and everyone erupted in competing cries of disappointment and promises to take good care of Caroline and Gabriel, their resident mama and baby. For the rest of the weekend Adam was a paragon of engaged fatherhood, handling diaper blowouts and burying tiny toes in the damp sand at the water's edge. On Sunday, he even took Gabriel after his five a.m. feed, and a couple of hours later when Caroline finally opened her eyes to the seams of pale light along the window shades, she could tell by the silence that she was alone.

She left the house and followed the boardwalk south, uphill to the ocean. The morning was overcast, misty and milky. From the top of the stairs she saw them standing in the surf, their figures anonymous in the haze, illegible save for the baby-size bundle in someone's arms and the balletic leaps of the black dog as it ran from its people to the water, chasing down a ball and bringing it back. Caroline watched for a while before descending to join them.

WHEN ADAM LEFT ON THE LAST BOAT SUNDAY EVENING, THEY all went to the dock to see him off. The crowd was a harried caravan once again, an exodus of the indentured souls who were expected back in their offices for the week. Sunburned faces grimaced as they summoned train schedules and meeting calendars on their phones.

Adam did not grimace. He hugged his friends, kissed his wife on the lips, rubbed his hands over his son's head once more. Caroline pulled Adam in for one more long embrace, as if to draw a last burst of sustenance from his comfortable, familiar body—her arms around his neck, Gabriel safely cosseted between the beating hearts in their chests.

Then Adam joined the line of people waiting to board. Caroline watched him, blinked hard as he appeared to sidle up to the same dark-haired woman in the crochet top from the ferry on Friday, stared as they disappeared through the doorway and into the hull together. But when her husband reappeared on the upper deck, he was alone.

"I'll call tonight," he shouted down to her.

"Okay."

"I love you."

"I love you, too."

They waved to each other as the boat eased away, groaning as it slowly turned out into the open water. Blaise, Perry, and Wynn stripped off their shirts; the women shrieked as the men cannonballed off the dock, vanishing in plumes of spray. The boat hummed toward the mainland, until it was just a silent dark spot against the deep pink and orange of the sunset and Caroline couldn't see Adam at all.

The men hoisted each other out of the water and shook themselves like sodden dogs. They all stood, for a moment, admiring the sky. Then Wynn wondered if they really had to stay completely sober all week or if they could each have one hard seltzer with dinner, Jane announced she was feeling anemic and wanted a burger on the grill, Taryn linked her arm through Caroline's, and they all went back to the house.

CHAPTER 4

The summer that Pantheon imploded after the suicide of one of its users, Caroline got to know three things very well.

The first thing was their banking portal. When Adam was gainfully employed, she'd never been in the habit of checking their balances, but now she did it three, four, sometimes five times a day. When she tired of the six-factor authentication process, she changed the log-in to facial recognition mode, which may have required her to glare into the screen at just the right angle, but also meant that she only had to answer three questions to access their account. There were many more red numbers than blue numbers. The largest ones each month were their rent and Caroline's student loan payment (her application for another deferment had been denied). Hour by hour, she watched Adam's meager savings dwindle. Her pathetic three-digit deposits from her assisting and nannying jobs couldn't keep up. The credit card balance, on the other hand, relentlessly ascended.

The second thing Caroline got to know well was the sources of those pathetic three-digit deposits. Devorah Auerbach's photo studio was on the top floor of her Chelsea town house, one block east of the Hudson River floodwall; she hired Caroline to help her complete the holographic renderings of her extensive documentary back catalog, but used her primarily as a secretary and nurse in practice. The Geller family lived sixty-two blocks north, in a penthouse with a view of the Roosevelt Island barrier beach. Eden and Boaz, the four-year-old Geller twins, were being raised screen-free, and required constant live human entertainment whenever they weren't sleeping off their twice-weekly vitality infusions. Caroline got to know both jobs very well, and yet even in their intimate familiarity they were indistinguishable from one another. Often, she would look up from a task—scrubbing the dried remnants of food out of a bowl, listening to the tinny jangles of hold music while trying to get through to a doctor's office, or speaking softly to someone sobbing on the other side of a slammed door—and forget if she were currently assisting or nannying. Her long days were bookended by increasingly harrowing commutes—in the darkness of early mornings and late evenings she was often followed from the subway station for at least a block or two, and even being alert and studiously minding your own business on the station platform could no longer guarantee that someone wouldn't scream in your face or grab for your bag.

The third thing Caroline got to know well was the vigilant and highly specific routines and rituals that this new life without money demanded. No nights out, weekends off, or takeout. Carrying yesterday's cold coffee to work in a mason jar, the lid screwed on tightly so it wouldn't spill. Running out of hair products and makeup and not replacing them. One hundred and one recipes requiring little more than a can of beans. The vast hours of silence when she finally got home to her husband, because he had nothing to talk about, and she was too tired to talk.

Adam didn't get to know any of these things, not the way she did. Adam spent that summer lying down.

He lay on their unswept floor (unswept because they couldn't pay for someone to come sweep it anymore, and Caroline was too busy working, and Adam was too busy lying down on it to sweep it). He lay on their couch, which Caroline began to think of as Adam's couch, because he was always taking up the whole thing. He lay in their empty bathtub, trying to keep cool without running the AC. He lay in their bed. On his back, his laptop sat on his chest like a pop-up compartment permanently stuck in the open position. He stared unblinking into its pane of light, typing first idly, then rapidly, then idly again. Caroline never knew what he was doing, and she was too exhausted and demoralized to ask. She had no energy— not for a fight, and certainly not for a pep talk.

A house centipede kept finding its way into their kitchen sink. Adam's most proactive gesture each day was to gently fish it out and send it on its way, only for another (or the same one) to appear the next morning.

The weather stayed hot until November that year, the leaves stubbornly retaining their green before unceremoniously browning and falling all at once. One afternoon, Caroline made a decision. Something had to be done. She slipped into their room and lunged into bed beside her husband, and before he could clap the laptop closed or click away from what he was doing, she saw the screen. Two armored knights played chess in a murky throne room, a glinting ax hovering over each of their heads.

"Adam."

He closed the laptop, but he wouldn't look at her.

"Look at me."

She waited. Finally Adam turned so she could see his eyes, soft and filmed over with tears. Strands of his hair were greased against his scalp; he hadn't showered in days. He looked away again.

"I'm sorry," he mumbled. She could hardly hear him.

"I don't want you to be sorry," she said. "I just want you to try."

He let out a long breath.

"I don't know what to do."

"Just apply for things. Anything."

He shook his head.

"I'm persona non grata," he said. "No company I would want to work for is going to touch me."

"But technically you weren't even found liable," she said. "The lawsuit was settled out of court."

"It doesn't matter. I was one of the founders—one of the faces. There was the whole fucking *New York Magazine* piece, for Christ's sake. 'Did Pantheon Promise Too Much?' That headline, right over the blown-up snapshot of the adorable little dead girl—"

"They didn't make you sound so bad in the article," Caroline lied. "They almost made it sound like you were a whistle-blower."

"Please. The writer basically implied we put the gun in that poor mother's hand and helped her pull the trigger."

"Well, you were the one who warned everyone that the mental health screenings weren't stringent enough, and that it had been a mistake to use the likenesses of dead children. Didn't they quote you on that in the article?"

"I'm just lucky the law hasn't caught up to the fine details of VR technology yet. Otherwise I'd probably be in jail for manslaughter."

Caroline had known from the beginning that Pantheon was risky. It had been Adam's brainchild, a VR experience that connected grieving people with their deceased loved ones in order to provide closure. He had been inspired by his own relationship with his father, a feckless and marginally employed journalist who had died of pancreatic cancer when Adam was an angry teenager, before they'd had a chance to repair their relationship.

"I just kept thinking," Adam would say, "if only I had a chance to bring him back and show him how I've turned out, who I've become. Apologize to him, tell him I understand him better now. Or just, watch a ball game together and shoot the shit. You know?"

Pantheon's resonance with photography had helped Caroline overcome some of her initial misgivings. How were the company's aims so different from her own goals for her artistic work? It was all about bringing back a moment that, without the aid of a captured image, would be gone forever. In those early, heady days, the project brought Caroline and Adam closer together. They spent many long nights drinking wine, listening to music, and discussing the theoretical underpinnings of their mutual fascination with resurrecting what had been lost—Adam had even wanted to name the company Winter Garden, after Barthes's *Camera Lucida*, which Caroline had introduced him to, but his cofounders said no one would get the reference.

The name Pantheon was Adam's cofounders' idea, and months later it was also their idea to relax the restrictions on who could sign up for the experience. They'd been the ones who decided to open up the previously adults-only VR likeness policy, so that parents could grieve their dead children. That was what Adam claimed, anyway—that he'd never wanted to do it with kids, that the others had gone behind his back, and that by the time he found out it was too late.

Caroline still wasn't sure how much Adam had really protested the change. She knew that he liked to be in control. It was unlikely that the shift would have happened without his knowledge, if not his involvement. And before the suicide, the new market had netted Pantheon an enormous amount of money. Surely Adam had been in support of *that*.

But despite everything—despite her anger and exasperation, despite her deep disappointment in how their life together was turning out—Caroline still believed in her husband's fundamental goodness. Pantheon had given him purpose, and he had earnestly believed in its therapeutic possibilities. He never would have hurt anyone intentionally. He was the type of person who couldn't even kill a house centipede.

Besides, she wasn't really one to judge. It wasn't as if she'd always practiced perfect ethics in her own work.

"Your real sin was that you believed in the wrong people," said Caroline. "You were too trusting."

"It doesn't matter what my real sin was," Adam replied, rubbing his hands over his face. "The fact is that no one will let me forget what happened. It's going to be the first line of inquiry out of any potential employer's mouth: 'What are your thoughts on the bereaved mother who killed herself after becoming obsessed with your product? What were your takeaways from that setback?' And that's if I ever get an interview anywhere, which, again, I probably won't."

"You don't know that. And the reason I know that you don't know that is because you haven't even tried."

His eyes grew hard.

"Don't henpeck me."

"Don't be so weak."

"I'm doing the best I can."

"Are you?"

For a long moment he wouldn't answer her. Finally he sighed again.

"I feel terrible," he said. "You don't deserve any of this. You should be working on your art, not slaving away for these rich fucks. I mean, the shit that you go through on your commute, the shit on the news about the machete attacks—what am I doing, letting you take the train by yourself?"

"What else am I supposed to do?"

"I should be there. Protecting you."

"Well, you're welcome to escort me to work if it will make you feel useful, but that's not going to help with our finances."

"See, you were always the more resilient one. You can actually get things done. I don't even know why you're with me."

"Adam."

"I've doomed us both," he said. "I knew this would happen. I'm turning into my father."

Caroline tried to control her face. She did appreciate whenever Adam recognized her talent and her resilience—whenever he acknowledged that she deserved better. But she knew that whenever he began talking about turning into his father they were sliding inexorably down the path of self-indulgent self-flagellation.

"It's like—it's like I'm watching myself from afar," he said. "Like I'm dissociating."

"Adam."

"Like I'm trying to climb the cliff face of a mountain, and rocks start falling from above and I'm just watching them rain down on me. There's nothing I can do but watch."

They'd been here before—when he did his data entry stint at Mosaic and hated himself; when he'd reconnected with his college girlfriend and flown into a tailspin of doubt and regret; when he couldn't decide if he wanted to marry Caroline or run away by himself to some imagined cabin upstate. She'd never wanted to be here again, on the cliff face. She shook her head.

"But that's not what's happening," she said. "You can be in control, if you want to be. Rocks aren't literally falling on you."

When he turned to face her again, he was almost smiling.

"The imagination is a powerful thing."

Her rage was like two fists pressed against her temples.

"You think the solution's just going to fall in your fucking lap?" she shouted. "Is that it?"

But in the end, the solution did fall into his lap, just like one of his imaginary rocks. There was never a listing posted for the Corridor job, and Adam never applied for it. Caroline came home one night in February after feeding the Geller twins their keto dinner and found Adam sitting at the kitchen table in the dark, their single functional space heater humming at his feet. Caroline turned on the light, and Adam told her he'd been contacted by a headhunter.

"They found my résumé."

"Where?"

"I don't know. It's just out there, I guess."

She waited for him to say more. He looked at his hands.

"And?"

"They wanted to know if I was interested in interviewing with them."

She let out a breath she hadn't realized she'd been holding in.

"That's amazing! That's great news."

There was a pause that went on too long. Adam kept looking at his hands.

"Well. I told them I needed to think about it."

In the longer silence that followed they could hear the clink-clank of someone rummaging through the recycling bin on the curb, the laugh track on their neighbor's television.

"I'm sorry, I guess I just don't understand," Caroline said finally, her voice even. "What is it that you need to think about?"

Adam wouldn't look at her.

"Here, I have some thoughts," Caroline continued. "Here are some things you can think about. You can think about our rent. You can think about our credit card debt. You can think about us needing to eat. You can think about the fact that you've been out of work for six fucking *months* and now someone's finally throwing us a lifeline."

"But it's Corridor."

"So what?"

"They're the biggest company in the world, and I'll just be a cog in the machine. I won't have any control, or influence. They say they're about making the world a better place—the 'maximization of human potential' or whatever their marketing says—but I just know it's going to be the absolute most boring day-to-day grind you can possibly imagine."

"Boring is fine," said Caroline, trying to make him see reason. "Boring is a paycheck. Boring is health insurance. Boring is no lawsuits. I would kill for boring right about now, Adam."

"But I need to have a purpose!"

"Aren't I purpose enough?" she snapped. "Did you or did you not mean what you said about how I didn't deserve this? About how you wanted to protect me?"

"Of course I meant it."

"Then what else is there to think about?"

He sighed again.

"Okay," he said. "I'll tell them I'm interested. Even though I'm not."

"Are you interested in staying married to me?"

"Yes."

"Well then."

She got up and took a glass out of the cabinet, then went to the sink to fill it. She had already turned on the faucet when she noticed the jittery brown squiggle of the house centipede trying to scramble up the steel wall of the basin. The flood of cold water washed the creature down; she turned back to Adam before she could see it disappear into the drain.

"I'm sure it won't be as bad as whatever you're imagining," she said.

THERE WERE FIVE ROUNDS OF INTERVIEWS. THE FIRST FOUR rounds took place online; Adam would emerge from the bedroom afterward, sometimes drained, sometimes ebullient. When he left the apartment for the final interview, which took place at the Corridor headquarters and lasted an entire day, he still didn't know what position he was being interviewed for. Caroline had fallen asleep on the couch by the time he barged in their door.

"I got it," he belched.

His breath smelled like the syrup at the bottom of a recycling bin. Arms wheeling, he stumbled into the bedroom. She followed and found him kneeling on the floor, his head and upper body resting on her side of the bed, as if he had fallen asleep while praying.

"I got the job. They want me."

Caroline gasped and tried to hug him, but Adam shook her off. With a groan he hoisted himself up to lie diagonally across the bed, his shoes on her pillow.

"La, la, la," he sang to himself. "La, la, la. Whew. La, la, la."

And then:

"I don't know if I can do it."

Not this again. Not this, when they were so close to safety and comfort, so close to everything being okay. Caroline told herself to stay calm. No henpecking.

"You can do it," she said, joining him on the bed, rubbing his shoulder. "I believe in you."

He shook his head.

"I do," she said. "I love you so much."

"I love you, too. It's just—" He belched again. "What if—"

"What if what?"

He looked like a drowned man—pale, clammy, flabby in the face.

"What if I hate it?"

"You won't hate it. Nothing can be as bad as you sitting around all day."

"Or—what if I make the same mistakes?"

"What mistakes?"

He wouldn't answer. He thrashed his arms suddenly, then went slack again. He whimpered.

"You're not going to make the same mistakes," Caroline said, still not knowing what he had meant. "This is a fresh start. A new beginning."

He was already shaking his head. She hated when he did this.

"It's a job," she pressed on. "A job in your industry, which you spent years training for and working in, and up until very recently you claimed to love. A job at one of the biggest, richest, most successful companies in the world."

"La, la, la," Adam sang again, his eyes squeezed shut. "Whew. La, la, la."

There was a long silence.

"You said we would have a family," Caroline whispered. "You said you wanted that."

"I do," said Adam. "You're my family."

"That's not enough," she said, tears coming into her voice. She knew what happened to childless couples and small families. "That's not what we agreed on. You said we would have children. At least two."

He didn't answer for so long that she thought he'd fallen asleep. Then he lurched into a sitting position and looked at her.

"Okay," he said finally.

"Okay?"

"I'll do it."

"Do what?"

"What do you think? I'll take the job. For us."

Relief washed over her. She felt dizzy with it, shivery all over.

"Really?"

"Yes."

He fell backward on the bed with a grunt, made no move to help her as she untucked his shirt and undid the buckle of his belt. She had long suspected that he enjoyed making her do all the work.

Not anymore, she thought. *Not anymore.*

She was on top, throwing her hips back and forth the way they both liked, when he grabbed her by the ribs—a move so rare and exciting that she almost came right then, until she realized that he was gagging, retching. He heaved her off him, then careened into the bathroom—naked, doubled over, cock flapping helplessly like a spring-loaded doorstop—and vomited all over the floor.

FOR THE FIRST FEW MONTHS HE WORKED AT CORRIDOR, ADAM continued to be miserable. He no longer had the time to lie on their floor, but he took every opportunity to make his unhappiness known. They'd be wrapping up a silent dinner, the bottle of wine finished; Adam would set down his phone with a sigh and begin to complain about yet another NDA or some new contract he'd had to sign—one with names and figures blacked out, another that stipulated he submit to medical testing at any time—and Caroline would nod and reach for his hand and tell him everything was going to be okay.

Then, that spring, around the time Adam was put on the research and development team with Noa, Perry, and Blaise, his depression lifted. Suddenly, he had friends—closer friends than he'd had in years. Late nights at the office turned into late nights out. They all seemed intensely bonded for the relatively brief amount of time they had worked together, but Caroline had been to art school, and she knew that high pressure in close quarters was a recipe for fast intimacy.

Caroline was rarely included in these late nights out, and when she was, she found she had little to say to these new friends. But what did any of that matter? Adam was working hard, and he was happy. Not just happy, proud of the work he was doing, filled with newfound purpose, even though to Caroline the work sounded just as deadly boring as Adam had originally feared.

Then again, what did she know? He couldn't go into much detail, not with all the NDAs he'd signed.

Adam began to wear his Corridor gear on weekends, slate-gray high-performance T-shirts and ball caps emblazoned with the black half-open door of the company logo. Caroline stopped assuming his long silences were depressive sulks, stopped being surprised when, after one of these long silences, he'd speak to her in an upbeat tone. They paid off their credit card. They paid off the rest of her student loans in one cathartic swoop. The balance in their account kept growing, the deposits accumulating faster than they could spend them. They opened new investment accounts, and those balances grew even faster. Caroline stopped checking them every day. She put in her notice with Devorah and the Gellers and returned to her own creative work. They weren't on the cliff face anymore.

At least she thought they weren't. It would be a few more months before she found out about the texts with the college girlfriend, and the meetings—in bars, in the college girlfriend's apartment—that resulted from those texts.

Caroline forgave him. They'd never really discussed non-monogamy in any practical terms as something they might do, but she knew that Adam's new friends were involved in that kind of lifestyle, and that it was actually pretty common these days. Once Caroline and Adam really talked about it after the fact, they concluded that it wasn't the sex so much as the secrets that had hurt her.

He was truly sorry for that, he said. He'd been deeply confused. He had made a mistake.

She let the cool water carry her downstream. They would stay together. The late-night theoretical conversations had reentered their routine, and even if they weren't quite as frequent or quite the same as before, at least Caroline felt like she had some version of the old Adam back.

She loved him. They were each other's family, after all.

A year passed. They started therapy, and Adam only saw his college girlfriend once more that winter, and only for one drink—to say goodbye, he said. Caroline believed him. Adam made it abundantly clear that he was choosing her, his wife—coming home from the bar and kissing her, undressing her, asking over and over again how he could be such an idiot, when this was all he had ever wanted.

They stayed married, and the following summer they spent a week on one of the lesser-known Cycladic islands. When Caroline thought of that trip she would remember the colors blue and yellow, Adam's great amusement at the contrast between the endless ultramarine ocean and the cups Caroline filled with her urine each morning, testing for peak fertility.

They felt lucky it all worked the way it was supposed to on the first try.

CHAPTER 5

Birth. White light, small hands reaching into a void that resolved as a blue-masked face, then a mobile of cumulus sheep and clouds overhead. Suddenly crawling, walking, then time sped forward even faster. Crayons and a kiddie pool, the kick of a soccer ball into a net, a flock of mortarboards in the air, a faceless bride and groom clinched at an altar, more births, a house, a puppy aging into a dog with a grizzled muzzle, reading glasses and a recliner, hair snowed over in seconds, blue-masked faces dissolving into a void again as a life blinked out into white. Delicate text appearing as the fog cleared:

Life goes fast. Get more of it.

And then:

MOSAIC.

Another blink, and a computer-animated redhead stood weeping at a graveside, holding a baby in her arms.

My husband! a pink speech bubble screamed. *Oh, my husband!*

The cemetery became a house with holes in the walls where the windows should be, the woman and baby shivering as snow piled on the sofa.

Add curtains? a pop-up asked brightly. *Or start a cozy fire?*

A fire roared to life in the hearth, and the baby flew from the mother's arms into the flames, grill marks appearing instantly across his belly.

My baby! Oh, my baby!

A giant check for one million dollars crashed through the wall, knocking the woman and baby to the ground, where a puddle of blood began to spread. Game over.

Think you know how to help a mother? Think again!

Caroline could not remember if there had always been a television in the living room. She could not remember seeing it there on the wall when they had first arrived at the house. But her memory was faulty, and she suspected that if she had asked anyone else in the house, they would have told her it had always been there.

Perhaps it *had* been there since Friday, just muted, or turned off all together. It was on now, playing a loop of fever dreams. Caroline sat on the couch, stunned from lack of sleep, nursing. She knew she had seen these ads at least a few times now. *Get more with Mosaic. Think you know? Think again. Get more.*

The redhead was a character in a different story now. Drenched in mud, she spied on her Lazarus husband, who was now fondling the spherical tits and ass of a naked blond cyborg.

Suffer in silence? screamed the speech bubble. *Or seek revenge?*

"Oh, I love this one," said Noa between mouthfuls of hard-boiled egg. She lay belly-down on the couch closest to the screen. "I know the developer and she's an absolute sicko. The best."

The redhead's arms turned into chain saws; she hacked at cheating husband and slut cyborg, cleaving their bodies into pieces, their mingled blood a firework display of red and black. Then the show they'd been watching came back on—a compilation of viral footage of violent customer meltdowns, some recent, others vintage. Noa sighed as they watched a mother with two crying toddlers hurl a chair at a teenage girl behind a fast-food counter.

"Remember when there used to actually be shows on television?"

"No," said Taryn from the other couch, her cheek resting on Nori's flank.

"Of course you don't," said Noa. "I meant Caroline."

"Sure," said Caroline, patting Gabriel's back. She still needed to burp him, even though he was supposed to be outgrowing the need to be burped. "I even remember when people worked in fast-food restaurants."

"And now we get this," said Noa, gesturing at the screen, where the teenage girl had taken out a gun. "Entertainment made from the fraying of the social fabric."

She swallowed the last of her egg.

"I fucking love it."

Hello, said the television, startling them. *I'm glad to hear you're enjoying yourself. Can I do anything else for you?*

"No thanks!" said Noa. "All good!"

Suddenly, Caroline felt hot spit-up flow down her shoulder blades. Too abruptly, she tipped Gabriel back so she could look at him. His lips were white with curdled milk; she could have sworn he looked satisfied with himself. He was supposed to be outgrowing the reflux, too. The bite on his cheek looked worse today, more like a rash. Maybe it was getting infected. Caroline didn't have a towel. The spit-up began to dry and congeal on her back.

"Fuck!"

I'm sorry, said the television. *I didn't quite get that. Did you mean—*

"Oh let me, let me!"

Then Taryn had taken the baby from her, and Noa was handing her a dish towel.

"Go clean yourself up," said Noa. "We've got him."

Caroline hesitated.

"Really! Go!"

All the way upstairs and into her bathroom, Caroline worried about leaving Gabriel alone with them. What did they know about babies? Taryn was practically still a baby herself. How would they manage if he spit up again? If he started to scream?

Then she let the worry go. It would be fine. And it was so lovely to take her time, so luxurious to shower without listening for sounds of distress, to let someone else handle the baby for a little while.

When she came back into the living room Gabriel was sitting in Taryn's lap, his back against her breasts, cooing and chirping. On the screen, a kaleidoscope of teenage girls in silver bikinis and head-to-toe blue body paint performed a choreographed dance of deranged pop-and-locks, their arms and hips slipping in and out of their sockets.

"Come into town with us," said Noa. "We need to stock up on some things."

Caroline considered the offer. Taryn lifted Gabriel to hide her face behind his butt, spoke in a cloying nasal ventriloquist's voice.

"Come on, Mama," she squeaked. "Say yes."

Caroline despised the cuteness, and she hated being called Mama. She also wanted to leave the house.

"You think so, Gabe?" she asked, forcing a hysterical brightness into her voice. "You think we should say yes?"

INSIDE THE GRAY-SHINGLED MANSION OF THE GROCERY, TARYN stood open-armed before a wall of greenery, her eyes shut as mist from hidden sprinklers and an acoustic remix of "Umbrella" emanated from somewhere behind the kale and chard. Noa filled her basket with stone fruit and tins of fish, then eyed the vast terrarium filled with sweets. Caroline watched as a pale, tattoo-laden hand reached into the display case to remove a cake iced with the melting globes of red and gold rosebuds, their green leaves so dark they looked black against the white base.

"Is that everything?"

"Didn't Jane ask for parsley? Or purslane?"

"And Wynn wanted more cheese. Burrata and blue."

"Maybe we should get more eggs. I keep craving hard-boiled eggs."

Noa and Taryn went on like that, until they'd been wandering the store for almost half an hour. Caroline lost track of them. Alone with Gabriel, back in the produce section, she watched her own severed hand burrow itself into a heap of jade grapes. She popped one into her mouth, then bent to the stroller to check on Gabriel.

He was quiet, but not asleep. His eyes were wide, staring into the overhead lights. Caroline palmed several more grapes and crushed them against her back teeth.

"You shouldn't steal."

Caroline looked up and saw a towheaded boy, one of the children from Camp Haven. There were dappled red stains all down the front of his romper, as if he'd been lying in a berry patch.

"I'm not stealing."

"I saw you." His voice was husky, a poor match for his cherubic face.

The boy narrowed his eyes at Caroline. Caroline narrowed her eyes back.

"You're right," she said finally. "Stealing is wrong. I shouldn't do it."

"It's bad for your baby," the boy said. "It's evil."

Before Caroline could respond, the boy had vanished behind a pyramid of pyramid-shaped watermelons. She blinked after the boy, trying to decide if she'd heard him correctly.

"Little shithead," she muttered.

Something made Caroline look to her left; for a moment, she thought she was looking in a mirror. A blonde with a body like hers, the same bug-eye sunglasses, the same watchful stillness. Only this woman didn't have a baby in a stroller. She had a toddler by the hand, a miniature copy of herself who was just as still, just as watchful. Mother and child stared at mother and child. Caroline scowled and bent to the stroller.

"That's right, Gabe," she said under her breath. "Everyone has an opinion, don't they?"

She found Noa and Taryn in line for the checkout. As Caroline got closer, she saw that their register was staffed by the teenage heads—the blond brunette, the black-haired redhead, the redheaded blonde, still in their heavy makeup and oversize T-shirts, their jaws working wads of gum as they struggled to ring up someone's bag of bagels. Caroline looked at the other registers and saw that they too were manned by at least two or three teenagers each. It was meant to be quaint—a historical re-enactment of low-skilled summer jobs, before the self-checkout kiosks were everywhere. It seemed excessive to have two or three people working the same register. Then again, these teenagers were so obviously out of their depth, so hesitant and confused even with the headsets and holographic screens to help them, that Caroline figured the whole operation would fail if they didn't have each other for support. She braced herself for the girls to recognize her and Gabriel. They did, their painted faces riven by manic smiles.

"Caro!"

"Gabey!"

Noa and Taryn turned to Caroline, puzzled. Caroline shook her head.

"We met the other day."

"We were on the beach, pretending to be dead," explained the blond brunette. "Just cutoff heads, you know, like you do?"

"Right," said Noa. "Of course."

"And Caro found us," said the black-haired redhead. "She was going to let us babysit for little Gabey Baby."

"Until he got bitten by something," added the redheaded blond. "And Caro had to go—"

Caroline shot them a look. The girls smiled.

"I told you," said Caroline. "How can I trust you to babysit if I don't even know your names?"

"That's right," said Taryn, playing along with the interrogation, even though she was clearly charmed by the girls. "How can we trust you?"

"You can trust us," said the black-haired redhead. "Promise."

Suddenly the register lit up and began to shriek, the holographic screens dissolving into blue-and-white fireworks. The girls bounced on their bare heels and clapped their hands.

"Oh my god! Y'all are our *one thousandth* customers of the summer!"

The girls began to dance, their self-contained yet coordinated pop-and-locks mirroring the holographic figures that emerged to dance on the conveyor belt, which themselves recalled the dancers on the television at the house. In the stroller, Gabriel thrashed his head from side to side, trying to see what was happening. Caroline gritted her teeth.

"Have we paid yet?" she asked. "We need to go."

"You're all set!" said the girls. "See you later!"

"Maybe."

As they left the store Gabriel began to complain. Caroline thought that if she pushed the stroller fast enough, she could outrun the meltdown, that the rumble of the wheels on the boardwalk would lull him to sleep. No such luck. The midday sun was oppressively hot, there was no shade, and Noa and Taryn were moving too slowly, taking their time with the bags, laughing about *kids these days*, and *oh my god*, don't you just feel *so fucking old* when you see them, the *clothes* and the *dancing*, and oh *please*, Taryn, you're what, twenty-*two*? Twenty-*five* next month, and I'm still a rotting *corpse* compared to those girls, well we're *all* rotting corpses, aren't we, and now Gabriel was screaming, again. Caroline closed her eyes and brought her hands to her temples. Then Noa and Taryn were on either side of her.

"I—I just—" Caroline stammered, eyes beginning to spill. "I don't know. He's normally better than this in the stroller. I mean, he's normally better than this in general. I have no idea why it's been such a struggle out here."

"Look," said Noa, putting her hand on Caroline's shoulder. "All I know is that you're doing a great job, okay? I don't think women get to hear that enough."

Caroline nodded tearfully.

"Seriously, I couldn't do what you do. You're killing it, as far as I'm concerned."

Taryn leaned down, peered into Gabriel's red, distorted face. He cried louder.

"Does he want to be held?" she asked.

"Probably not."

"Can I try?"

Caroline could tell that Taryn was one of those people who thought she had some kind of magic touch with children. She would have explained that it was something in her nature, despite her total inexperience and total disinterest in ever having children of her own. A manic pixie dream aunt.

"Okay."

But sure enough, as soon as Taryn picked him up, Gabriel stopped screaming, stopped crying. It was beginning to seem like everyone in the house could calm her son, except for Caroline.

Taryn beamed. She wasn't holding Gabriel the right way; one hand clasped on the curve of his butt, the other on his neck, his face smushed into her collarbone, the rash on his cheek angry and raw. Caroline the mother was concerned and wanted to correct her; Caroline the photographer liked the weirdness of the pose. They were all wrong together, and she loved it. She wanted Taryn to keep holding him, just like that.

Caroline the photographer won. Back at the house, she asked Taryn to keep holding Gabriel out on the deck while she got her camera. She photographed them together in their perfect awkwardness, moving them in and out of patches of sun and shade, directing Taryn even as her grip grew more tenuous and Gabriel began to struggle, taking frame after frame, shooting as Taryn's smile stretched wider and wider, well past the moment Gabriel began to cry again.

THERE WAS NO CELL SERVICE DOWN AT THE OCEAN. They realized it one by one, a series of frustrated epiphanies rippling down the row of chairs and towels that they'd arranged just so in a spot just far enough from other beachgoers, whose folding shelters and cabanas were crowded between the flapping red flags of the swimming area.

"Ha!" crowed Taryn, triumphant. "See? The universe is telling us something."

"What?" said Jane. "That I need to suffer more on my vacation?"

"That we're meant to be unplugged out here!"

"The universe isn't telling us anything," said Wynn. He wore a white baseball cap, *Unprecedented Times* embroidered in red cursive above the brim. "Other than the fact that someone fucked up when they designed the infrastructure out here."

"Maybe it was intentional."

"Even worse."

They gave up on their phones and stashed them away in their tote bags. Blaise and Wynn began a game of paddleball in the surf. Perry remained in his beach chair, reading a paperback he'd found in the house, some pop psychology nonsense about the history of humankind and evolutionary imperatives.

"Well, *I* think it's good," said Taryn. She lay flat on her towel, her tanned stomach stretched concave between her hip bones. "I promised Blaise I wouldn't be so, you know, *content*-driven out here. That I wouldn't post."

"You *promised* him?" Jane scoffed. "Okay, Serena Joy."

"I don't know who or what that is. Anyway, what I really meant was I promised *myself*. I want to be present. Like, why would I be on my phone when everyone who matters is here? You miss everything important when you're just focused on documenting it."

"Well, I certainly don't feel the need to share my vacations with the world anymore," said Noa. "But I need to keep up with what's happening out there. I don't need to unplug, because I'm always unplugged from what doesn't matter. Escapism is just another word for ignorance."

Taryn sat up and took a deck of cards out of her bag, shuffled them, and began to deal them out to herself, Noa, and Jane on their patchwork of towels.

"I'm not playing," said Jane, standing up. "I'll be in the water."

"Sorry," said Taryn. "I forgot."

She turned to Caroline.

"Play?"

Caroline hesitated when she saw that the cards were unlike any deck she'd seen before, their faces decorated with strange images: a family gathered around a table with a winged eye at the center, a man in a top hat and a woman with the head of a cat holding each other in a bed, a baby's face contained in a blazing black sun.

"I don't know this game."

"Wynn taught us," said Noa. "He found a deck in the house the first night we were here and got really excited. Apparently it's a traditional island thing, or something. He called it Fortunes."

"It's actually really easy," said Taryn. "You start with all the cards you're going to have. Each card has a value, and you count down from highest to lowest on each hand."

"But the highest number has the lowest value," said Noa. "The baby face is most valuable, and there's only one."

"Your goal is to be the first one out."

"How do I go out?" asked Caroline, confused.

"You get rid of all your cards."

"If you have the baby, you can end the game immediately, but only if it's your last card."

"And if someone else gets rid of all their cards while you still have the baby, you automatically lose."

"What happens when you lose?"

"Nothing," they said at the same time, then looked at each other.

"You just start over," Noa clarified.

They either didn't explain the game well enough, or Caroline was just no good at it. After the third botched hand they gave up. Caroline had ended up with the baby each time, unable to get rid of it in time to win.

Noa and Taryn ran for the water, whooping as they threw themselves into the explosion of cold spray, drifting out beyond the breakers to where Jane floated on her back.

Caroline didn't go with them. She couldn't. Gabriel was sleeping on the big towel under the shade of the umbrella. She couldn't remember how long he'd been asleep. If the nap stretched much longer than two hours, he'd be a mess for the rest of the day, and she'd be in trouble at bedtime.

It had probably been longer than two hours. Almost definitely.

She didn't wake him. She lay beside him and pretended to doze as well, listening to the irritating plock, plock, plock of the ball as Wynn and Blaise passed it from paddle to paddle. She kept opening her eyes to glance at Perry, who was still reading beside her. After a while Perry put his book down, took off his sunglasses, and ran to the water. Caroline watched him dive in, the tight dark arc of his body swallowed up by a wave. She closed her eyes again. Plock, plock, plock.

Then she gasped, shocked by the cold wet torso beside her. Perry laughed.

"Now you're *trying* to startle me," she said.

"Who said I wasn't before?"

"You're getting my towel wet."

He rolled away from her and into the hot sand, coating himself in a sugary crust.

"Better?"

"Better."

"Good," he said, propping himself up on his forearms. "I aim to please."

This was too much. Caroline sat up and faced him.

"I know this game," she said, her voice even.

"How do I win?"

"You can't."

"Why not?"

She sighed.

"Look," she said. "I'm sure if we actually tried to have a real conversation, we'd have nothing to talk about. That's always how these things go."

"You haven't even given me a chance."

She didn't know how to answer him. He stretched an arm toward his sunglasses and put them back on. They watched the others frolicking in the waves and surf. Plock, plock, plock. An older couple was walking down the beach toward them, holding hands. The woman was thin and frail, her flesh so mottled with veins that it looked like gray stone, mummified by the loose bandages wrapped around her shins. The man was short and stocky, with a discreet zippered scar down his breastbone.

"I can't believe your husband left you out here all alone."

Caroline shrugged.

"He has to work."

"Well, I would never. No matter how high-profile the assignment."

"Maybe that's why they don't trust you with the high-profile assignments."

"Maybe."

The older couple lay their towels just past Caroline and Perry, then lay down on their backs. After a moment the man rested his hand on the woman's inner thigh, palpated her there, as if to check that she was still breathing, still alive.

Rotting corpses, all of us, thought Caroline.

She lay down again and closed her eyes. Plock, plock, plock. She dozed again, allowed herself to drift into thoughts of Perry's palm on her waist; her palm on Perry's thigh. In a dream—she was sure it was a dream—she lifted her hand, only to bump her knuckles against Perry's. They drew away from each other.

"I was just—"

"Yeah?"

"—my camera."

She rolled over in the opposite direction to retrieve it from her bag, then stood on shaking legs. She took a few photographs of the baby that weren't very compelling. His bug bite was getting better, no longer visually interesting. Perry took off his sunglasses and looked up at her with frightening sincerity.

"Should I pose?"

"No."

CAROLINE REMEMBERED A COLD AND BLASTED WINTER DAY, the city sidewalks white with salt. Nothing to photograph. The man taking a smoke break beside his halal cart saw the camera hanging from her neck like a medal and invited her up to his apartment, just upstairs—that window, right there.

"Your loft?" She laughed. "What about your cart?"

He waved to a man on the corner, who nodded back at him.

"My cousin. He'll watch for me."

She didn't believe him, not even as they ascended the tenement stairs. But it was his apartment, or at least he had keys to it. She stopped worrying about the details once they were inside. She had always wanted to see what wasn't available to her, what she wasn't supposed to see, to capture the moment and inhabit it later, alone: This happened, now it's gone. Light poured in from the window that he'd pointed to from the street; its frame soft with layers of paint, its lower pane cracked, the breakage in the arcing shape of a distant bird. He took off his clothes. Deep surgical scars segmented his chest into the territories of an unknown country, evidence of a primordium implant done on the cheap. He lay down on the mattress on the floor.

"Tell me what you want me to do."

The pictures were no good; she'd been too excited to pose him, to compose. But there would be others.

Some of them she found in bars, on the subway, at parties. Out in the world. Some of them she found online.

this is unusual, but...

actually you're the third woman to ask me this week

ha
thinking about hiring an agent, actually
that might be wise
hey, you can say you knew me when

When he arrived at her apartment, he was shorter than she'd expected, but he'd brought a bottle of Sancerre. They drank it on her fire escape and told each other their best stories—his childhood clinging to the lower-middle-class rung of an upper-middle-class suburb of Boston, her slightly more precarious upbringing on an even lower rung just outside of Minot. Their fathers were dead (cancer, both), and their poor mothers were crazy (hypochondria, religion).

"How do I look?" Adam asked, pouting and contorting himself ridiculously against the flaking iron of the fire escape, until Caroline was afraid that he would fall. "Should I pose?"

She shook her head, laughing. She wasn't getting anything good—it was all a joke to him, a game—but back then she didn't care.

He'd been more serious once they were inside again. Even after she'd stripped down to her bra and panties, he lingered over the smattering of prints tacked on the corkboard over the folding table that passed for her desk.

"This one's great," he'd exclaimed, peering at a double portrait of two shirtless teenage boys, one standing and one sitting. Black shadows sliced up their bodies as the standing one, snarling slightly, ran a rough hand through the hair of the seated one, who looked beseechingly at the viewer. "Reminds me of a Caravaggio. Wait, don't tell me—David and Goliath?"

"Exactly," said Caroline. "That's the reference."

"I'm sure all your dates get it right away."

"They don't, actually," she said. "You might be the first."

"First and last?"

"Let's not get ahead of ourselves," she said, pulling him down into her bed.

She saw too late that she'd gotten too close, standing over him, feet inches from his waist. Perry grabbed her by the ankle and held on; she pressed the shutter, recording the desperate grip, the frame hardly composed. This happened, now it's gone.

"Tonight," he said.

"You can't be serious."

"I am."

Caroline kicked her foot free with a forced laugh and walked down to the surf. She thought she would photograph the others at play, but there was nothing interesting to capture.

The children from the camp were in the ocean, crawl-stroking westward. Caroline watched them bob up and down, their torsos appearing suddenly as if under glass in the clear green wall of the waves. The water seemed too rough for them to be training like that. On the horizon, she could just make out the uncertain smudges of container ships—there was a long line of them, all waiting for permission to come into port. A seagull floated by, some creature wriggling desperately in the trap of its beak.

"Where's your baby?"

It was the woman from the grocery store, the one who looked like her. She held her daughter by the hand; they were dressed in matching white cover-ups, the thin fabric wet and translucent at the hem. Caroline frowned.

"He's just up there," she said, gesturing vaguely up the beach. "Napping."

"How old?"

"Three months. Three and a half months."

"Ah," said the woman. "Goodbye newborn stage."

"Thank god."

The woman laughed ruefully.

"You'll miss it," said the woman, adjusting her grip on her daughter's hand and inclining her head up the beach, toward where Caroline had gestured. "She's too old now for me to just leave her like that."

"I haven't left him," said Caroline.

"When she wakes up, she always comes to find me, wherever I am. She'd follow me straight out the door and into traffic in the morning if I wasn't careful. Her father says we should drug her, but I don't know. I don't want to take any chances with this one."

Caroline waited for the woman to laugh, to say that she was joking. She didn't.

"Well, not my baby," said Caroline, chuckling awkwardly. "He just lies there and screams."

"I can't even remember those days. They disappear so fast."

"I wish they'd disappear faster, to be honest."

The woman turned to look at Caroline, and for a moment Caroline clearly saw her own face. Then the moment passed, and the woman looked like herself, a stranger, again.

"They will."

WHEN SHE CAME DOWNSTAIRS AFTER PUTTING Gabriel to bed that night she found Taryn, Blaise, and Jane in the living room. The television was on, tuned to a channel that was programmed entirely with old commercials.

Your money is also under attack! Not by fireballs, but by bills and inflation!

Nori lay under the glass coffee table, nostrils flaring and tail thumping in erratic bursts as she dreamed.

"Where's everyone else?" asked Caroline.

Jane looked up and arched an eyebrow.

"They went out to the yacht club," said Blaise. "You just missed them."

"Oh." Caroline tried to hide her disappointment. "I didn't know they were planning to go."

"I don't think there was a plan," said Taryn. "They just went."

"Drink?" asked Blaise. "I made daiquiris."

"Okay."

Jane was watching Caroline, smiling a little. Caroline chided herself for being foolish. Even if she'd known they were going out, what would she have done? Asked Perry to stay at the house with her? Gone with them? How could she, when she had no babysitter?

She sat down next to Taryn, who yawned, stretching so that her fingertips grazed Caroline's shoulder. She giggled, then seemed to yelp in pain, but it was only a hiccup. Blaise returned from the kitchen with Caroline's drink and sat down next to her on her other side, closer than he needed to. He smelled of cloves and organ meat.

Two years ago, she was the physician who admitted me into the psych ward. Tonight, we join forces on Dancing with the Stars!

Taryn inched closer to Caroline. She was wearing her robe, but Caroline could see she was naked underneath. She and Blaise were looking at each other, over Caroline. Blaise had his arm on the back of the couch, behind Caroline's shoulders. Their bodies were warm. It would have been so easy to lean into their embrace, to let whatever was about to happen just happen. Caroline closed her eyes for a moment, then opened them again. Jane was still staring at her from across the room.

Caroline stood up.

"Actually, I think it's bedtime for me," she announced, yawning theatrically. "I'm so tired."

She thought the others might protest, but they only shrugged. As she turned to go upstairs Taryn and Blaise poured themselves onto the other couch, on either side of Jane, beneath the television screen. The Mosaic ad was on again. Birth. White light, small hands reaching into a void that resolved into a blue-masked face, then a mobile of cumulus sheep and clouds overhead. Blaise licked Jane's neck. Crawling, walking, crayons and a kiddie pool, the kick of a soccer ball into a net. Taryn's hands eased Jane's sweatpants over her hip bones. A flock of mortarboards tossed in the air, a faceless bride and groom in a clinch at an altar, a puppy aging into a dog with a grizzled muzzle. Hands and mouths, opening and closing. Hair snowed over in seconds, blue-masked faces dissolving into a void again as life blinked out into white. Jane's body was limp, yielding and resigned, her gray eyes closed now, no gaze to confront the viewer.

Caroline told herself to look away and go up to her room. She told herself over and over again, even as she remained motionless for several more minutes, hovering there on the stairs, watching.

SHE HADN'T BEEN ASLEEP FOR LONG WHEN SHE thought she heard a baby crying. Her baby, of course. For Caroline there were no other babies, in dreams or otherwise. Just her Gabriel—drooling, cooing, crying—in all his maddening perfection. That dark hair, those dark eyes. Sometimes she still couldn't believe she had made such a perfect creature. And he was right there, crying for her and only her—his mother.

"Gabriel?" she murmured groggily. "Gabey?"

Smiling to herself, still dreaming, Caroline opened her eyes and looked straight at the shadow of a man looming in her doorway.

No. She wasn't dreaming. She was in the spaceship house on the island, and there was a man in her room.

A man she didn't know.

She screamed.

The shadow lurched forward, then back, turning and vanishing down the hall as a thunder of footsteps swelled up the curve of the stairs. When the women came running in, Caroline was kneeling on the floor, clutching Gabriel, pressing his face into her neck. Someone turned on the light, and they all blinked in the sudden glare of the illuminated white walls.

"Caro!"

"Oh my god!"

"What the fuck!"

They crouched beside Caroline and kept their hands on her as they listened to the racket of bodies blundering through the rooms below, shouts chasing the intruder out the side door. In another moment the men arrived, out of breath but grinning.

"It was just some drunk guy who got lost and thought it was his house," said Wynn as he burst in, tossing his head to flip his hair out of his eyes. "Totally harmless."

"He could hardly make it down the ramp," said Blaise. "Slid down on his ass, went away singing and yammering to himself."

Perry stood in the doorway, as if to guard it. Of the men, he alone seemed concerned. He looked at Caroline.

"Are you okay?"

She had to be okay, for Gabriel's sake. After the shock of his mother screaming and grabbing him from his bed, he seemed to have cried himself out. He was resting his head against her chest, peering at the others, his eyelashes matted with tears. Caroline took a ragged breath and tried to quiet the banging of her heart.

"I think so," she said.

The others looked at each other.

"We have to stay with her," said Noa.

"Duh!" said Taryn.

"Protect her."

"And Gabey."

The men nodded then, suddenly sober with responsibility.

"No one is leaving this room for the rest of the night!" said Blaise.

Jane rolled her eyes.

"Nothing gets you guys off like being the hero," she said. "It's pathological."

"Exactly," said Wynn. "I almost want him to come back so I can be the hero again."

"Well, you can station yourself outside, then," said Noa, putting her arm around Caroline. "Because he's not getting anywhere near Caroline."

Caroline smiled then, grateful. Maybe Adam had been right about his friends. They were her friends, too.

Someone suggested they watch the sunrise. They dragged blankets and bedding out onto Caroline's deck and lay down on the chaises and dew-soaked planks. Gabriel slept on Caroline's chest. Darkness gaped above them, the vault of the sky spattered with stars.

"So has that always been a regular thing out here?" Jane asked. "Drunk people wandering into each other's houses?"

"I mean, kind of," said Wynn. "In the town where *I* spent summers, definitely. There were lots of wild parties, especially on the weekends, and no one locked their doors. I don't know about Haven, though."

"Seems unlikely, based on what you've told us," said Perry. "You make it sound like they were more the pearl-clutching types."

"Nah, they had their own kinds of parties," said Wynn. "Weird shit."

"Like what?"

"Oh, I don't know. All we heard were rumors, which were probably made-up. Although—no, never mind."

"What?"

"You know that big wilderness area we saw on the ferry coming in? It's a national park. When my uncle was a teenager, he swore that he and his friends saw some kind of ritual or ceremony in the woods there. Like, naked people sitting in a circle around a fire holding cups of blood, streaks of it all over their bodies. Some kind of drawings on the ground."

"Seriously?"

"That's what they said, but no one believed them. They were tripping their faces off, which was more or less the norm for them."

"Still though," said Noa. "That's a *very* specific vision."

"Come on, babe," said Wynn. "Want me to share some of the visions *you've* had on your ayahuasca adventures?"

"Not particularly."

"It's creepy, though," said Taryn. "I mean, should we even be playing that card game?"

"Fortunes?"

"Yeah. It's almost like it summoned something."

There was a longer silence. They all looked up at the sky, waiting for the moment it would begin to pale at its lower edge.

"It was just some drunk idiot." Wynn yawned. "Trust me."

It was still much too early for the sunrise. The dark and empty spaces between their words expanded, their voices fading into the night as, one by one, they fell asleep. Caroline looked over at Perry and Jane, who were bundled together in one of the chaises, their unconscious faces stacked one on top of the other like discarded masks. She crept back into her room and laid Gabriel carefully in his bassinet, her hands on his torso until she was sure he hadn't woken up. Then she lay down on the bed and waited for sleep to take her.

But she couldn't sleep. Her thoughts were a maelstrom of anxiety, a storm that wouldn't subside. If an intruder could get in, what else could happen? Was this town, this island, even safe? She remembered what Wynn had said, about no one locking their doors. She sat up.

Had anyone locked *their* doors?

They really should, shouldn't they? Now that people were wandering in? No matter what the island tradition was.

Should she check?

She was afraid to go downstairs, but she knew she had to.

She should check.

Just to be safe.

Caroline got out of bed. She looked at the dark pile of Gabriel, the dark piles of dirty clothing and wet towels that had accumulated on the floor. Gabriel was still asleep, breathing evenly. The piles on the floor did not move.

The house was lightless, silent; glass walls let the night in. She moved through the huge blue darkness like a fish in a tank, trying each sliding glass door.

Locked.

Locked.

Unlocked. The door slid open easily, as if in relief, as if it had been waiting impatiently for the touch of her hand.

Good thing she had checked.

She should have locked the door and gone back upstairs to bed, but something invisible in the night beckoned to her, calling her outside. She stood on the deck and looked up to the moon emerging from behind the clouds.

"'Mother!'"

She froze, her heart pounding.

"'*My* mother,'" whispered a different voice. "It's '*My* mother.' Try it again."

"'My mother!'"

"Keep going."

"'During the night I wandered about in the midst of omens, and there came out stars in the heavens.'"

Caroline followed the sound of the voices down the ramp, her feet moving from the deck to the soft, cold sand. In the moonlight she could see the children in their pajamas—some sitting cross-legged, some standing and facing each other, their small forms grouped in careful arrangements on the proscenium of the cove.

"'He fell upon me,'" a child said, pointing at the sky while the others watched. "'I bore him but he was too heavy for me. I summoned the land to assemble unto him, that heroes might kiss his feet.'"

"What are you doing?"

The children stopped and looked at Caroline. A girl with long white-blond hair spoke.

"It's rehearsal."

"For our play," another child added.

"You have to come," said the first girl. "It's tomorrow night."

"It's—" said Caroline. "What time is it?"

"We don't know."

Caroline didn't know either.

"It's so late," she said.

The standing children turned back to face each other. The girl with white-blond hair nodded once, and the children who had been sitting got up and began to run in figure eights, bringing their arms up and down, as if their limbs were lifted and dropped by a breeze only they could feel.

"'Heroes kiss his feet,'" they cried, some of them snickering through their lines. "'Thou shalt spare him. Thou shalt lead him to me.'"

"Where are your parents?" Caroline asked.

They ignored her. The dancers halted, stretched their hands toward the girl with white-blond hair.

"'My mother, I have seen another dream,'" she said, looking directly at Caroline. "'I beheld my likeness in the street.'"

Caroline shook her head. Maybe she was the one dreaming.

Closer to the bay, past the child actors, she could see the shape of an animal. It was the doe again with her twin fawns, one with the missing eye. The doe stood at the water's edge, waiting, tasting the air, listening. Then, satisfied, she crossed the beach, vanishing into a thicket of reeds. Her fawns followed, tripping along on uncertain legs, tethered to her shadow. Their three eyes glowed pale and murky in the moonlight.

Caroline turned back to the house. There was something at the foot of the ramp—a plastic cup filled with a dark, warm-toned liquid, balanced on one of the lights embedded in the wood. The cup glowed, gemlike. Around it, there appeared to be some kind of etching, dark lines burned purposefully into the wood.

Caroline didn't want to look any closer. She decided she would pretend she had never gone outside at all.

Enough strangeness for one night.

Caroline ascended the ramp and heaved open the sliding

glass door. She didn't see the person standing in the living room until she was already inside.

Time stopped. It was the intruder again, a shadow that did not move or speak. Shifting smudges of light stained the walls. Caroline caught her breath.

No. It was Jane. She stood in the living room in her sweatpants and oversize T-shirt. She had clearly not been waiting for Caroline. Her gray eyes were half open; her head was cocked to the side, as if she had tried to shake a trickle of water out of her ear and had broken her neck. Caroline thought of her on the couch earlier, the slackness of her body, how she'd looked almost dead.

Oh, Caroline realized. Jane was still asleep.

"Jane?"

Jane moved closer, until their faces were almost touching. Her hands sought Caroline's and grasped them. When she spoke her words were incoherent, almost inaudible.

"What?"

Jane smiled faintly, lost in her dream.

"Tell me," said Caroline. "Please."

Good evening, said the black face of the television. *Can I help you find something?*

"No," said Caroline. "No thank you."

Jane was silent.

Still holding Jane's hand, Caroline led her up the stairs. She wasn't sure which bedroom belonged to Jane and Perry, but before she could decide what to do next, the door to her own room opened and Perry emerged, smiling sleepily.

"There you are." He yawned. "The both of you."

For a long moment they looked at each other. Tonight, he'd said on the beach. She hadn't imagined him saying that.

But clearly it had only been part of the game. And the night had been so long already. Jane's limp body passed from Caroline's hands into Perry's arms, a sleeping child carried to bed.

"I've got her from here," Perry said, leading Jane down the hallway toward their room. "Good night."

"Good night."

Back in her room Caroline felt for Gabriel in his bassinet, touched a hand to his upturned chest to assess its gentle rise and fall. Later, she would have liked to describe the serenity of his sleeping face—the drool-damp lips, the paintbrush lashes, the curve of moonlight on his slowly healing cheek—but it would have been a lie. It was far too dark in there to see anything at all.

CHAPTER 6

It was Caroline's fault that the evening began with an argument.

The day had dawned cool, gray, and rainy. Wynn had been the first to leave the house, heading to the store for provisions, and he'd found the cup of urine at the foot of the ramp. He took a picture on his phone and showed it to everyone once they were all gathered at the table for breakfast. One by one they drew back in disgust, as if he were sprinkling the piss itself over their bagels and lox.

"Who does that?"

"A parting gift from our night visitor?"

"How sweet."

"He really shouldn't have."

"Weird."

"Super weird."

Wynn laughed and whisked the phone away, palming it back into his shorts pocket before Caroline could get a good look at the photo. What she had seen looked ritualistic—a tourmaline amulet melted into a vessel of clouded plastic, left as an offering for some lesser god. She had caught a glimpse of the drawing as well, a rectangle surrounding a jagged, six-point star.

"Still think it was just a drunk guy?"

"It's just piss," Wynn said. "Not blood."

And when Caroline stepped outside later, the drawing on the ramp was gone.

THE RAIN DIDN'T LET UP UNTIL LATE AFTERNOON. CAROLINE had been stuck inside for hours, yet she was in a playful mood. Playful and relaxed. It didn't make sense that she would feel so relaxed with the bad weather, and without Adam there to help her with the baby, and yet she'd been surprised to discover there was something liberating about handling Gabriel on her own, in her own way, without having to expend the energy to ask Adam to do things and explain how she wanted them done, without Adam there to appraise what he might have considered her lapses in judgment. Letting Gabriel skip a bath, giving up on his nap schedule, shortchanging tummy time, handing him off to Taryn so Caroline could take a long shower, letting him cry himself out while she sat on the deck with a second glass of wine, not doing anything about the fly bite besides photographing it while it healed on its own.

Caroline allowed all of these things, as if what happened on the island didn't count in their real life.

The Corridor employees had been sequestered in their bedrooms the entire day for some kind of all-hands video call, followed by the fevered tackling of associated tasks, keyboards clicking behind closed doors. Caroline, Taryn, and Jane had occupied themselves by watching reruns of a British dramedy about sexually promiscuous teenagers. At their feet, Gabriel lay on his back surrounded by expensive, influencer-approved toys that were supposed to spur his cognitive growth—the floppy bunny, the mirror, the black-and-white rattle, the interlocking rings. Caroline kept forgetting to encourage him to reach for them.

He hadn't rolled again since that first night. It must have been a fluke, a sneak peek into a future development, before he was fully ready.

She wasn't really thinking about the intruder anymore, even though she probably should have been.

It had just been some drunk guy.

There was no sunset, just a gradual dimming of the gray sky. As the light began to fade and Wynn, Noa, Perry, and Blaise finally left their rooms to collapse on the deck furniture, Caroline was genuinely pleased to see them. Even though Jane and Taryn had kept her company, it turned out that neither of them had much to say. The long day was finally over, and she was desperate for adult conversation.

But the others seemed distant. Occasionally the members of a couple would whisper a few inaudible words to each other, but mostly they all just stared into their phones while drinking.

Caroline was disappointed. She thought by this point she and the other members of the household had reached a certain level of intimacy. Not the kind of intimacy that some of them shared in shifting combinations after dark, but an intimacy all the same. She didn't understand why they were being like this, suddenly.

She leaned forward in her Adirondack chair, flushed and warm with the glass and a half of wine she'd already drunk.

"You all work so hard."

The others looked up at her.

"I mean—what's it all for?"

It came out wrong. She had meant it to be a joke, sympathetic even, but it just sounded combative. The others went back to staring into their phones. Caroline tried to recover.

"Like, I mean, you all seem so stressed," she continued. "And the work just seems kind of, I don't know—like, what is it even good for?"

Wynn met her eyes. The corner of his mouth twitched.

"You mean what is it good for, aside from our salaries? And your husband's salary?"

"I mean, a way that it helps the world."

The others exchanged glances. Taryn and Jane wouldn't look at her. Wynn got up to refill his empty glass.

"Well, what about your work?" asked Noa finally. When

she'd first come downstairs, she had lain down on the longer of the outdoor couches like an invalid, her arm draped over Nori's heaving torso, but now she was sitting upright. Both she and the dog were looking at Caroline.

"My work?"

"Yes," said Noa. "How would you even describe it?"

Caroline thought for a moment. Her eyes wandered to her phone, to the surveillance footage. She had set up the camera carelessly that night—she thought she could make out the tip of Gabriel's foot, maybe a bent knee. The picture flared white for a moment as it shifted to night vision, as if capturing the detonation of an atomic bomb.

"It's about motherhood," she said. "Motherhood as praxis."

Someone stifled a laugh.

"Well, how is that meaningful?" said Noa. "How does that help the world?"

Caroline normally had an answer for this—she had written artist statements, had even secured a few small grants—but now she found she had nothing to say.

"It's political work," she replied lamely. "Motherhood is a political act. It complicates and refracts issues of bodily autonomy, the self—"

"What, so you become a new person just because you push a smaller person out of your vagina?" Noa countered. "And we're all supposed to be interested in that?"

"That reminds me," said Blaise. "Is there any of that roast beef left?"

Taryn swatted at his shoulder.

"You're disgusting," she said, delighted.

Blaise got up and went into the kitchen. From his own Adirondack chair on the opposite side of the deck, Perry watched Caroline, amused. He did not defend her.

"You know," Caroline tried again. "In times of despair we turn to art."

Jane laughed openly. She had moved to sit on the couch with Noa, as if to get a better view of Caroline's discomfort.

Caroline had thought that she and Jane had been getting along that day—that the threat of the intruder had bonded them, somehow—but she supposed it had just been the exploits of the wayward teens on the television keeping them together. How could she have mistaken Jane for a friend?

"I know a filmmaker," Jane said. "An artist, I guess. That's how she describes herself."

"The one we saw in that raw space on Canal Street?" asked Noa. "Who did the spoken-word rap about polyamory and the internet while filming herself getting filmed by everyone?"

"No. Different person. This filmmaker—this quote unquote *artist*—it's all just beautiful films of her beautiful friends in beautiful nature. There's absolutely no substance—none—but she does really well for herself because people are suckers for beauty."

"She probably says her work is political, too," said Noa, rolling her eyes.

"She does! She says it's all about denying mortality—a rejection of the abyss. And the effects of climate change, of course."

Blaise returned with a single oven sheet loaded with scraps of cold cuts, orange squares of processed cheese-like product, and some stale chunks of baguette. He set it down on the central coffee table and waited to be thanked by the others.

"Wasn't there anything else?" asked Taryn as people began to pick at the spread. "What happened to all those pickled artichokes? And my tinned fish?"

Blaise shrugged and sat down on the shorter couch. For a few moments everyone gnawed on whatever fragment of sandwich they had managed to cobble together. Caroline refilled her wineglass. She couldn't understand why everyone was in such a sour mood.

"Well, I used to make different work," she said finally. "It was about masculinity."

Perry was looking at her again, still smirking. He seemed to enjoy watching her twist in the wind like this. Maybe it was a turn-on for him.

"I would wander around photographing men, or I would find them online," Caroline said. "Men I had an interest in, and who I could tell had an interest in me. I liked the tension in the exchange."

"So why did you stop?" asked Noa.

Caroline hesitated.

"Partly because life got in the way," she said. "You know, once Adam and I got serious. But partly because of this one man—"

"What?" Noa pressed. "Someone get too friendly?"

"No," said Caroline. "Someone died."

They all looked at her.

"Really?"

Caroline nodded.

"This man—we met by chance, at a museum. He was only in his late forties, but he was really sick. I don't know with what, exactly. Something that did weird things to his body. Whatever it was, he was essentially in denial about it.

"We saw each other a few times. He was divorced, no children. He had a lot of money, and I think he was hoping for some kind of sugar daddy, sugar baby situation. By that point I was with Adam, so I wasn't really available for that kind of thing. But I let him believe it could happen, because I wanted to keep photographing him. I was just so fascinated by what the illness had done to him—he looked like an ancient wax figure. Elegant but decayed.

"One night I'm over at his apartment, and he collapses. I help him get into bed, but I could tell he was dying. Even though this man was nothing like my father, in that moment he reminded me of him—he looked exactly the way my father had looked when *he* was dying, which was a moment I hadn't been allowed to photograph. I should have called 911 immediately, but instead I got out my camera."

"Sounds exploitative as fuck," Jane interjected.

"It was," said Caroline. "I know it was."

She didn't care what Jane thought of her, not now—not when she could see Perry leaning forward, listening to her story with such obvious fascination. She could have gone further—could have told them about the way the man's pleas for help had turned into wordless moans, the way that, moments before death, she felt she could suddenly see the secret work of every organ, vein, and bone, straining against his wax skin—but she thought that would have been overkill.

"Eventually I did call 911, but it was too late," she said. "He died before the ambulance arrived. And I kept taking pictures."

Jane shook her head. The others just stared.

"I think I knew even then that I would never use them, and that they would be the end of the project," said Caroline. "I felt disgusted with myself. I had always thought photography was about seeing things I shouldn't see. I didn't realize there were things that I would regret seeing."

"It's too bad you gave it up," said Perry, examining the tips of his fingers, as if checking to see if they were soiled. "That work. It sounds interesting."

Jane shot him a look, which he ignored.

"It was," said Caroline.

More interesting than her work about motherhood. That morning on the beach, she had hovered over Gabriel, babbling at him, trying to get him to react to his name, to anything. He had stared at her blankly, almost wearily, and she wondered how many pictures she could take of him looking like that before it stopped being interesting.

Perhaps it had already stopped being interesting. Perhaps she had been bored for a while, and she hadn't wanted to admit it.

What if she never made an interesting photograph again?

"Anyway," Caroline said, self-effacing, "everyone has some kind of traumatic story like that. Something that marks a before and after."

"It's true." Noa yawned, prone on the couch again, her feet

in Jane's lap. "Only my story is that I was at the exhumation of a mass grave."

"Oh god," said Blaise. "Here we go."

"Near Volintiri, when I was in the Peace Corps," Noa said. "Steps from the southern border of Ukraine. I wasn't supposed to be there, but I'll never forget it. The experience was so traumatic that I had to resign from service."

"And you fled to—where was it? Paris?"

"Marseille," Noa snapped. "Then, when Russia invaded Bulgaria a few months later, it was so crazy because I'd just started dating this guy from Sofia. I was teaching myself the language and everything. He left France to fight for his country and I never saw him again."

"Ah yes, the invasion of Bulgaria," said Perry. "It was actually all about Noa."

"It's true," Blaise agreed. "Every geopolitical catastrophe is just the backdrop to some white woman's tragedy."

"Well, what's your tragedy, Blaise?"

"I was sexually assaulted."

"You were not."

"I was," Blaise said, his knees bouncing. "This older couple—I met them through one of the more exclusive apps, and we'd been messaging a lot. Remember Winter Storm Kenan?"

"No."

"Well, it was the afternoon before, and they invited me over to their house to be blizzard buddies. I was living in that awful illegal warehouse space, remember that place?"

"No."

"Getting out of there sounded like a pretty good idea. This couple had a fireplace, wine, drugs—a whole fucking carriage house in Brooklyn Heights to themselves! So I went over, and I thought everything was going well. Everyone seemed happy. He was happy, she was happy, I was happy. I'm not sure who these people were, but they were really loaded. I feel like one of them might have been in politics? They kept joking about having me sign an NDA. And I remember thinking all the art in their house was really weird, even though I can't picture any of it now.

"So we're partying, and at some point I blacked out, and when I came to, I was on their stoop. I was naked except for the used condom still hanging off my dick, and their door was locked."

"No!"

"I'm pretty sure it was part of the kink for them, discarding me like that. There I was on the street corner, on drugs, totally naked, at two in the fucking morning in two feet of snow.

"It was so cold, like, so fucking cold. You don't remember that storm? I can't believe you don't remember that storm. I've never felt cold like that. I thought I was going to die. I kept banging on their door, screaming, like, *Let me in, let me in, open the fucking door, please, please, please,* but they wouldn't answer me. No one heard me, no one let me in.

"Thank god the bodega around the corner was open. The old Pakistani guy working there screamed like a woman when he saw me. He said he thought I was a ghost."

Blaise had told his story in a rush, as if he couldn't get it out of his body fast enough, his words flowing too quickly and thickly for anyone to interrupt. When he finished there was a shocked silence, a moment of suspended horror. Then Wynn snorted.

The others looked at him. Wynn tried to compose himself.

"I'm sorry," he said to Blaise. He pressed his knuckles to his lips, tried and failed to hold in another laugh. "Just, the image of you out there. And the guy at the bodega screaming like that."

Wynn snorted again, brushed his hair out of the watery slits of his laughing eyes. Blaise stared at him, tremulous, blinking hard.

"It's not *funny*."

His voice broke. Grimacing, he rubbed his eyes with the

heel of his palm and sniffed. The others were still silent, still horrified.

"People always do this," Blaise choked out. "They always laugh when I tell the story, because they think I'm just some fucking himbo, that everything I do is a fucking joke. But it's not a joke. It's not funny. I could have died."

He sobbed suddenly into his hands, and the sob released the rest of them from their suspended state. Taryn joined Blaise on the couch and held him. The other women made sympathetic sounds. Wynn brushed his hair out of his eyes again, stood up and sat down again, looking stricken. Perry got up and went into the house.

"It's not funny," Blaise repeated, snuffling into Taryn's breasts.

"You're right, baby," she soothed, rubbing his back. "It's not."

Perry returned, brandishing the brown glass medicine dropper. The others unhinged their jaws like baby birds, waiting their turn as Perry came around and dispensed a dose of Q into each gaping mouth. Then he was standing over Caroline, grinning, dangling the dropper above her head, but before she could accept or refuse, he snatched it away.

"Sorry," he said lightly. "I forgot. None for Mama."

"But—"

They all looked at her. The argument had been her fault to begin with. But if she took the Q, maybe they would see that she meant well, that she truly wanted to be part of the group.

That she was one of them.

"Just a tiny bit," she said.

She could tell it was the right decision when the others exchanged smiles. Lips parted, eyes closed, Caroline didn't even feel the drop dissolve on her tongue.

Though it seemed impossible that the Q could take its effect so quickly, a sense of calm descended. They all relaxed into the surfaces that held their bodies, listened to the crinkling of the wind in the reeds, the catlike licking of the bay against the shore. For a long time nobody spoke. Finally Wynn sat up and looked at Blaise.

"I'm sorry I laughed."

Blaise nodded.

"I think I laughed because I recognized myself," Wynn continued. "I've been the person in the apartment and the person out on the street. I've hurt people before, and, well—"

He paused, searching for the right words.

"I guess—I guess I just have to kind of—live with the memory of those mistakes. The therapist I saw for my sex addiction blames it on my fear of death."

"I hope you stopped seeing her," said Blaise. "She obviously didn't cure you."

"Okay, okay, maybe I deserved that," said Wynn. "Though I'm far from the only one, present company *not* excluded."

Blaise nodded again, as if to say they were even now.

"Anyway, that's not what an analyst does. Right, Jane?"

"Right," said Jane tartly. "They enable your addictions by allowing you to blame everything on your parents."

"What I meant is they don't cure you," said Wynn. "They help you understand yourself. And she helped me understand that because I'm so afraid of getting old, getting sick, and dying, I feel compelled to live, like, as recklessly as I possibly can. And because I'm afraid of the people I love getting old, getting sick, and dying, I do things to push them away. If we can't rise above frailty and decay—if we can't solve death—then what's the point? I don't know if I can bear to know or love anyone."

Something snagged at Caroline. She could have sworn she'd heard those exact words before, or at least something very similar.

And then she remembered. Adam bare-chested, Gabriel a red coil of flesh against his body—their first moments together, skin to skin, before he was whisked away again, back to the NICU to fix the problem of the fluid in his lungs. Adam had looked over at Caroline propped up on the hospital bed, his eyes shining with tears.

"I hate how fragile he is," he said. "I don't know how I can bear it."

She glanced at her phone again. Gabriel had moved completely out of frame.

"That's why you have children," Caroline said, suddenly recalling something she'd once put in an artist's statement. "So in a way, you can live forever."

"Having children and living forever are not even remotely the same thing," said Jane. "Though I guess mothers tell themselves they are."

"I'm not just a mother," said Caroline. She didn't know if it was true.

"I'm probably a mother, too, actually," said Noa. "I mean, in a strictly biological, genetic sense. I sold so many of my eggs in my twenties—at least a couple of them must have made it."

"You sold your eggs?" asked Taryn, wide-eyed. "All of them?"

"That's not how it works," said Jane.

"They took as many as they could, and then I got the rest of the equipment taken out once I got the Corridor job," Noa said. "Best decision I ever made. I was not meant to be a parent."

Wynn was staring into the middle distance, his jaw set. Jane had moved away from Noa to the other end of the couch they shared.

"Of course, it's not without its risks," Noa went on. "Selling your eggs, I mean. I knew this one girl—she did it twice a year, all through her twenties *and* thirties. Paid off all her debt, finally. Then when she was in her forties, all these kids came looking for her. Like, what a nightmare, all those children, and they're all *yours*!"

Jane had gone pale, her eyes burning in her face. Noa brought her hand to her mouth.

"Sorry, Jane," said Noa. "I didn't mean to. I wasn't thinking."

"It's fine."

Jane closed her eyes and took a breath, gathering herself.

"After the seventh or eighth miscarriage you get kind of numb to it," she said. "It's why the motherhood debates don't interest me. Can't do it, so I'm not going to think about it."

"There are things you can do now," Taryn tried. "New therapies, treatments—you wouldn't believe what's possible. My friend, she—"

"*Not me.*"

Jane was shaking now, her fingernails digging into her palms. Caroline thought someone should go to her, comfort her. No one moved.

"Anyway, I really didn't want to talk about any of this," Jane said. "Thank you all for bringing it up."

She got up and went into the house, yanking the glass door shut behind her with a sucking whoosh and thud. Perry watched her go but did not follow. Caroline tried to catch his eye, but he wouldn't look at her.

"I was just never interested," Noa said, refilling her glass. "It's not worth it. To see all the trauma that Jane went through—why make the choice to put yourself through that? As we've already established, it's not like it makes the world a better place."

"Well, you know what they say about women and dogs," said Perry, fondling Nori's ears.

"What do they say, Perry?" asked Noa. "Enlighten us."

"If a woman has a small dog, it means she wants a baby. If a woman has a large dog, it means she wants a man."

"The fuck does that mean?" Wynn demanded.

"You understand yourself so well," said Perry. "I'm sure you can figure it out."

"Y'all need to stop this right now," Taryn said. "I mean it. Listen, remember when I got into aspirational theory?"

"I thought it was affect theory."

"No, aspirational," she said. "Anyway, all this bad stuff—you can manifest it by worrying about it. You attract what you fear."

"Babe," said Blaise. "Excuse me, but. What?"

"It's true! Especially in a place and time like this, where we're all so spiritually lubricated."

"I don't believe this," said Noa. "I'm not hearing this."

"Being so vulnerable with each other," Taryn finished, though she sounded less certain now. "It's not easy. It requires a lot of—of intentionality. You know, care-processing."

The mood had curdled again, perhaps irretrievably. To Caroline it seemed that everyone had managed to alienate everyone else, that for the last hour or so they had not been giving of each other but only talking past each other. They had careened through space like doomed astronauts cut from their ships, only connecting when they collided in accidental, glancing junctures of mutual damage. The Q wasn't enough anymore. They needed something else. Then Caroline had an idea.

"A walk!"

The others looked at her.

"Let's go for a walk," Caroline repeated. "Come on."

The idea settled on each of them, dissolved into their bloodstreams, its own narcotic. They each repeated it, so that it became an incantation, first soothing, then rousing. A walk, a walk, a walk, a walk! A walk!

A walk was exactly what was needed. The problem was that they'd been cooped up all day, and they needed to get out. Stretch their legs, see what else was going on out there. Maybe they would even make it all the way to the yacht club this time. Why not?

But first, another dose of Q. The dropper went around again, its contents dribbled into waiting mouths, until they had emptied it. Perry left to check on Jane and returned, shaking his head.

"She's not coming."

Taryn and Noa made their sad faces. Caroline kept hers

under control. The sky was thick with mist. The clouds grew heavier and sank over their heads.

UPSTAIRS IN HER BEDROOM, SHRUGGING A SWEATSHIRT OVER her dress, Caroline decided to skip her medication. Better not to mix anything with the Q, even though it didn't seem to be affecting her very much at all. Maybe a bit of a fluttery feeling, a trickling and skipping through her veins. She turned around to see Gabriel awake, watching her with her husband's dark eyes. She could hear Adam now, berating her.

You forgot *him? You were just going to leave him there, by himself? Are you crazy? What kind of mother are you?*

No. *No.* Caroline shook her head. She hadn't forgotten Gabriel. She hadn't! It was impossible to forget your own baby. She wasn't crazy. Crazy! What kind of mother, indeed.

Gabriel smiled, as if he could read her thoughts. His fly bite looked like the remnants of a lipstick kiss. Caroline lifted him out of the bassinet and held him tightly, as if she were a child hugging her favorite stuffed animal, breathing in his wonderful Gabriel smell and swaying as love—it was love, she reassured herself, not the drugs—surged through the softness of her body, until she almost laughed aloud. Maybe she did laugh aloud, that's how happy she was. Her child. He was perfect. She loved him so much.

Maybe she could ask Jane to watch him, if she was going to stay back at the house. She could set her up with the surveillance feed, assure her that the baby would sleep the whole time and she wouldn't have to do anything at all.

No, that would never work. Poor Jane and her seven or eight miscarriages. She couldn't ask Jane to watch her perfect, healthy baby while the rest of them went out and had fun. It would be too cruel.

She would have to bring him along.

She nursed him first, even though she wasn't sure if he was hungry, and she was even less sure if she should be nursing with the Q in her system. She attempted a half-hearted search on her phone (*can you breastfeed on Q*), but there weren't any results. Perhaps she had typed the query incorrectly.

It was fine, probably. The wildly popular data scientist Caroline had followed on social media all through her pregnancy—the one who enthusiastically sanctioned a nightly cocktail after the first trimester—would almost certainly have said it was fine.

Sitting on the edge of the bed, Caroline took off the sweatshirt and wriggled out of the straps of her dress, the loose bodice falling like a curtain over Gabriel's face. *Peekaboo.* She flicked her wrist, snapping the flap of thin fabric over his face, hiding and revealing him, hiding and revealing him, smiling all the while. *Peekaboo.* He was still too little for any sense of object permanence. She stopped playing with him and he settled his mouth on her.

Caroline felt a hand lift her hair, exposing the back of her neck. She turned around.

"Hey."

It was Perry.

"Hey."

He leaned closer.

"Is this all right?"

Normally, she didn't like being touched while she was breastfeeding, but she decided that events had already proceeded to the point where she didn't mind. She nodded, and Perry brought his mouth to the bend where her neck met her shoulder.

"Still okay?"

She nodded again. His hand reached in and brushed against the velvet head in her arms.

"Ready?"

The fluttery feeling was faster now, a scrabbling of tiny, winged things inside her, trying to take flight. She wondered if Gabriel could feel them, if the flying things were flowing out of her and into him, connected as they were.

"Almost."

CAROLINE SOBERED UP ONCE THEY WERE ALL OUTside again. At least she thought she had sobered up. How else to account for the sudden sharpness and clarity of everything around her—the innumerable gradations of silver, steel, and aluminum in the wood of the boardwalk and the wood of the trees, the polygons of lighted windows and the pulsing red bulbs of the Public Safety and Public Health bungalows hanging like ornaments in the leaves, the sting of salt in her mouth and lungs?

Gabriel was quiet and agreeable in his wrap, an extension of her body once more. The others had cheered when she'd emerged with her camera and the baby and announced he was coming with them. If anyone noticed Perry slinking down the stairs behind her, they hadn't said anything.

Let them believe what they wanted to believe. All he had done was check on her, help her get ready.

No one else seemed to have sobered up. If anything, they were even more giddy and antic, laughing errantly at nothing and hugging each other. Caroline thought they must have taken something else, while she and Perry were upstairs.

The amphitheater was an illuminated barge floating in the darkness, its striped gold-and-silver backdrop a beacon in the night. The rows of benches were mostly empty, save for a few anonymous figures grouped in twos and threes. By unspoken agreement, Caroline and the others paused on the boardwalk to watch the performance, which seemed to just be starting.

Without introduction, a broad-shouldered drag queen strode onto the stage, the sharp ridges of her cheekbones smeared with glitter, the hem of her yellow-buttercream ball gown hissing against the boards. She curtsied deeply, then straightened, slit open the black pillow of her lips to show a palisade of white teeth.

"Who's on Q right now?"

On the boardwalk they whooped and hollered. The rest of the audience was silent.

"I'm not, actually," Taryn whispered to Caroline, hands cupped around her ear. Caroline frowned.

"You're not?"

Taryn laughed.

"You're not, either."

"What was that, then? In the dropper?"

Taryn shrugged.

Onstage, the drag queen was still grinning, pacing and prancing, her head and torso flung back behind her and trailing her legs like a banner.

Let your freak flag fly, thought Caroline, swallowing down a giggle at her own joke. She could still have fun.

"I'm Oona Vita," said the drag queen. "Anyone celebrating anything?"

"Life!" shouted Wynn.

"I'm celebrating life, too." Oona laughed. "Every day I wake up and I'm like, wow, this again?"

She plummeted to the stage in a death-drop dip, regarded them with a sparkling wink.

"Fortunately, this is America," she cooed. "If I dream hard enough, I can trade my dirty old meat suit for a brand-new meat suit!"

She paused to allow for cheers and applause, but none came. She sat up with her legs splayed out in front of her, revealing pumps the color of liver, and gave a winsome, aw-shucks shrug.

"Weird," said Noa.

"I like her," said Blaise.

"Don't threaten me with a good time," said Wynn.

"And now, the moment you've all been waiting for," Oona cried, clambering onto her pumps again. "The lights of your lives, the apples of your eyes, your frozen champagne-and-caviar embryos, your best and final offer for the future—your Camp—Haven—Child—Players!"

The audience remained silent as two children dressed in brown-paper-bag tunics ran onstage. Caroline recognized the girl with white-blond hair, though she was wearing a battle helmet in the shape of a conch shell that covered one of her colorless eyes. The other child was a smaller boy with dark hair; a pair of twisted shofar horns sprouting from his scalp. Their faces were striped with black paint, daubed with glitter. They were followed by the undulating, six-legged skeleton of an enormous bull, crepe streamers of flesh dangling from its bones as it snuffled and snorted, flapping black feathered wings, its googly eyes rolling and red with rage. The child warriors' tennis shoes lit up with hectic, bouncing rainbows with every step as they dodged and circled their prey.

"'Don't you want to live forever?'" screamed the white-blond girl. "'Kill him now!'"

The boy produced a bamboo fishing rod and thrust it into the bull's innards. The animal broke apart into six shrieking children who ran circles around their killer before fleeing offstage. The boy with the horns collapsed to the ground.

"'There is the house whose people sit in darkness,'" he gasped. "'Dust is their food and clay their meat. They are clothed like birds with wings for covering, they see no light, they sit in darkness. I entered the house of dust and I saw the kings of the earth, their crowns put away forever.'"

He coughed once, closed his eyes, and died. The white-blond girl threw off her helmet and tore open her paper tunic with both hands. Bare-chested, she doubled over, keening, then lifted her head to regard the audience with an expression of quivering wonderment.

"'I must begin the search for everlasting life!'"

Caroline lifted her camera and snapped a picture of the moment, even though she was too far away to capture the sparkling pixels coming out of the girl's eyes.

"Weird," said Taryn.

Once again by unspoken agreement, the group on the boardwalk moved on, leaving the lights of the theater and the silence of the audience behind them as they headed farther into town, toward the yacht club.

"What *was* that?" asked Taryn.

"*Gilgamesh*," said Perry.

"Huh?"

"The search for immortality. Oldest story on earth."

"I think I was supposed to read that in middle school and never did," said Wynn. "What happens at the end?"

"He fails," said Perry.

INSIDE THE GAZEBO OF THE YACHT CLUB THERE WAS A VAGUE smell of sewage and bleach; the tile floor was slick and shiny with it, faintly reflecting the fairy lights that hung from the rafters. Tables and chairs had been stacked into precarious childhood forts along the walls to make room for a dance floor. The crowd was all jailbait and silverbacks, and they were all dressed in white. Young girls and old men circled each other, their eyes gleaming with flirtatious intelligence.

"Drinks?"

"Drinks!"

The others danced over to the mirrored bar, leaving Caroline standing on her own. Everyone in the crowd had the red bull's-eyes of bug bites on their arms and legs.

"Caro!"

"She's here!"

"And she brought Gabey!"

The three girl heads came minnowing up to Caroline, white shirts down to their knees, their thickly painted faces dented with happiness. They celebrated by breaking into the coordinated pop-and-locks of their favorite dance from the grocery store. The redheaded blonde clutched a sleeve of crackers that looked like a stack of golden coins; she held it to her chin like a microphone.

"You were supposed to wear white," she said. "It's the white party."

"I didn't know," said Caroline.

"She didn't know!"

"How could she have known?"

"How could she *not* have known?"

Caroline held out her hand, and the redheaded blonde emptied a few gold coins into her palm. Crumbs fell on the baby's head, gilding him with a fine dust.

Her friends returned holding gemlike drinks, blue and red and green, their mouths open in laughter to reveal purple tongues. Too many colors.

"We were supposed to wear white," Caroline told them, but they weren't listening. Someone handed her a dark garnet drink that she hadn't asked for. She took a sip, tasted honey and pomegranate. She drank the rest of it. The music got louder and they all began to dance.

Before the baby, before Adam, Caroline had nights where things came in flashes. The flash of a throat bent backward in laughter. The flash of interlocked joints. Faces flashing in and out of sight, hidden by hair, by arms, by shoulders, by other faces.

This was different. She was wide awake, noticing every small detail of everything around her. A girl in a man's shirt open over a white cotton bra-and-boy-short set, her mouth stained red with grenadine. A man with a fly perched in the steel bristles of his hair, a light-up ice cube clamped between his teeth cycling through its colors: blue, red, green, blue, red, green. A man and a girl playing catch with a tiny iridescent gift bag festooned with trailing cellophane ribbons. Two girls whispering to each other, looking on imperiously as two men performed a choreographed dance in front of them. Two men and two girls sitting on the sticky floor, a deck of cards spread before them: a family gathered around a table with a winged eye at the center, a man in a top hat and a woman with the head of a cat holding each other in a bed, a baby's face at the center of a black box, a door opening to darkness.

Caroline felt wide awake, and it was this clarity, this alertness, that made her so sure of what she was doing when she undid her wrap and handed her baby to the heads so she could be alone with her camera.

Everyone else was dancing, kissing. Blaise and Wynn were kissing. Noa and Taryn were kissing. The blond brunette was holding Gabriel; the other two girls were holding their phones, filming while they danced. Other people were filming, too. Caroline photographed it all. The others danced around her, their bodies close, circling, closing in.

Then Perry was taking the camera away from her eye, and he was kissing her. She gave herself up to him, but only for a moment. She had wanted it for days—better to prolong it. She backed away from him, smiling, opened her mouth, and threw up.

Everything came out of her—the red drink, the gold coins, all over the white tile floor. She spit, spit again. Coming back up, it tasted like blood. Gabriel began to scream. The sound was unbearable, not human. Caroline covered her ears. She was on the floor now, kneeling.

"Oh, Caro!"

"It's okay, Gabey. It's okay."

"Do you want us to take him back to your house?"

Caroline looked up to see Adam standing by the bar, holding a plastic cup filled with maraschino cherries, his mouth pressed into a thin line.

You just gave him to them? Those girls? Are you crazy? What kind of mother are you?

No. *No.* Caroline shook her head, and Adam vanished. He wasn't on the island, she reminded herself. He wasn't in Haven. He wouldn't be back until tomorrow.

"We'll be right behind you," said Noa. "We just need to clean her up."

They were outside on the patio now. Caroline was lying down on her side, watching as Noa and Taryn plunged their hands into the neon pool, filling them with bright water. A pulse of rainbow undulated through the windows of the yacht club. Caroline closed her eyes for what felt like a long time and when she opened them again she was still there, lying on the deck.

The pool began to come apart, fizzing and disintegrating in tiny popping bursts. Through the boards against her ear, Caroline could hear bodies tumbling into the shallows of the bay.

"Oh my god." Someone laughed. "Oh my god."

She didn't have her camera. She didn't have her baby.

Then someone was lifting her up, and they were running through a wall of rain, back to the house.

NORI WAS HOWLING FROM BEHIND THE GLASS WALLS. AS THEY ran up the rain-slicked ramp, the dog stood on her hind legs to greet them, her anvil head thrown back to show a white lightning bolt slicing down her throat and belly that Caroline had never noticed before.

The girls were in the living room, arrayed on the couches. Their hair and clothing were dry. The television was on. A drone was following a pair of foxes through the lush, overgrown ruins of a nuclear power plant. Butterflies flitted through blown-out windows, alighting on beds of moss.

The girls beamed at Caroline.

"Gabey's upstairs."

"He went down so easy."

"He's such a good baby."

"We told you," someone said. "We told you it would be okay."

Caroline rushed upstairs. The bedroom was dark—too dark to see anything at first—but she could hear the soft sound of her son's breath, could see the dark shape of him in the bassinet.

She was so relieved that she thought she might throw up again. She had wanted to hold Gabriel, but instead she lay down on the bed and waited for the sloshing in her body and the room to stop and settle. She looked into the light of the open door and saw the looming shadow of an intruder.

She wasn't dreaming. There was a man in her room, again. But this time she knew who it was.

"She's passed out."

Caroline thought he was talking about her. She shook her head.

"No I'm not. I'm awake."

"Not you," Perry said, leaning over her. "Jane."

"Is she okay?"

Perry laughed.

"No. She hasn't been okay in a long time."

"Oh."

Poor, poor Jane, Caroline thought as Perry shucked her out of her wet dress. It was cruel to inflict pain on someone who had already suffered so much, whatever their arrangement was. But all those dead babies had nothing to do with Caroline and what was happening in her room now.

"She was right after all," said Perry. "She knew even before I did that it wasn't going to be her. She didn't have it."

"What?"

"Never mind."

"No, not never mind," said Caroline, the words like chunks in her mouth. "Didn't have what?"

Perry grinned.

"She's not a bad girl, like you."

Caroline frowned.

"I'm a bad girl?"

"You told us yourself."

Caroline tried to consider what he meant by this, but she was distracted by the black mask Perry was holding to his face. He kept making clicking sounds with his tongue and teeth.

"My camera," said Caroline.

"*My* camera," corrected Perry.

"I thought it was gone."

"It was safe with me," he said, tossing the camera onto the bed and climbing in, pinning her down. "Just like you."

Rain spattered on glass and wood. Once, Caroline turned her head to the side, and could have sworn that she looked into Gabriel's open eyes, even though the mesh of the bassinet hung between them like a veil.

Then Perry was prodding her, trying to get her to move.

"Come on," he said. "You're still a mess."

"I thought you cleaned me up."

He drew her to her feet and kissed her.

"I need to do it again."

The shower was a glass elevator hanging over a void. Perry finished fiddling with the knobs and turned to face her, his hands on her upper arms. His penis was the same size as her husband's. She thought about telling him as much but decided not to. Her husband would be there tomorrow. Caroline turned her face away from the warm spray coming from the nozzle and looked out at the black sweep of the bay below them. She began to laugh.

"Do you know what I did? The first day we were here?"

"Yes."

"You do?"

"You promised yourself that you'd let me fuck you before this vacation was over."

"No," Caroline said, shaking her head, still laughing. "No. I took a shit in the bay."

"What?"

"I had to go so badly, and I knew if I went in the house everyone would hear me, so I walked out into the water and took a shit out there."

She kept laughing. He was laughing, too, and then he was gently bending her arm behind her back, breathing against the nape of her neck, calling her dirty and bad. One leg folded awkwardly, one foot falling asleep. Caroline pressed her palms and forehead to the glass and looked out over the bay again, until it was too fogged over to see.

CAROLINE DREAMED SHE WAS GIVING BIRTH ALL over again. Adam was by her side, holding her hand through the pain of each contraction and telling her not to worry, that no, this wasn't what they had expected, and no, it wasn't ideal, but they had the best doctors in the world, and everything would be okay.

But we already did this, she said. *This part is over.*

Caroline opened her eyes. In the unfamiliar room, it took her a long moment to recognize what she was looking at. A bright wet eye became a gleam on rounded glass, her uncapped camera lens staring at her from its resting place on the night table.

There was a moment of the familiar, disoriented panic before she began to come back to herself, regaining a sense of her body on the mattress. Nothing and no one beside her, nothing and no one in her arms.

The baby was not in bed with her, thank God.

Still half asleep, still disoriented, Caroline turned her head toward where Gabriel was supposed to be. But something wasn't right. She must have been back at the amphitheater. The show was over, and the gold-and-silver backdrop had come down, revealing a wall of white light. Then the stage wall resolved itself into the mesh panel of the portable bassinet—pale and glowing, its perfect shape perfectly empty, uninterrupted by the smallest shadowed mound of her son's body.

She whispered his name into the dark.

CHAPTER 7

Babies weren't supposed to die anymore, but they still did.

When Caroline was pregnant, she'd become obsessed with dead babies. She'd gone down a social media rabbit hole of neonatal death, spending hours perusing the profiles of women who'd given birth to babies without skulls, women whose preemies had fallen out of them, women who'd lost their full-term baby after a home birth gone wrong. There were cord accidents, there were cessations of heartbeats, there were fatal diseases that developed nine weeks after birth that were catalyzed by a simple fever. Many of the people with dead babies were Christian; they posted colorblock illustrations of Jesus holding a swaddled bundle, captioned *My story, His glory.* Caroline could not stop watching their videos of waxy purple faces peeking out over knitted quilts, parents cuddling a graying death mask, babies that looked like shrunken totems.

Our angel went to be with Jesus. The biggest miracle has happened, she is FULLY and PERFECTLY healed!

There was a before you, and a during you, but I never thought there would be an after you.

God reminded us that He is the author of time.

Occasionally, old Pantheon-related footage would surface. A little girl in a pink galaxy-print snowsuit pranced around a snow-covered backyard, shrieking with laughter as soft flakes landed on her nose.

Mommy, I miss you, too, said the virtual girl, turning to face the viewer. *But please don't cry anymore.*

This cute video KILLED a woman, the caption read.

Caroline couldn't look away. Not even from the content-creator mother who did a sponcon post with a leisurewear company two weeks after the stillbirth of her baby:

Where is my award for getting out of bed and getting dressed today? Just kidding, this adorable twinset is actually pajamas!

It ruined Caroline's algorithm forever.

One account stood out. They were bereaved parents who were able to spend over a week with their stillborn son, thanks to the pilot of an advanced cryopreservation crib developed by Anima, Corridor's health-care subsidiary. The parents bathed the dead baby, held him skin to skin, read stories to him, and took his corpse outside for a walk in the sun. They were grateful for the technology that had allowed them to spend so much time with their child. Once he was finally in the ground, they continued to proselytize about it, until they became paid Anima influencers, raising money and awareness for future initiatives to not only end infant loss but also expand cryopreservation offerings to adults, so that all deaths could be grieved the way they deserved to be.

GABRIEL HAD SURVIVED BIRTH. BUT FOR ALL OF ADAM'S ANXIety about his own clumsiness, Caroline had been the one to drop their son. Not drop him, exactly. But it had been her fault that he fell.

Eight weeks after bringing him home, two episodes into the third season of yet another brooding Scandinavian detective series, Caroline had laid Gabriel down in the dead center of the couch so that she could grab her half-gallon steel water bottle off the coffee table, and he had somehow slipped and fallen onto the floor. She would never forget the sound his head made when it landed on the thin rug over the hardwood, the endless half second before he began to scream.

While they waited for the car that would take them to the emergency room, Adam had self-soothed by searching online to determine the worst-case consequences of Caroline's carelessness, narrating his increasingly hysterical queries aloud: *how dangerous is dropping baby, dropped baby screaming, dropped baby ten weeks old, skull development ten weeks, dropped baby survival rate, will i go to jail for dropping baby, celebrities who dropped babies, did i just kill my baby, worst things for baby.*

"Look at this," he said. "'Getting Oral Sex While Pregnant Could Mess with Baby.'"

"Well, we never needed to worry about that, did we?" she snapped.

At the hospital they checked Gabriel over, held him for observation for a few hours, and finally pronounced him okay.

"So is his skull unusually strong or something?" Adam asked the attending physician. "Do we have a future in the NFL?"

"*Adam!*" Caroline clutched Gabriel against her body with both hands, as if he were in danger of slipping again.

"He must get it from me," said Adam. "Being thick-headed, I mean."

The attending physician showed Caroline and Adam the tiny scar near her temple where her own father had knocked her into a cabinet.

"Almost everyone injures their baby at some point," she said. "It's a rite of passage."

Far worse was what Caroline had done before Gabriel was born, even though it hadn't been her fault at all.

At thirty-three weeks, Caroline had flown to Bismarck to move her mother, Darlene, into the Golden Sunset Homes. Her mother said she was being involuntarily committed, but this was not technically true. She could not afford to care for the farmhouse anymore; she was underwater with the refinanced mortgage, and Erestor had purchased the land for far less than it was worth. After settling up with the bank, they would use what was left from the proceeds of the sale to move her into the facility. Darlene had signed the paperwork and everything, but two weeks before the closing she'd refused to leave.

Adam had flown out to deal with it. He called from the crumbling front porch of the house Caroline had grown up in, which they had never visited together.

"She says you need to come."

"Well, that's lovely. Tell her I can't."

"I did. She says she won't budge unless you come. And I quote, 'Tell my daughter I'm not leaving my house with a Jew.'"

"Then we'll have her committed! Jesus fucking Christ."

"I already asked the lawyer."

"And?"

"We can't."

Caroline groaned.

"He said with HEOL there's a lot of gray area, but without a diagnosis and doctor's note—"

"I don't want to *kill* her, Adam."

"No one is suggesting that."

"I just want her to be taken care of."

"I know you do, babe. It's what anyone would want."

"What if—"

Caroline hesitated. Months of rehearsing had brought her no closer to knowing how to ask him for what she wanted, which was to move her mother to New York.

But she knew what Adam would say. He would have crunched the numbers already. Caroline could see him gesticulating, explaining that while it might be *possible* it certainly wasn't *smart*, and certainly wouldn't be fair to their child. Their children.

"What?" he asked. "What if what?"

"Never mind."

There was a taxidermied mountain lion on display in the bank downtown where they had the closing. Years ago, a farmer had shot the great cat in the heart when she charged at him through a field of tall winter wheat. He said his instincts had taken over.

Caroline gripped her mother by the hand—she had lunged for the door when they first arrived, and she now stood sulking at the window, petting the lion's head. They had already emptied the house. Everything had been carted away to be burned.

"'The young lions suffer want and hunger,'" her mother said, eyeing the swell of Caroline's belly. "'But those who seek the Lord lack no good thing.'"

"Darlene. Stop it."

"Gus would have never let this happen," she said. "He would have fixed everything."

Caroline couldn't hold back.

"Dad wouldn't have fixed shit," she snapped. "He never took care of us. It's because of him you're—"

Her mother began to sob. She would have dropped to her knees if Caroline hadn't held her up by her wrist, the way a parent would hoist a small child.

"Was I no good?" her mother cried. "Lord, was I no good? What kind of mother was I, that my daughter would do this to me?"

Caroline's vision blurred.

"I'm sorry," she whispered.

Caroline and Adam made it home. In the car back to Brooklyn from the airport they'd fallen into a reverent silence as the lights of the skyline came into view. Over pizza in their living room, they'd made promises to never go back, had vowed to raise the baby Jewish, just to piss off the crazy bitch.

But as she lay in bed that night, Caroline thought of her mother petting the dead lion in the bank. She thought of her mother in her new room—her cell—lying curled on the bed, weeping as Caroline and Adam tried to say their goodbyes. The tears came again.

What kind of mother was I? What kind of mother was I?
The next morning her water broke all over the kitchen floor.

CAROLINE HAD BEEN GUILTY OF MUCH MORE IN THE MONTHS since Gabriel's birth. Not almost killing her baby. But small crimes all the same. For so much of Gabriel's life she'd been unable to live in the moment. It had always been about endurance, willing herself through each endless wake window, each numbing cycle of feeding, diaper change, tummy time, and bath, so that she could get on to the next thing, get on to the brief hours of the day and night when he would be asleep again, and she could be alone with herself once more.

"So she's saying he was never alone?"

"Correct."

"Not even for a moment?"

"She says he was asleep in the crib, and she was asleep in the bed next to him. When she woke up, he was gone."

"She woke up when?"

"Call came in at four thirteen."

"And when did she go to sleep?"

"She doesn't know."

"Not even a ballpark?"

"She said it was around when the rain started."

"And she never once left the bedroom?"

"She says no."

"And she says no one else came in?"

"It was just her and the guy."

"Her husband?"

"No."

There was a long pause, and then a low whistle.

Caroline sat on the white couch with her head between her legs. She could hear the pair of public safety officers conferring on the deck. They went on bantering, telling their version of her story to each other.

There were other people in the room with her. Someone was sniffling softly on one of the other couches. Someone was pacing, the thunk of their feet moving closer and farther, closer and farther. A pair of muffled voices pressed against a closed door.

There was a weight on her back, someone's arm draped over her spine. Slowly, nauseously, Caroline tilted her head to the side, expecting to see Perry sitting beside her, holding her.

It was Blaise. He gave her a weak smile. Caroline squinted back.

"Where are the real police?" she asked.

Blaise brought his hand to the back of her neck, traced a rectangle there with his fingertips, over and over again.

"These *are* the real police."

Caroline hung her head again.

An upside-down face swam into view, small white grapes of eyes in sucking dark holes, rimmed at the bottom by caterpillars of russet hair. It was too much, too grotesque. She let her gaze fall and catch on a pale blue shirt collar, ornate nautical badge, navy shorts, pink calves. The black joystick of a holstered gun. Meaty, hairy hands clutched a small, faintly glowing panel—a digital notebook, the screen already stained with words.

Her words.

"We need to ask you a few more questions, ma'am."

"Why?"

"Just to make sure we're getting it right."

Caroline closed her eyes.

"Okay."

"Can you take us through it again?"

"Through what again?"

"Tonight."

"Last night, he means."

"The whole thing?"

"As much as you can."

"But I already did."

"We'd like you to try it again."

Caroline took a breath, kept her head down.

"We all went to the yacht club."

"Your son as well?"

"Of course! I wouldn't leave him here by himself."

"No one's suggesting that."

"I would *never* do that. I'm not *crazy*."

"So he was at the yacht club with you?"

"Yes."

"Notice anything out of the ordinary there?"

"It's all out of the ordinary to me," Caroline said. "I've never been to this place before."

This seemed like the wrong answer, but she had no other to give.

"And then?"

"Then when the rain started, we went home."

"When the rain started you went straight home?"

"Yes."

She remembered the cold drops beginning to fall on her upturned face, the bodies in the shallows of the bay. She didn't have her camera; she didn't have Gabriel.

"When the rain started you came home with the baby?"

Caroline shook her head.

"The others—the girls. They carried him home. I was right behind them. They got to the house first with Gabriel and put him in his bassinet. I already told you all of this."

"So you got home and put him in his crib?"

"No. He was already in his bassinet when I got home."

"So you saw him in his crib."

"His bassinet. Yes."

"And then?"

She was lying down and she was naked. She would have liked to pay attention to what was happening to her body—she had known it would be important—but now she couldn't remember anything.

"It's important you tell us everything, ma'am. Every detail."

Why were these men still talking to her? These pigs, these

sickos, wanting to know about her sex life. If it was between two consenting adults, what did it matter?

Something was wrong. There should be many, many more police here by now. They should be searching the house, taking more extensive notes, canvassing, gathering evidence. Fingerprints, forensics. Strands of hair, flakes of skin. Whatever. She had watched more than enough procedural television to know what real police should be doing. None of this was happening. None of this was right.

"I want the real police," Caroline said again.

There was another long pause, a sigh.

"We are the real police, ma'am."

She lifted her head and sat up then. They were all there, the other members of the household, watching her with soft frowns of pity.

"No, you're not."

"Ma'am."

"She's in shock," said Noa. "I'm not sure how helpful this is."

"It is very helpful for us, ma'am."

"Doesn't seem helpful for her right now."

"We need to know everything."

"But she's told you everything already," said Blaise, his arm still around Caroline's shoulders. "We all heard it."

"Sometimes things resurface in the repetition. Things she didn't remember at first, or things she didn't think were important."

But she remembered it all! That was the thing—she knew it was all important. She'd known from that moment on the cove with the heads that there was something she needed to know, that those girls were trying to tell her something and she had missed the message.

She tried to sharpen the details of the night's pictures in her mind. The dancing. The kissing. The foamy red waterfall of the drink spilling out of her, the rainbows undulating through the windows, the hands catching light in the disintegrating pool.

Further back. The mirrored bar, the old men and young girls all dressed in white, the heads circling. The playing cards fanned out on the floor—the winged eye, the head of the cat, the baby in the box.

I mean, should we even be playing that card game? Taryn had said. *It's almost like it summoned something.*

"Wait," Caroline said. Everyone looked at her with renewed interest.

"Last night," she said. "I mean, the night before last. Someone got into the house. An intruder."

Caroline knew this was a significant detail if not an essential clue, so she was alarmed when the officers continued to gaze at her blankly. Maybe they were just trying to keep their expressions under control. Not give too much away. The integrity of the investigation could be at stake.

"We assumed it was just a drunk person who was lost and wandered into the house," Caroline continued. "But maybe—maybe it was someone trying to take Gabriel."

The officer holding the digital notebook made a quick jot, but that was all. No follow-up questions, nothing. Caroline didn't understand.

"There was a cup of piss," she said desperately. "At the end of the ramp. And this weird drawing, like some kind of cult thing."

The officers frowned.

"And?"

"Well? Isn't *that* out of the ordinary? Couldn't that be a lead?"

"Perhaps," said one officer. "But not likely."

"Usually when a baby disappears, the kidnapper is someone known to the family," said the other officer. "Someone with access."

"But if a stranger could get into the house, wouldn't they have access?" Caroline pressed.

"Are you sure it was a stranger, ma'am? That it wasn't one of your group?"

"We're sure," said Perry. His voice was strained, and seemed to come from far away. "We all saw him. It was a stranger."

"We weren't asking you, sir. You'll be questioned separately."

"Why?" Wynn interjected. "Why the fuck is he going to be questioned separately?"

"Sir, I'm going to ask you to remain calm, or we'll have to—"

"Wynn," said Noa, warningly. "Stop. You're not helping."

"Look, I just—" Wynn sighed. "I guess I just can't help but notice the racial dimension of what you're suggesting."

"Sir?"

"Look at him, he's got the darkest skin of anyone here."

"All due respect, sir, that's not why we're asking him about—"

"The heads, then," Caroline interrupted.

Everyone looked at her.

"If it's not the intruder, then you need to find the heads."

The officers frowned again.

"What heads?"

Caroline sighed, exhausted, exasperated.

"The girls, I mean."

"The girls?"

"I—told—you," she said, spitting out each syllable. "The girls who brought Gabriel home. The ones from the yacht club."

"You didn't tell us about any girls, ma'am."

She had told them. She was sure of it.

"I did," she insisted. "I did tell you."

"You told us you saw your baby in the crib. Your only child, your only son. You told us you got home from your night of drinking and doing drugs and you all went to bed with each other—the women went to bed with each other, the men went to bed with each other, you went to bed with this man who is *not* your husband—and your baby was asleep next to you the whole time, watching you while you were getting fucked, is that right?"

Caroline shook her head. He hadn't said any of that. In her guilt she was imagining things.

"Isn't that what you said, ma'am? That you saw him in the crib, and he was never alone once you went to bed, not even for a moment?"

She had never left Gabriel alone. Never. She had turned her head to the side and met his dark eyes—her husband's eyes—through the veil of the bassinet. She had seen for herself that he was there, accepting, forgiving. She'd been so focused on him being there beside her that she hadn't noticed anything else.

The shower.

She remembered how long they had taken, Perry cleaning her and dirtying her again. She looked at Perry now—she thought he'd been the one pacing the room before, or maybe one of the muffled voices behind the closed door, but now he was sitting directly across from Caroline on the opposite couch, watching her, and he was so very handsome, and though usually his skin was such a lovely, rich brown it now seemed flat, drained. What would he say when the fake police talked to him? *You were the one with her, weren't you? Yes, I was.* Or, *No, I wasn't.* Would he tell them everything? Would he tell them nothing? Had Gabriel even been in the bassinet at all? Had she imagined the whole thing? Caroline covered her face with her hands and let out a garbled moan.

"Ma'am? Can you repeat that?"

"I said I *don't know.*"

CHAPTER 8

They finally got through to Adam. In the hour that had passed since the police arrived, he must have been asleep. Caroline imagined the throb of his silenced ringer on their bedside table infiltrating his predawn dreams.

Finally, he answered. Someone handed Caroline her phone, and she held her husband's bleary face in her palm.

"Caro—what's wrong?"

She dropped the phone and looked up at the others.

"I can't," she croaked.

Perry bent and retrieved the phone from where it had fallen face down on the floor. He held it up to his own stern face.

"Something happened," Perry said into the phone. His eyes cut away. "Gabriel is gone."

"What?"

Perry handed the phone back to Caroline. Adam's face was in her palm again, green-gray and blurred.

"I don't understand," said Adam. "What did he say?"

"Gabriel is gone," Caroline repeated. "Someone took him."

Now it was Adam's turn to drop his phone.

The officers made Caroline go through the story again, for Adam's benefit—the excursion to the yacht club, the drinks, the retreat home in the rain, the girls, the baby asleep in the bassinet, the black gaps in Caroline's memory. There was something almost corporate about this latest repetition, as if they were discussing branding strategy. Let's just make sure we're all on the same page, build consensus. Circle back. No silos.

They questioned Adam, too, of course, though he knew nothing. He hadn't even been on the island since Sunday evening. The officers asked him about his night in the city, the contours of the two days leading up to his son's disappearance, though he hadn't been anywhere near his son. Had he noticed anything out of the ordinary? Had he received any strange phone calls? Trouble at work? Suspicious strangers spotted? Anyone who might have wanted to hurt him or his family? Their questions were surface-level, stupid; they seemed to be making them up as they went along, imitating detectives they'd seen on television.

Adam answered each inquiry with a neutral denial. No, nothing out of the ordinary. No, nothing strange. No trouble, no strangers. No one had a reason to hurt them. Nothing. The officers nodded in response, pretending to take notes.

The cell service was awful. Adam's face kept breaking up, pixelated growths sprouting on his forehead and chin whenever he moved.

"May I speak to my wife alone?"

Caroline took the phone upstairs and into their bedroom, shutting the door behind her. She lay down on the bed.

"How soon can you be here?" she asked.

Adam looked away, his face frozen in profile. For a second she thought the call had dropped.

"Adam?"

He came back to life, moving on the screen again.

"I can't come out until tonight," he said. "I need to stay here and fix this."

"Fix it?"

"You need to trust me."

"You can't leave me here by myself," said Caroline. "I need you. Gabriel needs you."

"That's why I need to stay and fix this!"

Adam began to cry, his face disintegrating. Caroline gripped the phone tighter.

"Tell me what the fuck is going on, Adam. Right now."

"Not so loud."

"Tell me!"

"Not on the phone."

"Then how?"

"End the call and open your laptop. Then wait two minutes while I log us in."

The phone screen went dark. Caroline opened her laptop. Soundlessly, the screen blinked into white. Not a static white—it seemed to move and breathe, like fog. She waited. In another minute the screen resolved into Adam's face, still bleary but no longer pixelated, the tufted headboard of their bed at home visible behind him.

"This is safe," he said. "Or it should be. It's end-to-end encrypted."

"Fine," said Caroline. "Now talk."

"I haven't been honest with you," said Adam. "I know that. This thing I've been working on—remember I told you I couldn't tell you anything, that it was for your own safety? And you asked me if it was legal?"

"Yes."

"Well, it was a complex question, and that's why I didn't answer. We're sort of beyond the realm of legal versus illegal with this work."

"I don't get it."

"What we're doing—this infrastructure—it could be world-changing. It *will* be world-changing. We've done our absolute best to keep it a secret—and believe me when I say that the level of security around this project is like nothing I've ever seen—but even with all of our safeguards in place we can't be sure that intel hasn't made its way out there. In fact, we're almost positive it has.

"Only a handful of people at Corridor even know about the project, everyone on the team only knows about their own isolated part of it, and our NDAs have been fucking ironclad, but these people—the ones who've been watching—they have ways of being very persuasive. They have hackers and technologies that we believe can bypass the most advanced encryption."

"So they might be listening to us now?" asked Caroline.

"Probably not," said Adam. "Not on our home devices."

"I still don't understand," said Caroline. "Who's been watching you? What are you doing?"

Adam dropped his voice to a whisper.

"The military—foreign governments—Mosaic. They get people to talk, they get people to do what they want. Or they kill them and their families."

Caroline blinked.

"You sound crazy."

"I know, I know, I sound crazy, but I promise I am telling you the truth. I swear to you on our son's life."

"Don't," she warned. "Don't say that."

"Too many powerful people are paying attention. Some of them want to stop us, and some of them want to get a piece of what we're doing. There have been threats. And because I'm at the heart of it, I have a target on my back. I know this—I've been followed, I swear. I didn't tell you, because I didn't want to scare you. I have access to information that these people want, and I think that's why—that's why someone, why they—Gabriel—"

He couldn't bring himself to say it. Caroline studied his flat ashen face, mind reeling. Ever since his start-up days, Adam had alluded to a vast, hidden world of wealth, power, and conspiracy that abutted the sphere of tech. He'd spoken often of a thousand-armed creature casting its alien shadow, forever trying to pierce the membrane of ethics and rationality. Entities who thought of themselves as gods, who had the power to rearrange the building blocks of humanity to suit their own insatiable desires, who used the bones of the poor to build their ladders to the stars, their cities in the heavens. There was a seed of truth in this, Caroline knew. But she also knew Adam to be dramatic, a man with a mind that loved a good story and an ego that needed to be reassured of its supreme importance.

Besides, the Corridor job was supposed to be boring! That's what Adam had said, that he would just be a cog in an enormous machine, grinding through the humdrum days in pursuit of a paycheck. When had it become cloak-and-dagger, life or death?

"You swear this is true?"

"I swear."

"Then we need to tell someone," said Caroline. "The real police, the FBI. Someone."

But Adam was already shaking his head.

"We can't," he said. "If the police get involved, that's the end of it, we'll never—"

"This isn't some fucking movie, Adam. You're not—I don't even *know* which fucking action hero you think you are. We need to tell someone who can actually do something about this, *if* it's anything remotely like what you're saying."

"We can't trust the authorities not to make the situation worse! We can't trust them at all. Who knows who they're really working for. If we go that route, then he never comes home."

"Adam—"

"I know what I need to do. It's my fault this happened, and I swear to you that I will fix it."

"But *how*?"

"Just *trust me*."

He was out of breath, almost retching, his face filmed with sweat. Caroline was sweating, too. It was hot in there with the door closed, the air like broth.

"I thought you would both be safe out there on the island," Adam said. "I really and truly did. I will never forgive myself for being wrong about that."

"I need you to come here now," she said. "I can't do this without you."

"I'll be there tonight. I promise."
"What time?"
"The last boat to Haven is at nine. I'll be on it."
"Adam, that's too late! You need to come now!"
"I'll be there as soon as I can."

The call ended and the screen went dead before Caroline could say anything else. For a moment she stared at the alien shadow of her own face, as if looking out a window at night. Then she shut the machine.

ONCE CAROLINE RETURNED TO THE LIVING ROOM, the officers finally left with assurances that they'd be in touch in the next few hours and redundant instructions to call them immediately if anything came up. The people in the house listened for the receding booms of footfalls down the ramp, waited for the silence that signaled the police had well and truly gone.

Even then, they did not speak or move. Gray morning light had begun to leak through the windows. The television was on and muted. Handsome sailors huddled together on the deck of a polar explorer ship run aground in a vast sea of ice. Caroline took a breath.

"Adam says he'll be here tonight. He can't leave yet."
She hesitated.
"I don't know what he's going to do, but—"
They watched her, waiting for her to say more.
"He thinks—he thinks he can fix this."
She wasn't sure if she was supposed to tell them. Then again, Adam hadn't told her that she couldn't.
"He thinks it has to do with Corridor," she said. "I mean, not Corridor, but whatever it is that he's been working on. He

said he has a target on his back. Someone wanted to hurt him, so they took Gabriel."

They were staring at her. Caroline kept going. Now that she had started, she found that she couldn't stop.

"He says we can't trust anyone, that he has to fix it, but I don't know—I don't—"

Perry stood up. He was the first to reach her and embrace her, to stop her from talking.

"Oh Caro," he said. "I'm so, so sorry."

Then the others were on her as well, hugging and rocking her, passing her around like a doll. Caroline let herself go limp in their arms. It felt so much better not to do anything, to not have to decide or explain anything else as she was led to a couch, laid down, and tucked in with a soft blue blanket. She sank into the cloudlike cushions. Nori trotted over, snuffling wetly, and sat on her feet.

"You need to eat, Caro," said Taryn. "What can I get you?"

Caroline shook her head.

"Just water," she said.

"I'm on it," called Blaise from the kitchen. He brought over a tumbler of water. Caroline sipped it slowly and sank deeper into the couch. On the television screen two sailors were talking closely, their bearded faces pressed together as if to kiss.

"All right," said Noa. "What now?"

Everyone waited for someone else to speak.

"We knew Adam was working on something that he couldn't tell us about," said Perry finally. "But we had no idea—"

"We had no idea it was so dangerous," finished Blaise.

Relief washed over Caroline. So she wasn't the only one who hadn't known. More importantly, they didn't seem to think that she was crazy.

"So you believe him?" she prodded. "You think it's possible that someone might have taken Gabriel because of the work that Adam has been doing?"

"It's definitely possible," said Perry. "Though we don't really know for sure. It's new territory and all under lock and key. I've seen them be paranoid about leaks to competitors and the media for new launches before, but not to this extent. Whatever it is must be revolutionary, and they must have put the fear of God into Adam about talking about it because he never so much as gave us a hint about what he was working on, even when he was drunk, which isn't like him. Now I can see he must have been trying to protect us by keeping us in the dark, but going it alone made him vulnerable to something like this. I can't believe the company didn't take the risk of something like this happening more seriously."

"Well, he's definitely right about one thing," said Wynn. "We can't trust the police."

"Local cops in places like this are always useless," Noa said. "All they do is issue drink citations."

The group nodded.

"It's more than that," Wynn said quietly. "They exist to serve the locals, and the locals want things to be a certain way. They feel a certain way about us. All of us."

"What do you mean?"

"I mean, I don't even think it's Adam's project that put the target on his back. The fact that Adam works for Corridor—that everyone in this house is somehow connected to the company—puts us all at risk. Because of who we are and what we represent, I don't think we can trust anyone on this island."

He stopped suddenly, then cocked his head, as if listening for something.

"Shut the doors," he whispered.

Blaise and Perry jumped up and slid the glass doors shut. Caroline flashed on an image of the illuminated glass box of the house, imagined what it would look like from the shore of the private cove. They were vulnerable in there, on display like zoo animals. Corridor's CEO had been wise to put his compound underground.

As if she could read her thoughts, Taryn curled up against

Caroline, shivering in apparent fear. On the television a giant clawed paw snatched a sailor off the ship's deck and into thick fog.

"This place used to be different," said Wynn.

"You told us," said Blaise. "The covenants or whatever."

"No, it's more than that," said Wynn. "The families went way, way back. Like, all the way back to colonial times. They were the ones who wiped out the Indigenous population. Slaughtered whole families, women and children. Said it was self-defense, but we all know that was bullshit. They were also involved with piracy and the slave trade."

"Jesus."

"For the entire history of the community, its members were obsessed with exclusivity and the purity of their bloodlines. Supposedly they betrothed cousins to each other as children in elaborate ceremonies, shit like that. And I know I said the blood rituals in the woods were just rumors, but a lot of people really believed they were true."

"Fucking rich people," said Taryn, shuddering. "Even worse than Catholics."

"You really did not go into *nearly* enough detail about all of this before bringing us here," said Noa.

"It's not exactly the most appealing pitch for a vacation spot," Wynn admitted. "But I really thought for sure that those days were over. I mean, *everyone* in big tech vacations here! Haven is practically a Corridor summer camp.

"But now I see there's no fucking way the descendants of the old generation would have given up without a fight. This—this kidnapping and cover-up—it could be their way of reasserting their dominance and warding off strangers. Telling us that we aren't welcome, or safe."

"But why Gabriel?" asked Caroline. "Why my baby?"

Wynn hesitated.

"There were other stories," he said. "Other rumors. The blood, in the rituals—most people said it was from animals."

Wynn paused. When he spoke again his voice was a whisper.

"But some people thought it was blood from children. Babies."

There was a long silence. Black smudges stole across Caroline's vision, like hands covering her eyes. She shook her head to clear them.

"No," she said. "No."

"Come on, Wynn," said Perry. "That's obviously not true."

"I didn't say it was true, I'm only repeating what I've heard."

"You brought us to *Infant Sacrifice Island* for a vacation?" Noa hissed. "Are you fucking insane?"

"Calm the fuck down! I never believed it, I swear! I still don't—not really. But a small minority insisted. They said the insecticide spraying that happened when I was a kid was really a test to see how much the neighboring communities would tolerate. A test to see how much Haven could get away with, especially when it came to other people's children."

"The worst, most violent and repressive tactics practiced abroad always end up being used domestically," said Noa authoritatively, as if quoting from something she'd read somewhere.

"Listen."

Perry had taken out his phone, its screen shining on his glasses so that Caroline couldn't see his eyes.

"Tons of weird shit has happened out here. Just do a cursory search and see what comes up."

Everyone took out their phones, except Caroline. She thought she had brought her phone downstairs with her, in case Adam tried to get in touch, but as she felt around in the folds of the throw she realized she didn't have it. She watched the others as they conducted their own research.

"Listen to this," said Blaise. "This is from the Unaesthetic Facts wiki: 'Relations between Haven and its neighbors have always been uneasy, and tensions were brought to a head during the Spanish flu pandemic. Fearful of the spread of the disease, Haven instituted a strict curfew and no outsiders policy. Riots erupted when a child from a neighboring town accidentally wandered into Haven and was shot. State troops were called in to suppress the violence.'"

"Fucking hell."

"But that was so long ago!" Caroline protested. "And it's from Unaesthetic Facts—I mean, graffiti in a bathroom stall would be more reliable."

"There's no Community Note," said Blaise. "So it must be at least somewhat legit."

"Hold on, there's more," said Noa. "This is from *The Guardian*, and it's much more recent. A decade ago, a few days before Christmas, the body of a young nanny was found in the oceanfront house of the family she worked for."

"How'd she die?"

"Shot in the head. Execution style. Then beheaded."

"Yikes."

"No one else had been at the house since Labor Day," Noa continued. "No one knew why the nanny was out there. In the living room they found a television that didn't belong to the family, and under the house they found a dead deer that had *also* been shot in the head and buried in a shallow grave. Police wouldn't say whether the nanny and the deer had been killed by the same weapon.

"And here's the even crazier thing. You all remember Erestor, right? Not you, Taryn, it's okay, I know. Well, this nanny worked for the family of the CEO of Erestor, and the murder happened right before the company went under. Coincidence?"

"Obviously not."

"*Obviously* not," Noa declared. She seemed almost giddy. "Erestor's primary focus was analytics for nanotechnology, and the company was deeply involved in the defense industry. Like, as deep as you can get. They were super-powerful and well-connected, but the nanny's murder was the start of the company's unraveling. It's like they met their match out here, on the island."

"Oh!" cried Taryn. "I found something, too! Back in the late aughts, there was a town a couple miles to the east that burned down. A bunch of people died. They never rebuilt."

"I remember that!" said Wynn. "There were theories that Haven was involved. There'd been some kind of dispute about something. Land or water use, or something with the national park."

"They'd kill people over something like that?"

"That was the official story," said Wynn. "Who knows what the fight was *really* about. This was right around the time when the Haven association was losing its power. They were worried about the next generation opening things up to outside development and control. Some people said the town that burned down had evidence of Haven's rituals, and were threatening to expose them."

"Maybe not just the rituals. Maybe the infant sacrifice, too."

"*If* such a thing exists."

"If such a thing exists."

"Which it almost certainly doesn't."

"Of course."

Caroline didn't want to believe any of it—especially not the infant sacrifice—but she had to admit the evidence was piling up that something was deeply wrong with Haven.

"I guess I have been noticing things ever since I arrived," she said. "People like, I don't know—*watching* me. There's something off about those kids in the camp. They definitely seem like they're part of some cult. And those girls—"

"Those three girls from the grocery store!" Noa gasped. "You're right!"

"They were always trying to take Gabriel from me," said Caroline, her voice rising. "I never agreed to let them take him. Never."

"And there was the intruder."

"Those rent-a-cops didn't want to pursue that angle at all."

"That's the most obvious sign that there's something to it."

The men began to leap up and roam around the room, chattering about other conspiracies they'd come across. Nori whimpered and whined. Caroline felt her heart speed up.

"I don't understand why Adam thought we would be safe out here," she said. "What was he thinking?"

"How could he have known?" Wynn shook his head. "If he thought the greatest risk was from whatever he's been doing at work, I could see the argument that he thought the island would actually be the safest place for you, that you'd be better off here than in the city while this project is in whatever critical stage of development it must be in now. He didn't know—"

"None of us knew," Perry said. "But now it's our responsibility to find out what's going on. We're all in this together."

"We'll retrace our steps. Everywhere we've gone since being here. The store, the beach, the theater, the yacht club. We need to see what we can find."

"We need to find whoever it was who came into the house that night. Or whoever it was who sent them."

"And those girls."

"One hundred percent."

"They could be the key to everything."

"Just—please just promise us no stupid male heroics," said Taryn. "Please?"

I didn't quite get that, said the television, making them all jump. *Could you repeat your request?*

"I don't get this fucking TV," Noa snapped. The stress seemed to be getting to her. "Sometimes it talks, sometimes it doesn't. I have no idea what triggers it."

"The system is probably corroded from all the salt air," said Wynn. "Not working how it should. Everything rots out here."

But though no one could say what triggered the television, it had sparked a memory for Caroline. She thought of the last time she'd heard it speaking, and she remembered a shadow in the living room that did not move or speak, the half-open gray eyes of a sleepwalker.

Jane. Caroline looked around now and realized that Jane was not among them.

"Where's Jane?" Caroline asked.

The others held still, but only for a moment.

"She's in our room," said Perry. "In bed."

"In bed?"

"She said this was all too hard for her," Perry explained. "Then she self-medicated too much, and well—I don't know if she'll make it out of bed at all today."

"Too hard for her?"

"She has her own history, you know."

Right, Caroline remembered. The seven or eight miscarriages. The same reason why Jane didn't come out to the yacht club with them the night before, and why Caroline couldn't ask her to watch Gabriel.

An ugly thought came to her. She pictured Jane digging her nails into her palms, talking about how she'd never be a mother, radiating a bitterness so intense Caroline could taste it like smoke at the back of her throat.

Caroline looked down at herself and saw that she was still in her soiled dress from the night before. She must have grabbed it from the bedroom floor and put it back on when she realized Gabriel was gone. Pale drips striated the black linen, and the neck had been yanked out of shape. She hadn't meant to hurt Jane, but she couldn't blame Jane for hating her.

She hasn't been okay in a long time, Perry had said.

What could pain like that do to someone? What could it make them do?

"I need to change," said Caroline. "Then we'll go."

UPSTAIRS CAROLINE FOUND HER PHONE WHERE SHE'D LEFT IT, face down on the bed. It was hot to the touch, and the charge was at seventeen percent.

She was dizzy, suddenly. Her breasts were beginning to hurt, heavy with milk that had nowhere to go. She lay down on the bed to rest for a moment, and felt a little lump pressing against her back. Snaking an arm beneath the bedding, she felt around for whatever was buried under there. She touched something soft and shaggy, brought it out in front of her face.

Gabriel's floppy bunny.

Caroline crushed its stinky, marled fur against her mouth and began to sob. She allowed herself, finally, to imagine where Gabriel, her baby, might be, and it came to her all at once, an awful cascade of snapshots, a stack of glossy prints falling to the floor.

Gabriel crying alone in a strange room. Gabriel crying alone in tall dune grass, Gabriel crying alone in the darkness of the woods. Gabriel crying in the arms of a stranger. A hand over his mouth, suffocating him. Gabriel screaming into the gusting wind, in the arms of a stranger, on a boat in the night.

Or worse. Even worse. Gabriel tossed overboard, mauled by propellers, sinking in pieces. Gabriel floating face down in the bay. Gabriel hit by a truck on the beach, the vehicle's headlights rising and dipping over the swells of sand, blood trailing behind its wheels. Gabriel buried in bracken under a raised boardwalk. Gabriel washed up in the white lace of the surf, sucked in and out and in and out again.

She'd been careless. She'd ignored him. She'd resented him. Maybe she had even gone so far as to wish him away. Maybe he'd been taken from her because she didn't deserve him. She knew this was what her mother would say, that Caroline's ingratitude had opened the door to her suffering. Surely there was a line from scripture to explain it, damning her.

There was that feeling again—that she was being watched. How else to explain how suddenly she roused herself, how quickly and purposefully she turned and stared directly into the unblinking, vacant eye of her uncovered lens?

Caroline reached for the camera and examined the front element glass for scratches. Had she really left the lens cap off? She never did that. Never. She'd learned her lesson long ago at a crowded party, when a hookup's belt buckle had scraped against the 25mm Zeiss borrowed from the college equipment room. Her work-study stipend had been docked almost three thousand dollars to replace the precious piece of plastic and glass. And the hookup had been totally forgettable.

Perry, she remembered. Perry had taken her camera.

Not only had he taken her camera. He'd taken photos of her.

She switched the camera to play mode and peered at the LCD screen. There she was, a bolt of flesh on the bed, her thighs huge and white in the foreground, her breasts sagging to either side, her head cut off at the neck. She wound the wheel backward, watched the stop motion stuttering of her body writhing, frame by frame, until suddenly her body disappeared and was replaced by the body of her baby, the pale blowfish of his belly straining against the tan forearms bolted across his chest and hips.

Caroline stopped short, her heart knocking. She stared at the picture of Gabriel, the fragment of him held by one of the teenage girls. He was struggling. He was trying to get back to her, his mother. He had known that something was wrong. The fly bite on his cheek was as red as ever, as if he'd been marked by an angry god.

She continued to wind the wheel, much more slowly now, and studied the images that went by, carrying her backward through time. A few more of Gabriel, held by the blond brunette, a sea of arms and faces around them. A few of the black-haired redhead and redheaded blonde coming into the frame, phones in hand, the three girls arranged like Botticelli's three graces. Pieces of her friends—Wynn beatific in profile, Blaise's tender hand brushing corn-silk hair back from Wynn's sweaty brow. Taryn and Noa's noses touching, lips parted in whispers. Other, more carnivorous faces looming, watching Caroline with nefarious intent—a man with bared teeth, a girl's slack mouth bloody with grenadine. The blackened soles of bare feet—two pairs young and pedicured, two pairs old and gnarled—bordering a spread of playing cards.

Of course. Caroline had taken all these photos—had handed

Gabriel off to take them. They were some of the last images of what was happening around her before it all went wrong, before Gabriel disappeared. A trove of potential clues. She almost laughed out loud.

The photos would help her.

Caroline gathered her tools on the bed: camera, card reader, laptop, portable printer. Then she popped the memory card out of the camera and into its reader and downloaded the files to her laptop. She waited impatiently as each blank rectangle suddenly flickered full with color and form, like lights turned on in the windows of a skyscraper, one by one. Caroline clicked and clicked, highlighted the ones that seemed important, the ones she wanted to look at more closely.

Send to print. Send to print. Send to print. Send to print. Send to print.

There were many, and she printed them all, the little compact inkjet whirring dutifully beside her, until the bed was blanketed with three-by-five pictures, rustling and shifting like feathers.

Tacks. Had she brought tacks? She had! There they were, rattling in their little silver tin in her camera bag. Oh clever, clever Caroline.

The wall at the foot of the bed would be perfect. All she had to do was take down the one poster—that spooky robot lady, such a bizarre choice for a beach house. Caroline propped the frame against the bedside table and set to work tacking up her photographs in a deranged salon-style hanging, until the tips of her fingers stung and her upper arms ached.

She sat down on the bed and studied her work. There was so much to see. She knew that if she kept looking—if she just looked hard enough—she would see everything. She would see it all, and she would find her son.

"There you are."

Perry appeared in the doorway, blocking the way. Her heart hammered as he came toward her. He held out another glass of water.

"Here."

Caroline hesitated, then took the water and drank it down. It reminded her of what water had tasted like in the early days of her pregnancy—slightly metallic at the tip of the tongue, like licking an old coin.

"You still haven't changed your clothes," Perry observed.

"I don't need to. I'm fine. I'll just put on my sweatshirt."

Perry moved closer, his face grave, until they were almost chest to chest and she could feel the heat of his body. His chin hovered over her shoulder as he gazed past her, at her photos on the wall.

"Look," he said.

She turned around. He pointed to a print of Gabriel in the teenage girl's arms, the belly straining against the dead bolt of the arms.

"Look right behind her," he said. "Look at that guy's face."

She looked. A thickset man stood right behind the girl, leaning toward her and the baby. The soft focus of the background couldn't hide the unmistakable leer on the man's face, or the glint on his gray teeth.

"And here," Perry said. "Look at this one, and this one."

He kept pointing, moving his finger too fast for Caroline to see everything he was pointing to.

"I know those girls are important. But in each of these photos, there's a man in the background looking directly at either Gabriel or you. Do you see what I mean?"

"I think so."

"Maybe you photographed something you shouldn't have," he said. "Like, part of a ritual that the island people didn't want you to see."

"At the yacht club? I know the girls are definitely not legal, but it was just dancing."

"Maybe what happens at the yacht club is a prelude to something darker. Who knows."

"Maybe."

Caroline took some of the prints down from the wall and laid them on the bed.

"I'll bring these with us," she said. "For reference. Maybe they'll help."

Caroline put on her sweatshirt. Perry encircled her in his arms from behind, cupping her elbows in his hands.

"Ready?"

It was a friendly hug, meant to be comforting. But something felt off. Caroline felt her gut shift. A knotting, then a loosening.

The water hadn't tasted like water.

"Just a second," she said. "I just need to pee."

Alone in the bathroom, behind the closed door, she knelt in front of the toilet and threw up with the same quiet, brisk efficiency of every morning weeks nine through twelve of her pregnancy, the quick purge between putting her herbal tea mug into the dishwasher and brushing her teeth.

When she came out again Perry was sitting on the bed, studying her photographs. He looked up as she approached, his eyes gentle.

"Everything okay?"

Caroline nodded, gathered up what was there and tucked the sheaves into the pouch of her sweatshirt.

"Ready."

She took her phone, too, even though there had been no time to charge it.

CHAPTER 9

Downstairs, it was decided: the women would go out and look for the three girls, and the men would stay back and search the immediate surroundings—the cove, the woods, and the area under the house.

Inside the grocery store, Caroline stared into the lush green wall of kale and chard and pictured the men rooting through the tall grass, ducking under the deck, their bodies hunched with awful purpose. She saw what they would see—the suspicious mound in the sand, silent and unmoving, a child buried.

"Caro?"

She flinched. The glitter in Taryn's wide eyes was gone. Her undercut was suddenly institutional, a marker of ill health.

"We found someone to ask," said Taryn, her voice low. "Someone who might know."

Caroline stared at Taryn, then stared at the rest of the produce section behind her. A pile of jade grapes. Corn heaped like firewood ready to be set ablaze. Homely tomatoes hemorrhaged from an overturned basket, some of them split and oozing. Flies buzzed.

"Caro? Did you hear me?"

She looked past Taryn to the dessert case. The severed hand was still in there, ink-stained fingers reaching for a white mound crowned with melting red roses.

"Someone who knows?" Caroline asked. "Knows what?"

Taryn looked at her sadly.

"Where those girls are. Look."

Caroline followed Taryn's pointing finger and saw Noa conferring with a middle-aged man in a polo shirt, his furred arms crossed over his wide chest. Noa was speaking too softly for Caroline to hear, but Caroline could sense the urgency in her tone and could see from the concern in Noa's Bambi eyes that she must have been telling him some part of the story. The man looked up and smiled as Caroline and Taryn approached.

"How can I help you, ladies?"

Caroline met the man's static, practiced smile with a frown.

"Who are you?" she asked.

"He's the manager, Caroline," said Taryn.

She recognized him, but she couldn't place him. He watched Caroline expectantly, holding his smile in place, waiting for her to tell him what she needed, so he could be the hero.

"The manager?" she repeated. "Are you sure?"

"We're looking for three girls who work here," interrupted Noa. "Probably thirteen or fourteen, heavy makeup, hair is blond, black, and red."

"They're always together," said Taryn. "We need to talk to them."

The manager was shaking his head. He'd started to shake his head before Noa had even finished her sentence.

"I'm sorry, ma'am. You must be mistaken. We don't have any girls working here."

Caroline let out a laugh, like ejecting a small bone stuck in her throat.

"Of course you do," she said. "We saw them. They rang us up at the checkout."

The man was shaking his head again, beckoning them to follow him through the narrow aisles. When they reached their destination, Caroline brought her hands to her open mouth.

They were at the front of the store. All of the registers were automated self-checkout kiosks, the full-length mirrors of their holographic screens burbling blue-and-white fireworks as they waited for their next customer. There were no workers at all.

"When did you change it?" Caroline demanded.

"Five or six years ago," said the man. "We updated the holographics just last summer. It's all top of the line. You won't find a better system anywhere else on the island."

Now Caroline was the one shaking her head.

"No," she said. "No. It wasn't like this."

"Ma'am?"

"We were here just the other day, and none of this was here," Caroline said. "There were girls working all the registers. We were their thousandth customers of the summer. They *danced* for us."

"I don't know what to tell you, ma'am," said the manager, shrugging his massive shoulders. "The store has been fully automated for years. Before we had the kiosks we did have teenage employees during high season, but the last cohort of kids who worked here are all in college now. I'm not sure what you think you saw, but I promise you we don't have any girls working at this store."

"Bullshit," said Caroline. She turned to Noa and Taryn. They were squinting at the kiosks, their mouths open in shocked silence.

"You were here," Caroline said to them. "You saw them, too."

They nodded in agreement, suddenly alert again. They were with her on this.

"Absolutely," said Noa.

"One hundred percent," said Taryn.

The manager shook his head again, his smile beginning to unfasten itself and slither off his face.

"I believe that you believe you saw that," he said carefully. "But I'm telling you that you are mistaken."

For a moment no one said anything. The fireworks kept exploding and regenerating in an endless cycle. The manager sighed.

"Maybe they were customers? I might know who they are—my daughter is fourteen and she knows all the girls out here. Why do you need to talk to them?"

A fly landed in the steel bristles of his hair, its tiny legs rubbing together as it embedded itself in the man's scalp. It hit Caroline with a force that almost knocked her down. She saw the light-up ice cube clamped between his grinning teeth, saw his leathery, liver-spotted hand stroke a young girl's midriff.

"You were there, too."

The manager raised his eyebrows. The fly crawled down to his widow's peak before retreating to his crown again.

"Ma'am?"

"At the yacht club," said Caroline. "Last night. You were there."

Something clicked on behind the man's eyes. He almost managed to hide it from her. Almost.

"I don't go to the yacht club," he said. "It's members only, and I've never been able to afford the annual fees."

He chuckled painfully.

"Us townies," he said. "We may keep things running here in Haven, but we certainly don't run the place, if you know what I mean. Haven't for a long time. We're just not a part of that scene."

"But you were there!"

Caroline looked to Noa and Taryn, waiting for them to back her up as they had before. But they were silent, uncertain this time.

"You remember him, don't you? He was definitely there."

"We were so fucked-up, Caro," said Noa, gently. "If you told me Kissinger's reanimated corpse was there, I'd probably believe you."

Caroline concentrated on her breath, trying to smooth its rough edges. She wanted to scream but knew that screaming wouldn't get her any closer to her son. She had to be calm. She had to be sweet.

"I know you were there," she murmured in her best bedroom voice, gazing into the man's eyes. "I need to know what you saw."

The manager held her gaze for a long moment. His eyes were small and dark, sunken into heavy brows and sagging bags. She saw the flicker of knowing mirth pass through his features—the same way he would look at a fourteen-year-old while fondling her.

Or the same way he would look at a baby he wanted to steal.

"Wait," Caroline said. "Look."

She felt around in the pocket of her sweatshirt for her photographs. Hands shaking, she sifted through them until she found the one she was looking for.

"That's you, isn't it?" she said, thrusting the print at the manager, her thumb half-covering his leering face. "And these are the girls I'm talking about. You were all there."

The manager stared at the photograph, impassive.

"Even if it wasn't you," said Caroline desperately. "You said you're a townie. You know this place."

The man lifted his eyes to glare at Caroline.

"And?"

"I know there must be things you can't share with me, and I promise, I'm not trying to expose your rituals or anything. Whatever is sacred to you and the community, fine. It's none of my business, and I'm sorry if we've done anything to hurt anyone by being here. But—you said you're a father yourself. You have to understand—I just want my son back. My baby."

"How *dare* you accuse me," the manager snapped suddenly. "You have no idea what you're talking about."

Caroline felt her face grow hot. Her breath felt jagged in her throat.

"I'm not—I'm just—"

"I know exactly who you are," the manager interrupted.

"Me?"

"You people," he spat. "You come out here and buy up all

the land and build your goddamn mansions, and even that's not enough for you."

"I didn't—"

"We don't even want what you're selling, but you give us no choice. You force it on us. And you destroy everything you get your hands on."

"But that has nothing to do with my baby!" Caroline shouted. "He's innocent, how could you—"

She reached out to claw at the man's face and felt hands on her arms, pulling her back.

"I'm so sorry, she's very upset," said Noa. "Her son, he's—"

"He *knows* about my son," said Caroline. "He knows."

She pulled free of their grasp and stalked out of the store, blinded by the sudden hot glare of the sun on the sidewalk. She felt the manager huffing at her back, following close behind, menacing her. She turned to face him and held up her hands, trying to protect herself.

"Please—"

With a groan the man tore off his polo shirt, revealing a chest webbed by innumerable purple scars, the tangle of ruined tissue thickest around his heart.

"You see this? *You see this?*"

He slapped at the scars with open fists, then pulled at his pecs, as if to rip the old wounds open again.

"They told me I needed it. Told me I would die without it, that I would leave my family with nothing and no one to care for them. They didn't tell me what it would cost, or what I would have to do for them."

"I don't understand," Caroline pleaded. "I don't know who you're talking about."

"I'll be paying for it the rest of my goddamned life!"

Caroline stumbled backward. She was dizzy, spinning, coming apart into splintering fractals of white light. Then she was sitting cross-legged with her back against the bike rack. Noa and Taryn were kneeling on either side of her, trying to get her to drink from a plastic bottle. Caroline swallowed, then coughed.

"I don't want that."

Noa dumped the bottle's contents on Caroline's head.

"Too bad," said Noa. "You need it."

Caroline brought her knees to her chest and hugged herself, shivering. The manager was gone. Other people came out of the store cradling brown bags in their arms. They paused to stare at Caroline before remembering to look away.

"It's okay," said Taryn, gentle. "You're okay."

Caroline shook her head.

"I can't believe I did that," she said. "I shouldn't have said all that to him. What was I thinking?"

"You were upset, Caro," said Taryn. "You can't blame yourself."

"Still. I should have been more careful."

She saw a look pass between Noa and Taryn.

"You're right," said Noa finally. "We need to be careful. We don't know who might be involved. And we especially can't trust any townies."

"That man was in my photo," said Caroline. "He was there. He was watching us."

"I believe you."

"I don't even think he works here," Caroline continued. "I don't remember ever seeing him at the store. I think everything he told us was a lie."

"You're right," said Taryn. "I don't remember seeing him there before, either."

"But we *did* see the girls working the checkout," said Caroline. "We didn't make that up."

"We didn't make that up," Taryn agreed. "That was real."

The glass doors of the store were shut now, showing them their muddied, melting reflections. No one else came in or out.

"What do you think he was talking about?" asked Caroline. "When he was hitting the scars on his chest? He said something about being told he needed it, and that he'd be paying for it the rest of his life."

"Maybe it's something they make people do out here on the island," said Taryn. "Some kind of ritual mutilation. I mean, folk medicine gets *such* a bad rap, and frankly, most of the things people say about traditional healing practices are really racist and closed-minded, but I wouldn't put anything past these rich white freaks."

"He said he wasn't rich, though."

"That's what all rich people say."

"Yeah, I bet it's more cult shit," said Noa. "Like, the scars show everyone that you belong. That you're down with the sickness, willing to do the dirty work."

Two of the camp children ran by, one of them brandishing a red, white, and blue rocket ice pop. Caroline brought her fists to her eyes.

"I need to get off this island," she said. "I need Adam, and we need the actual police."

"The next ferry's not for another three hours," said Noa. "We're stuck here for now."

Caroline opened her eyes.

"That can't be right," she said. "Three hours?"

"That's what it says on the app, see for yourself."

But before Caroline could check Noa's phone, she looked up and saw that a girl in a bikini on a pink bike had stopped to watch them. Her tan thighs tensed as she held herself in place, balancing on periwinkle pedicured tiptoes. Cellophane ribbons were tangled into the brown strands of her hair, shimmering in the sunlight like wet entrails—ribbons that had come from a tiny iridescent gift bag.

Caroline recognized her. She had been in the yacht club, too.

"Hey!" said Caroline. "Wait—"

But the girl had already kicked off and pedaled away, disappearing with a clatter down the boardwalk, toward the bayfront and then out of sight.

Before Noa and Taryn could stop her, Caroline was up and running. She raced down the boardwalk after the girl on the bike, boards banging beneath her feet, tall reeds whistling on either side of her, until she reached the bayfront.

Had the girl turned left or right?

Right, Caroline decided. She'd turned right.

She ran on, farther and farther away from the heart of the town, past the last house, until there was nothing but beach grass on either side of her. The bayfront walk dead-ended abruptly in a potter's field of boats, holes smashed into their hulls.

Caroline stood heaving, her hands on her knees. The water sucked and slapped against the shoreline bulkhead in time with her panting, though she couldn't see the shore through the wall of grass, the greenery as lush and impenetrable as the wall of kale and chard in the grocery store.

But there—almost hidden amid the green—a scrap of pink.

Once Caroline uncovered the bike's haphazard hiding place, she could see there was a clearing. Not a clearing—a path. She followed it only a few more yards until it spit her out onto a lip of sand, a hidden and private beach—the edge of the perfect circle of the cove. Across the water, Caroline could see the white spaceship of their house looming over its own pocket of shore. From where she stood, it was impossible to see if there was anyone inside.

"Oh shit."

"Goddamn it, Ash."

"It's not my fault, I—"

"You definitely forfeit the hand for that."

"Oh, *most* definitely."

Caroline turned and saw the teenagers. There were eight of them, four girls and four boys, dressed in bathing suits, bucket hats, and tattered crop tops, their bodies arranged in a lumpen, distended circle on the sand. She recognized some of the girls from the yacht club—one of them still had red smudges of grenadine around her mouth.

The heads were not among them.

Caroline looked closer and saw that the teenagers were playing a card game. She watched their hands as they began to shuffle and deal again. Their nails were painted different shades of purple, and beside each boy there was a stack of small bills, a mix of ones and fives and tens. Caroline recognized the deck of cards they were using—the family gathered around the winged eye, the man in a top hat and the woman with the head of a cat holding each other in bed.

It occurred to Caroline that she didn't know exactly where adolescents of this age fell within the hierarchy and history of Haven. Were they descendants of the old families? The offspring of the newcomers? A mixed gang of the two, the usual mingling of young townies and vacationers you'd find in any summer community, attracted to each other by the mutual promise of fresh blood?

What might they know, and where would their loyalties lie?

The fact that they were playing Fortunes didn't tell her much. It seemed as though anyone could learn the game, whether they were a local or not. They played silently, their faces grim, until a boy with eggplant-colored nails threw down the card with the baby in the box and let out a whoop.

The girl with the ribbons in her hair stood up, her eyes bright with tears, her voice cracking.

"It was supposed to be *me* next!"

The girl with the grenadine mouth laughed.

"That's not what the cards say."

"But I'm tired of being bait! They're old men, it's disgusting, it's supposed to be my turn to—"

"Tough shit."

The girl with the ribbons leaned forward and slapped the other girl hard across the face. With a cry the boy beside her lunged at the boy who'd won the hand, knocking him backward onto the beach, straddling him. In their struggle they kicked over their soft bricks of money, scattering a glitch of presidents' repeated faces over the pictures on the playing cards.

Caroline watched aghast as the other teenagers cheered and danced around the fight. They darted forward and back, getting as close as they dared, snatching up the bills and raining them on the heads and shoulders of the grappling boys.

"Hey," said Caroline. *"Hey!"*

The boys stopped fighting. From their nest of money and sand they looked up at Caroline, still holding each other by the arms. There was something loving about it. Erotic, almost.

Now that she had their attention, she didn't know what to say. She didn't know if she could trust them, or how involved they were. She thought of other teenagers she'd encountered in her past peregrinations as a photographer—all the boisterous boys on stoops whose teasing threatened to tip over into violence, all the preening, adultified girls naturally inclined to distrust an outsider. Even the ones who seemed hardened and unreachable at first were almost always willing to help her in the end.

She plunged in.

"I'm looking for three girls," said Caroline. "I think you know them. I've seen you all together before."

The teenagers stared up at her.

"Here," said Caroline. "Can I just show you?"

She knelt in the sand and spread out her photographs. In the clearest ones of the girls, they were holding up their phones, gazing intently into the glow of their screens as they filmed the chaos around them.

What exactly had they been filming, and why?

"These girls here," said Caroline, pointing. "I think they have something to do with my son's disappearance."

She paused again.

"I'm not really sure. But I need to talk to them. Please, it's important. I really need to find them, and I think you're the only ones who might be able to help me. Do you know where they are?"

The boys nudged one another, grinning in obvious conspiracy. Caroline tried again.

"If you don't know where they are, then maybe you can tell me more about the yacht club. What happens there?"

The boys snickered. One with violet nails and a single pearl earring brushed long dark curls out of his eyes and regarded Caroline with amusement.

"I mean, what does it look like?" he asked Caroline. "Didn't you see for yourself?"

Caroline looked at the girls, who avoided her gaze.

"It looks like underage girls partying with old men," she said.

"Well, there you go," said the boy. "What you see is what you get."

Caroline shook her head.

"But—I mean, does anything else happen? Like, after the bar closes?"

The boys broke into hard-edged, raucous laughter, falling all over each other as they mimed various stages of fornication. The girls stayed silent, sullen, staring into the sand. Caroline knew she was mishandling the interrogation, badly.

"I mean, is it just the drinking and the dancing?" she asked. "Why do you play the card game?"

"For fun!"

"Yeah, just for fun."

Caroline glanced at the spread of money, the still-pink slapped cheek of the girl with the grenadine mouth. The game couldn't be just for fun.

But the boys wouldn't say any more about the yacht club or the card game. They smiled at Caroline, stonewalling her.

And still the girls on the cove did not speak. Caroline could not account for their ongoing silence, unless it was just the universal ritual silence of teenage girls making themselves small around teenage boys. It seemed possible, even in a place as strange as this.

Caroline gathered up her prints. Then she decided to try one more time.

"These girls," she said. "Would they take a baby?"

She looked directly at the girl with the cellophane ribbons in her hair.

Please, Caroline thought. *Please.*

For a long moment they stared at one another. Then the girl uncrossed her arms and sighed.

"Yeah, they might," she said. "It's possible."

Conflicting emotions surged through her body—relief that someone was finally willing to talk, terror when she imagined what they had done with Gabriel. She saw hands lifting her baby, his body black against a flickering fire. A cup filled with blood.

"*They* wouldn't have hurt him, though," said the girl, as if she could see the images in Caroline's head. "They *love* babies."

The other girls nodded, backing up their friend. Caroline tried to control her breathing, to stay calm and think of what to ask next. At last, she was getting somewhere.

"Where would they take him? Where do you think they are now?"

But that was it. Just when she'd thought the dam was about to break open and they were about to tell her what she needed to know, the girls all clammed up again, thin lips tightly sealed. Perhaps the boys had given them some kind of signal.

In any case, no one else would speak, and Caroline gave up. She felt their eyes on the back of her neck as she made her way to the path and through the wall of grass, back to the bayfront.

Noa and Taryn were there waiting for her, perched on the hull of one of the abandoned boats. For a moment Caroline wondered how they had tracked her to that exact spot, but then decided they must have seen her running in that direction and had found the hidden pink bike.

"Well," said Caroline by way of greeting. "That wasn't very helpful."

"Where did you go?" asked Noa. "What happened?"

"The girl on the bike," she said. "I followed her. I thought she and her friends could tell me where I could find the three heads, but it was a dead end."

She found she didn't want to tell Noa and Taryn the rest—not about the card game, or the fight, or what the girl had said about the heads taking Gabriel. She didn't want to summon up those images again, and the thought of relaying the whole story exhausted her. Besides, there wasn't time.

"We just have to keep searching," she said. "Where should we go next?"

Noa and Taryn looked at one another, and then at Caroline, hesitant.

"What?" Caroline demanded. "What's wrong?"

"Caro," said Taryn. "Are you sure you can do this?"

"What do you mean?" Caroline realized that she was breathing heavily, hoarsely. "Of course I can do this. I don't have a choice."

"You haven't slept," said Noa. "You're overwrought."

"I'm not overwrought."

"We're worried about you," said Taryn. "Maybe you need to rest for a bit."

Caroline shook her head, trying to ignore the pain in her engorged breasts. She was wet all down her front where milk had begun to leak.

"I'm fine," she said. "I'll be fine. I swear."

Noa took out her phone and began texting.

"I just got a text from Wynn. The guys want us to meet them at the beach."

"Why?"

Noa and Taryn exchanged another look. A mutual reassurance, or a caution.

"What?" said Caroline. "Why do they want us to meet them there?"

"Caro—"

"They—they didn't find anything," Caroline choked out. "Did they?"

Taryn and Noa put their arms around her then. Caroline saw the men in her mind's eye, searching the dunes. She imagined clearing the sand away from where her child had been buried, revealing his bloodless face.

"They didn't find anything," said Noa. "But Blaise remembered something."

CLOUDS MOVED IN. THE SKY ABOVE THE OCEAN was streaked with gray, and a strip of ice blue balanced on the horizon, backlighting the husks of the container ships that waited, many miles out. The number of portable cabanas and shelters on the beach had increased since the other day, so that it looked as if a tent city had sprung up in either direction around the lifeguard stand.

The men were waiting for them on the stairs.

"There was no sign of anything near the house," said Blaise. "But looking around outside made me think of something from a couple days ago, when I went for my run on the beach.

"It was really early, and the beach was totally empty. I'd been running for about ten minutes when I saw this dark shape in the dune grass. I got kind of excited because I thought maybe it was some kind of animal, but then I got closer and saw that it was a rolled-up sleeping bag. Someone must have been camping there."

"And here's the thing," said Wynn. "Camping on the beach is illegal out here."

"I didn't know that," Blaise went on. "Even if I had, I don't know if I would have thought anything of it. Certainly not enough to mention it to everyone else. I mean, live and let live, right? I'm not a fucking narc.

"But searching through the tall grass near the house brought the memory back. And then I remembered what day I had seen the campsite, and what happened later that night."

Caroline knew what he was about to say, even before he said it. Her heart was pounding.

"It was the night the stranger got into the house," she said.

Blaise looked at her and nodded.

"Yes."

They were all silent for a moment. A Doppler siren of seagulls screamed by just over their heads, two birds clashing in airborne combat.

"Do you remember where the campsite was?" Caroline asked.

Blaise paused.

"Not exactly," he admitted. "Like I said, I'd been running for about ten minutes. Heading east."

"What landmarks do you remember?" asked Wynn. "What houses were around?"

Blaise thought for a minute, his face drawn in concentration as he tried to summon a memory, an image.

"There was a yellow house," he said finally. "A small house, with pale yellow siding. I remember thinking it was cute. A nice place to live."

"I know where that is," said Wynn. "It's in the next town over. Almost a mile away."

"Should we all go?"

"No," said Wynn. "Blaise and I will head down the beach and look for the campsite. The rest of you keep looking for those girls."

"I want to see the campsite, too," said Caroline. "What if—"

"We're going to run there," said Blaise. "I don't think you have the energy to keep up with us."

"I do," said Caroline. "Of course I do."

"She definitely doesn't," said Taryn. "She should be in bed, honestly."

Caroline tried to protest again, but Blaise and Wynn were already bounding down the stairs, down to the beach. She watched them sprint away, their muscled legs powering them over the explosions of sand kicked up by their feet.

"Trust me," said Perry to Caroline, his voice low. "You'll be more useful here with us."

THEY SPLIT UP AND WALKED AMONG THE BILLOWING SHANTIES. After a while, Caroline found herself alone near the water's edge. She could hear the plock of rubber against wood. A small, dark-haired boy who was not Gabriel in fast-forward was playing paddle ball against himself, tossing the tiny pink sphere in the air and whacking it with the wooden racquet. Plock, plock, plock. Miss. Plock, plock. Miss. The boy ran doubled over, as if in pain, racing to retrieve the fallen ball from the gray mirror of the surf.

Two figures were coming toward Caroline, one pushing the other in a big-wheeled beach wheelchair, the pair making slow progress over the humps of sand. Caroline recognized the elderly couple. The woman was sitting in the wheelchair, her legs wrapped in bandages to hide the bruises and decay. She looked even sicker than before. Her partner with the discreet scar gripped the push handles, driving the frail woman forward.

Finally the man came to a halt, and the woman hopped out of the wheelchair into a front handspring, her suddenly agile body arcing through the air. Caroline would have sworn to anyone that she saw it happen with her own eyes. The woman landed perfectly on her feet, raised her hands in a gymnast's salute; the man clapped and let out a shout of laughter. They set down fluffy white towels; on their knees, they reached for each other, their eyes crunched shut as their mouths fused together.

There was knowledge in that handspring. It defied all physical reality. They knew something, and Caroline needed to know it, too.

She approached the couple. They were lying down now, face-to-face, their gnarled, brown fingers working at the puckered elastic of their waistbands. The woman's top was already off, her pale breasts wrinkled and dangling, dusted by sand.

"Excuse me," said Caroline. The man and woman wrenched their lips apart and stared up at her.

"I've seen you here before," said Caroline. "I'm wondering if you can help me."

The man covered the woman's breasts with his hands, hoarding them for himself. Caroline thought of the woman's front handspring—the propulsion from the chair, the snap of the body into motion, the rotting corpse now a bird in flight. She'd had questions she meant to ask, questions that could help her find Gabriel, but none of them made sense anymore.

"I saw what you did just now," said Caroline. "How did you do that? I saw you just the other day, and you couldn't even walk."

She looked at the woman's legs. One of the bandages had slipped off, revealing not mottled flesh but platinum scales over flexed muscle, the limb both taut and iridescent. The woman saw Caroline staring and lifted the glowing leg in a showgirl's kick.

"You like them?" she asked Caroline. "Brand new."

"Only the best for my girl," said the man. "Top-of-the-line."

"They said it will make everything easier. Even with the side effects. They're supposed to pass, anyway."

The woman took in a deeper, more agonized breath, then coughed up a sputum of tiny red bubbles. The whites of her eyes were jaundiced. Blood pooled beneath her fingernails, turning them a dull purple.

"It's worth it," the woman said. "It really is."

"We wouldn't be able to come here anymore if we hadn't done it," the man added. "No one in our family would, even though we've been a Haven family since the beginning."

The woman patted the man on his thigh.

"It's all right, dear," she said. "It could have been so much worse."

"I know."

"At least we could pay for it with our own money. At least you still have your integrity."

"Yes."

"We have to enjoy the time we have."

Caroline's heart began to beat in a new rhythm.

"But who made you do it?" she asked. "And why do they make you do it?"

A whistle blew. Caroline turned to watch as children crawled out of the water like tetrapods, until they were all on the beach and the ocean fell still in a way that was both empty and not empty. It frightened her. She turned back to the elderly couple.

"What's going on?" she asked. "What's happening?"

"Must be something in the water," said the man.

Caroline got up and began to walk toward the children, who were watching the water, waiting for something to reveal itself. The two seagulls from earlier had taken their battle to the sand, their wings flapping erratically as they circled and screeched. One lunged at the other with its beak, and bright blood burst from its torn throat. Caroline looked away, hurrying toward the water's edge.

A tall woman in a white cover-up was coming the opposite way, striding quickly through the surf. Caroline recognized her, even without her daughter.

"Hey," said Caroline, catching her doppelgänger by the arm. "Hey."

The woman turned, looked at the hand on her arm.

"My baby," she said to the woman. "You were right. He did what you said. He disappeared."

The woman looked from Caroline's hand to her face. She observed her with her head tilted to one side, the way Caroline had seen some people regard her work in galleries, looking and waiting for a polite beat before moving on.

"You must be confused," the woman said brightly, showing perfect white teeth. "I don't think we've met before."

Slowly, soundlessly, a crowd of people was gathering at the shore.

"We did meet," said Caroline. "In the grocery store, and on the beach."

But the woman was already shaking her head. She shrugged her arm out of Caroline's grasp and touched the skin where her hand had been, as if she'd been scalded.

"I'm sorry," she said. "I don't think I've ever seen you before, and I've definitely never seen your baby."

The crowd continued to swell. More people than Caroline could have imagined were on the beach. They had abandoned their chairs and tents and umbrellas, the shantytown turned into a ghost town.

"But it was you," said Caroline. "I know it was you. You were with your daughter."

"It couldn't have been me," said the woman, looking into Caroline's eyes. "I don't have any children."

"Yes you do," insisted Caroline. "She looks just like you. A miniature you. You said you couldn't leave her alone. That she was too old to be left alone."

"No."

"Yes. She would just come find you, wherever you left her. You said your husband wanted to drug her."

The woman laughed.

"What do you know about me?" she asked. "What do you know about anything? You don't even know who they are."

"They? Who are *they*?"

The woman gestured toward the dark throng watching the water.

"There," she said. "Look."

"What is it?" said Caroline, afraid. "What am I looking for?"

"Go and see," she said. "You're better off seeing for yourself."

"Tell me," Caroline begged. "Please tell me what's going on."

"I'm sorry," said the woman. She walked away.

Caroline stumbled onward in the other direction, toward the crowd of people amassed on the shore. They were waiting for something to be dredged out of the water, or for something to wash up, and she knew what it was. The sun broke through the clouds, poking a dazzling finger into the shallows. Suddenly, she saw Adam standing amid the horde with his arms crossed. His eyes were hidden behind his sunglasses, his smile edging toward impatience. Then someone else's body moved in front of him, and when the other body moved away again Adam was gone. She shook her head. If only he were there with her.

Caroline looked from the crowd to the water. It was a pot about to boil, a curtain about to lift. There was a sharp whistling in her ears. Her heart beat faster as she forced herself through the crowd, watching as the gentle wave delivered the dark bundle from the shallows and onto the sand. The small body rolled as it touched ground, the same way her baby had rolled, just that once on that first night on the island. The white lace of the surf was a shroud over Caroline's feet.

The infant shark was no larger than a wriggling puppy. It thrashed and bucked, its gills swelling with each labored breath.

Caroline couldn't bear to watch it die. She moved toward the shark to take it in her hands and help it back into the water where surely its mother waited. But before she could reach it, a child had stepped forward and lifted the shark's body, raising it above his head to the cheers of the gathered crowd.

Someone shoved Caroline from behind. She fell face first into a breaking wave, her hands and knees scraped by crushed shells, her nose and mouth filling with salt and sand and foam.

"Caroline!"

"Oh my god!"

"Are you okay?"

There were hands on her back and arms. Her friends had found her—Noa, Taryn, and Perry. They pulled her out of the water. Still kneeling, Caroline lifted her head just in time to see her prints borne away on the rushing surf and the dead black rectangle of her phone fallen beside her, too heavy for the ocean to carry.

"Someone pushed me," she gasped, trying to catch her breath. "I don't know who, I didn't see—"

"Look!"

Perry pointed into the slowly dissolving crowd of onlookers. A few yards away, a figure was darting through the widening gaps between bodies, trying to escape. A man in dark clothes, not dressed for the beach. A menacing shadow of a person, slicing his way through a waking nightmare.

"That's him!"

And just like a nightmare, Caroline found that no matter how much she struggled, she could not get to her feet, even as the others ran off in pursuit.

CHAPTER 10

They lost him.

Caroline blamed herself. She had taken too long to stand up, and her delay had cost them everything.

If only she'd been up and running with the others! They wouldn't have had to hesitate and hang back to make sure that she was okay. They wouldn't have allowed the man in black to disappear into the crowd and elude them.

Moments, mere moments. It brought Caroline all the way back to the day they'd arrived, the precious, squandered minutes in their endless to-do list of new parenthood that had made them miss their ferry.

Moments, mere moments. Her fault.

She would give anything to go back to that afternoon. Adam beside her, trying to cheer her up and make the best of a minor inconvenience, their baby safe in her arms. Now she sat on the top step of the stairs that led down to the beach, sobbing into her hands.

"It's okay," whispered Taryn, her cool, sandalwood-scented arms wrapped around Caroline. "It's okay."

Caroline cried harder, her knuckles pressed against her eyes, taking great gulps of air, until she was almost screaming.

"Caro, it's okay."

"It's *not* okay! It's *not* okay!"

It would never be okay again.

After a while Caroline opened her eyes. Slowly, the blurred figures of Perry and Noa came into focus, sitting a step below them on the staircase. Perry reached up and rubbed Caroline's knee.

"Did you—"

They shook their heads, too crestfallen to speak. Caroline moaned and began to weep again, and Perry moved to sit beside her.

"Hey," he said. "Hey."

He wrapped an arm around her waist and hugged her to him, kissed her softly on her wet cheek. Caroline wondered briefly what Noa and Taryn must think, seeing Perry embrace her that way, but decided it didn't matter.

"There are other places we can look," Perry said, his lips close to her ear. "Other options. There's no reason to give up now. I'm not going to lie to you and tell you it's all going to be okay, but it's still too early to lose hope."

Caroline nodded. She wanted to believe him, despite how hopeless she felt. She wanted there to be other options. Perry clasped his hands on her wrists, and she allowed him to pull her to her feet.

"What about that Public Safety cabin?" Noa suggested. "They've got to have some kind of surveillance setup."

"Good idea," said Perry. "If we could get in and look at some of their footage, maybe we'd see something useful."

"Won't the rent-a-cops be there?" asked Taryn.

"Maybe," Noa admitted. "But maybe not. They could be out harassing other people. We might get lucky."

"It's worth a try," said Perry.

They didn't ask Caroline what she thought. She was worn out and depleted, her assent taken for granted.

Caroline looked down from the top of the stairs to the beach below. The baby shark had been taken away by the jubilant crowd, but the body of the exsanguinated seagull still lay splayed on the sand where it had fallen. Smaller birds, sparrows and sandpipers, had begun to surround it. They fluttered around the corpse, chirping and pecking, bloodying their tiny dancing feet in their own private ritual.

THERE WAS NO ONE ELSE IN SIGHT ON THE TREE-CHOKED boardwalk as they approached the twin bungalows of Public Safety and Public Health. As they got closer to the small white buildings, Caroline could see the handwritten sign posted on the door of the latter—*Haven Doctor's Hours, 11 a.m. to 12 p.m. and 5 p.m. to 6 p.m., Mon.–Fri. No Appointment Necessary.*

Judging from the single small window cut into each exterior, the bungalows were dark inside, evidently unoccupied. Caroline knew the doors would be locked, and they were. But Perry was undeterred. Pressing himself against the outer wall of the Public Safety building, he shimmied along the narrow ledge of its wooden platform, disappearing around the corner and out of view. The women waited in tense silence, listening to the hushed creaking of slender branches bending in the breeze, straining to hear footsteps on the boardwalk that never came. Finally the front door of the bungalow opened, and Perry stepped out.

"Back window." He grinned. "Wide open. These rent-a-cops really are fucking stupid."

Caroline wanted to be relieved, but she wasn't. The abandoned boardwalk, the open window—it all seemed a little too easy. As if the next step of the investigation had been planned this way, laid out for her like a fresh change of clothes on a bedspread. Doubts burbled in her belly, nauseating her.

Maybe she *was* just overwrought, as they all kept telling her. Well, she had every reason to be.

"You go in with him, Caroline," said Noa, nudging her forward. "Taryn and I will keep watch out here."

Caroline followed Perry into the bungalow, and he shut the door behind them.

Inside, they could see the bungalow was little more than a shed—a single, dim room that was mostly taken up by a wooden L-shaped desk and a few folding chairs. Three monitors rested on the desk's surface, and three hung on the wood-paneled walls, each screen divided into a flickering patchwork grid of views. Their cooling fans hummed and groaned with expended energy. Caroline and Perry kept the overhead lights off as they studied the teeming spread of images.

There was the ferry dock, deserted save for a few teenagers climbing onto the wooden pilings to launch themselves into the bay. There were several different views of the grocery store, both inside and out—the narrow, treat-crowded aisles, the automated registers, the sunstruck sidewalk and bike rack out front. There were even more views of the yacht club, its wraparound deck and turquoise pool crowded with people enjoying their afternoon, while the murky interior was mostly empty, just a few men hunkered down at the bar, watching a baseball game on the television. There was the leisure complex, its green field dotted by the bodies of white-uniformed children doing calisthenics while the camp cabins crouched nearby, as if ready to pounce on them. The wooden whale shape of the amphitheater, abandoned at this hour.

The majority of the views were of intersections of boardwalks and exteriors of houses that Caroline didn't recognize—a chocolate-brown wooden tower that reminded her of a grain silo; a long gray edifice that seemed to sink into the swampy ground, its facade composed of arches like a Roman aqueduct; another white house that looked like a spaceship but was not their house. There were even some unfamiliar interiors—someone's nautical-themed living room, an industrial kitchen with sliding doors that overlooked the ocean, a bedroom with walls that were covered in mirrors. Most puzzling were the views of what appeared to be random patches of wilderness, as if the camera had been misdirected or knocked away from its original subject, though there were too many of these to be accidental. Whatever the case, seemingly every part of Haven was here, on display.

Surveilled.

Caroline and Perry stared into each square, searching for the man in black. They saw various figures flitting in and out of the frames, many of them mysterious in their anonymity, but they didn't see the intruder.

"If only we could figure out how to rewind." Caroline sighed. "Go back and look. Then we'd find him. We could even find Gabriel, too. Some sign of him."

"We'd be here for hours," said Perry. "We don't have that kind of time."

They looked in silence for another moment. Caroline caught her breath at a sudden movement in a copse of pines, but it was only a deer.

"Why do they need so much of this, anyway?" she asked.

"What do you mean?"

"This footage," she said. "Why do they need a camera on every inch of the town?"

"It's like this everywhere," said Perry. "Most people just don't know about it. Or they sort of know about it, but they choose not to *really* know it, and they definitely choose not to think about it. And even what most people might imagine pales in comparison to what really exists. Most people could never believe how widespread, how deeply rooted and all-seeing the surveillance apparatus really is."

Caroline didn't know what to say. He sounded like Adam and his conspiracy theories.

"And really, they only have themselves to blame," Perry continued. "Decades ago, the citizenry allowed their ethics to be compromised for a promise of safety. Once you make that deal with the devil, there's no going back."

"But even here on the island?" Caroline pressed. "In Haven? Everyone keeps saying all of big tech vacations here. All their rich and powerful friends. I feel like they wouldn't allow it, that they'd find a way to make themselves exempt."

Perry laughed ruefully.

"Even here," he said. "*Especially* here. You know why, don't you?"

"To keep track of the cult? Like, keep the natives under control?"

"That, but also blackmail."

"Blackmail?"

"Sure. Every recorded image is a potential insurance policy against someone else. You never know when you might need it. If you can't opt out of the surveillance arms race, you may as well take advantage."

Caroline shuddered.

"It's almost scarier than a multigenerational island cult."

"Well, you must understand it on some level," said Perry. "Submission to the all-seeing eye."

She frowned.

"What do you mean?"

"What you told us about your work, your photography. How it was all about seeing what you aren't supposed to see."

"That's what my work *used* to be about."

"Right. And then someone died. But you kept taking photos anyway."

Caroline gaped at him.

"Why are you even bringing this up?" she asked. "Do you think I want to debate this right now?"

Perry shrugged.

"Just pointing out that your ethics can be compromised, too."

Caroline didn't want to talk about it anymore. She was tired. Exhausted to the point of collapse. Perry must have sensed it, because he snaked his arm around her waist again, just like he'd done earlier on the stairs leading to the ocean, as if to keep her from falling.

But this time something made Caroline flinch and pull away from him. It was involuntary, so sudden she couldn't even put a reason to it. They stood apart for a moment, just breathing, watching each other warily. Caroline thought of Perry pinning her to the bed, taking photos of her. She thought of the two seagulls on the sand, poised to begin their dance of death.

"Sorry," said Perry softly. "I didn't mean to—"

"Shh!"

Over the hum of the machines, she could hear voices outside. Noa's and Taryn's, lilting and light, trying to be casual. And others. Deeper, male voices, questioning them.

The rent-a-cops.

Caroline and Perry ducked down on their hands and knees. They listened, straining to hear what was being said on the other side of the door. Caroline couldn't make out words, but from the tone and volume it sounded like Noa and Taryn had stopped trying to play innocent and were now arguing with the public safety officers.

She and Perry didn't dare speak. Their eyes met, a simple message passing between them: *Don't move, do nothing.* They waited, listening as the argument outside escalated, the women's voices growing shrill, the cops sounding increasingly aggravated and impatient, until suddenly they could hear Noa's voice clearly.

"Take us, then!" she shouted. "Take us, and we'll show you!"

Caroline had no idea what Noa was talking about. Clearly it was some kind of diversion, designed to draw the officers away from the bungalow. It would never work. The rent-a-cops may have been careless, but they weren't completely moronic. Besides, wasn't this their center of operations? Caroline stiffened as she braced herself for the turning of the knob, the opening of the door. How would she and Perry explain themselves?

But it did work. Somehow, Noa and Taryn had convinced the officers to lead them away. Caroline heard their quartet of voices growing fainter and fainter, until all that was left was the hum of the monitors again.

Perry let out a breath.

"They're gone," he whispered.

"Are you sure?" Caroline whispered back.

Perry slowly rose to his feet, until he could peer out the small front window.

"Yep," he said. "Gone."

Caroline stayed seated on the floor. Though in theory the danger had passed, her heart was beating oddly again, unevenly. Her mouth and throat felt swollen and dry.

"I think it will be safer if we leave separately," said Perry. "Less suspicious if we walk in different directions."

Caroline swallowed hard.

"Okay," she croaked.

"You leave first," he said. "Head toward the house. I'll go into town and see if I can find out what happened to the others. Just don't let anyone see you."

She nodded, even as she remained where she was. Perry opened the door, and the warm daylight found her, spilling from the threshold into her lap as smooth and inexorable as the oncoming surf.

Then in the next moment Caroline was up and walking—away from the bungalow, away from Perry. Her heart was still pounding. The whispering trees closed around her, and she did not look back.

CHAPTER 11

When Caroline made it to the house she was relieved to discover that she was alone. She needed time and space to think, to collect herself and attempt to clarify the cause of the strange sensations she was having in her body—the dry mouth, the syncopated heartbeat, the recoil from a friendly touch.

She was in pain, too, her breasts filled with rocks. She needed to pump.

But she couldn't remember if she'd even bothered to bring her pump to the island. She hadn't used it since Gabriel's days in the NICU—he'd been so good at nursing, and back at home she'd never had to be apart from him for more than an hour or two.

Even if she had brought the pump, she didn't have the time to use it now.

She stood in the empty living room, the silence of the space echoing around her, and decided to conduct her own search of the house.

Who knew what she might find? An errant piece of physical evidence—a strand of hair or drop of blood, a scuff mark from an unknown shoe. A note. A body.

No, not that. Not a body. She wouldn't find that.

But she would be better off seeing for herself. She sighed as the impossible weight of the last few hours fell on her, with no one there to hold her up.

"I can't fucking believe this," she said aloud.

Hello, said the dark, blank face of the television. *Can I help you?*

Caroline was about to tell it no, no thank you, as she always had, dismissing what she'd unconsciously assumed was an irrelevant intrusion from one of tech's minor spirits. Her tongue was against her front teeth, the word of refusal almost formed, when she stopped herself.

"Actually, yes," she said. "Yes. I do need help."

Okay, said the television. *What can I do for you?*

Caroline thought for a moment. She felt foolish, but she decided to be direct.

"Where is my baby?" she asked. "Where's Gabriel?"

Classic television and movies available with your plan, said the television. *She's Having a Baby, Gabriel's Fire, Rosemary's Baby, The Trials of Gabriel Fernandez, The Boss Baby*—

"No, that's not what I'm looking for," said Caroline. "I'm looking for my son."

Okay, said the television. *The Good Son, His Only Son, Son of God*—

"No," Caroline interrupted. "I don't want to watch anything. I need information."

The television seemed to think for a moment, processing Caroline's words.

Okay, it said after a beat. *What do you want to know?*

Caroline looked around the living room. She thought of the teenage heads sitting on the white couches the night that Gabriel had vanished, their hair and clothing suspiciously dry as the rain pounded against the glass walls. She thought of the way they had grinned at her, proud of their caretaking.

"Who else has been here?" Caroline asked. "Who else has been in this house?"

I'm sorry, said the television. *That information is not available.*

"Why not?"

You do not have access. Please log in with your Employee Experience ID and password.

"But I—"
Access denied.
"No!"

She was crying again, making ugly and strangled sounds that she didn't recognize as coming from her own body.

"Please!" she shouted at the television. "Please!"

Suddenly, the screen sputtered to life, beats of blackness now interspersed with fast snippets of images: crayons and a kiddie pool; a computer-animated woman and baby shivering in a cemetery; masked men performing a choreographed dance; two teenagers making out on an unmade bed; a burning forest, blackened matchstick trees with leaves of orange light; a circle of people gathered around a fire in a glowing hearth, a little girl in a snow-covered backyard; black-and-white baby monitor footage of an empty bassinet; a fleeting glimpse of a room that looked very much like the one she was currently standing in, a glimpse so fast she thought she might have imagined it.

There was sound, too, seemingly disconnected from the quick, scattered spittle of pictures on the screen, an incomprehensible selection of options recited aloud by the television's voice:

Friends Summer Trip Playlist Volume 2, Party Time
Winter Retreat
Beta Test 037
The files are IN the computer

Caroline stopped crying and held still, trying desperately to take it all in, even as the parade of images seemed to accelerate beyond what the human eye could see and the sound grew increasingly garbled.

Retard Retreat Spring, Members Only LOL
Fuck Mosaic Playlist
Beta Test 052
Fuck
Fuck me
Stop

I'm out
I'm out
What are you doing?
What are you doing?
WHAT are you DOING?
PLEASE

The realization hit Caroline with a jolt. It wasn't just a menu of options—these had to be recordings.

But she didn't know how to control any of it.

Too soon, the glitching stopped and the television went black again. After a long moment, Caroline knew that it wouldn't restart on its own.

"Can you show me more?" she whispered. "Please?"

The television was silent.

"Please," Caroline begged. "Can you please show me?"

I'm sorry, said the television, calm and composed again. *Playback from that time is no longer available.*

And that was it. Bitterly disappointed as she was, Caroline decided to go on with her search of the house. There was still a chance she could find something.

She started in Noa and Wynn's room, which was down a curving hall and three steps up from her own room. The bed had been made carelessly, the comforter pulled askew over the pillows. When Caroline lifted it, she smelled sunscreen and sandalwood, an undertone of iron. A half dozen empty wine bottles were arranged in diamond-shaped clusters at each corner of the bed.

On the dresser there was a collection of miniature platinum hardware. Caroline thought they might be hard drives or power sources—their lights blinked blue, though they were not plugged into anything. Prototypes of something, perhaps. She had never seen pieces like them before. Caroline picked up a glowing egg and turned it over in her palm; she examined the laser-etched Corridor logo, the door opening into oblivion.

The other room on the same level belonged to Taryn and Blaise. The bed was unmade, and there was the ghost of a love seat at its foot, its form draped with damp white towels. A sliding door led to a small balcony, which was just large enough for two wooden folding chairs that faced in opposite directions.

Someone had written on the bedroom walls, a scrawl like black mold. Caroline read the affirmations.

Love flows to me.

Each day is another small step toward the fortune you deserve.

Run to the horizon. Jump and become the stars.

I am lovable. I am loved.

I will always get through this, somehow.

Life flows to me.

There were some small doodles as well. Caroline looked for rectangles surrounding six-pointed stars, but the ink had bled into the humid wood, smudging the details of the drawings so that it was impossible to see what they were.

She didn't like this, not at all. The drawings linked the house much too closely to the island cult. And the fact that her friends hadn't said anything about their presence on their walls—well, she didn't even know what to think about that.

The last door at the end of the hall opened on a short flight of stairs leading down, which led to another closed door. This had to be Perry and Jane's room, she realized.

Could she trust Jane? Would Jane help her?

What had she been doing shut up in the room all day?

Caroline knocked. No answer.

"Jane?" she whispered.

Then louder:

"Jane?"

Still no answer.

Caroline opened the door, expecting to find Jane sprawled in bed, on drugs or hungover or sleeping or some deadening combination of all three.

But the room was empty. The bed had been stripped down to its fitted sheet, and there was a dark oblong oval on one side that was wet to the touch. The windows were higher up on the walls than they were in the other rooms, broad rectangular bands close to the ceiling that Caroline couldn't see out of.

A monitor and keyboard were set up on the desk, both branded with the same half-open Corridor door. The screen was dark, asleep. Caroline prodded a key and waited for a response, but nothing happened. She felt around the back of the machine for a power switch but found nothing.

Suddenly the screen turned white. A moving and breathing white, like a wash of milk. After several long seconds the fog began to dissipate, unveiling a scatter of browser and finder windows jammed with incomprehensible text, still too faint to see.

The screen went black again. Caroline stabbed at the keyboard repeatedly, but the machine wouldn't turn back on.

There was a framed picture on the floor, facing the wall. Caroline turned it around and met the dark eyes of a toddler—his face a smooth plane of platinum, his skull and chest unraveling into a glittering mess of metal vines.

Her moving the frame had loosened it, and now she could see that something had fallen out of the back—a few small strips of paper, a series of what looked like charcoal sketches but were actually ultrasound images, tiny white blobs floating in the dark void of a womb.

Jane's dead babies? But why here, hidden like this?

The darkness in the corner moved, unfolding itself. Caroline shrieked. Nori stretched and trotted over, her pink tongue lolling. Caroline scratched the dog behind the ears with trembling hands.

"Where's Jane?" she asked. "Where is she?"

Nori didn't answer.

Back in her own room, Caroline climbed on to her bed and opened her laptop. First she searched for Mosaic. She scrolled past the official site, the Wikipedia page, the "People also ask" questions: *Is Mosaic a good company? Is it hard to get a job at Mosaic? Mosaic ad explainer.* She read the headlines under

"Top stories": *Mosaic Is Perfect Stock for Dangerous Times, Mosaic Scraps Proposed Pension Cuts After Employee Revolt, Mosaic Bets Big on Predictive Maintenance, Mosaic CEO Speaks at Brussels Summit: "Crossroads of Innovation."*

Then she searched for Corridor. *What does Corridor do exactly? How big can Corridor get? Is Corridor evil? Corridor Wins $335M Contract From Dept. of Defense, Corridor Buys Out NHS, Corridor Backs HEOL legislation: "We support freedom of choice for all."*

On the seventh page of results, she clicked a link that brought her to a message board she'd never heard of before. It was all in plain text, two-thirds of it in programming language. Caroline scanned the English that was there:

> thoughts on Corridor rumors?
>
> SIL works in SF office and says not true but don't believe her
>
> i heard beyond nano and cryo
>
> time to face the truth?

The screen went white. Caroline clicked refresh, then clicked the back button. The pages wouldn't load. Clicking each link again would only bring her to an *error: not found* message. Nothing further.

She needed to talk to Adam. But her waterlogged phone wouldn't turn on, and she didn't know how to call through the computer using the encryption. Trying to reach Adam wasn't safe.

Besides, it was possible that he was already on his way.

She closed the browser window and saw there was another window open behind it. A dark room, a streak of blue light, illumination on glasses. She saw the man watching her for only a second before he disappeared and was replaced by an undulating, dotted infinity symbol. Its edges hardened into right angles and it became a half-open door, a portal to darkness.

Caroline slammed the laptop closed.

She looked up at her prints that were still tacked to the wall, examining Gabriel struggling, the men leering in the background, the girls filming everything with their phones.

She got up to look closer. She studied the fragments of Wynn and Blaise embracing and of Noa and Taryn whispering. They were in more of the images than she'd initially realized. While Caroline had been photographing the silverbacks and jailbait dancing and playing cards, the others had been there in the background. They were almost out of frame, but they were unmistakable—the only other people at the yacht club who weren't dressed in white.

In every image, they were deep in conversation with three heads. Blond, red, and black.

She felt uneasy, unsure of whose side they were on. Could she even trust them?

Come on, she thought. She was being ridiculous. They were her friends, and they were helping her, *had* been helping her this whole time. Their sense of urgency matched hers. The way Wynn and Blaise had sprinted away to try to find that campsite—

Another epiphany, another jolt, this time so chilling that she almost bleated aloud in panic.

If the intruder was part of the island cult—a scion of the old Haven community, fighting back against the intrusion of newcomers like her—then wouldn't his family have a house? Or even if his family had been forced out, wouldn't he have friends who would take him in? Why would he need to set up camp on the beach?

Wasn't that something only an outsider would do?

Caroline didn't have time to think it through anymore—she froze as she heard the rumble of footsteps coming up the ramp. There wasn't time to take down any of her prints. Instead, she grabbed her camera and slung its strap over her shoulder. She knew all the images were in there, safe on her memory card, and that was all she needed.

Hurrying, her heart jiggling in her throat, she went out onto the deck off the bedroom. The cedar privacy planks walled her in, blocking her escape. She heard the others enter the house, just as her eyes lighted on the table positioned between the chaises.

It was just high enough. She scrambled over the wall, held on and let herself hang, then dropped down into the soft sand below.

SHE HAD TO KEEP GOING. THE PLAN HAD BEEN TO retrace their steps—the grocery store, the beach, the theater, the yacht club. Caroline wasn't sure if it made sense for her to continue, or if the plan had ever been a good one, but she didn't know what else to do. Perhaps going through the motions would kick-start her brain again and help her determine her own, better course of action.

If such a thing existed.

She decided to go to the amphitheater. There would be people there, other parents of young children. Maybe someone would help her.

By the time she reached the theater, Caroline could tell by the restless shuffling of the audience members arrayed on the benches and the haggard looks on the faces of the child performers that the early evening performance was almost over. From the boardwalk she could see the girl with white-blond hair kneeling on the stage, which had been transformed into the shimmering surface of a vast lake. Colored spotlights and lasers played over the backdrop and water, looping and skittering. Other children juggled bright egg-shaped balls of light, their necks layered with gorgets of glow sticks. Their mouths were open but they were silent. The girl who was Gilgamesh began to weep.

"What was it for?" she cried. "What use was the blood, life, and love flowing through my body? To what purpose the unfurling of my days, if they could not go on forever?"

The lights on the backdrop drew together to form a half-open door. Caroline blinked and the door disappeared.

Gilgamesh lay down with her hands folded on her bare chest. Her colorless hair streamed around her on the surface of the gently rippling water. The children who had been juggling dropped their glowing eggs into the water and stepped forward, holding hands.

"Oh, frailty of mortal flesh," they chanted. "Oh, fragile king! Oh, fortune, cruel! No haven here on earth for you. Oh, helpless hunter! Oh, questing prince! Pursue your quarry through the stars. Oh, heartless hero! Oh, mother, mine! Lift up your eyes and see!"

The light show became more frenzied and the children began to weep. More of them came from offstage, dressed as animals and imaginary creatures—rabbits in medieval armor, fawns with feathered wings, a boy in a tattered black cloak and top hat, a girl whose head was swallowed by the papier-mâché skull of a cat. Water sloshed at their ankles. The child supplicants approached bearing cups that seemed to flicker with flames. Offerings, thought Caroline. She knew with a sudden and terrible certainty that if she could view the children from above, she would see that their bodies were arranged around Gilgamesh in the shape of a jagged star enclosed in a box.

The stage lights went out. There was a long silence, then the sharp clop of high heels as Oona Vita strode out in her yellow-buttercream ball gown, high and dry at center stage.

"There you have it," Oona crowed. "Your Camp Haven Child Players!"

Caroline jumped down from the boardwalk and moved toward the audience. She lunged at the nearest couple, banging her knee against their bench. The man and woman shrank back, their white linen caftans like hospital gowns.

"Excuse me," said Caroline. "I'm sorry to bother you, but I'm looking for my baby and I need to find out what's going on here."

The couple kept staring, aghast.

"You must know something," said Caroline. "Aren't those your children up there? Don't tell me you don't know."

She pushed past them, down the aisle, accosting the other members of the audience as they began to rise from their benches, her camera thudding against the side of her body. One after another they recoiled. She thought she could recognize the grocery store manager, the elderly lovers from the beach, the woman with her own face.

Every one of them turned away from her.

THE YACHT CLUB, THEN. MAYBE THE THREE GIRLS would be there.

There was a crowd outside, the mass of bodies twitching and shifting like a sleeping animal, exhaling smoke, staring into the burning sun balanced on the horizon. Everyone wore pajamas—the girls in lacy slips and bunny rabbit onesies, the men in robes over cotton and flannel twinsets. Another themed party. On the margins, Caroline felt eyes set upon her, watching her as she approached. But by the time she got closer they had already looked away.

She pushed toward the entrance. Snatches of talk ricocheted against her ears as she wedged herself between fleece-sheathed shoulders and satin hips.

"I follow like, sixty-five plastic surgery accounts."

"Why do you do that to yourself?"

"It's just unfair to girls like me who are naturally stunning."

"But where would I get a brain scan? My doctor doesn't do that."

"Mine does every year. You just have to ask."

"I'm so glad they found each other."

"Found each other? He basically ordered her. He went to Mumbai and was like, you're mine, and brought her back."

The crowd became a wall, impenetrable. Caroline found herself next to a man in pale blue poplin waiting to get inside. Together they leaned against the clapboard of the building, as if they'd meant to meet there. The man cradled his phone in his hands, seeming to angle it so that Caroline could see what was on the screen.

The British royal family was standing on their viewing balcony, waving to the throngs below. As the camera zoomed in, the littlest prince and princess blinked twice with lizard eyes, the lids closing like elevator doors over yellow irises. The picture changed, and changed again, scenes blinking by with increasing speed, just as they had on the television in the house: a pendant swung back and forth before a man's blank face; a woman's hands kneaded a naked back, bubbling hives forming under French-manicured fingernails; masked faces peered at a gummy-smooth, skeletal purple infant hooked up to a spiderweb of tubes; a small figure that could have been a child sat on a stool with a bag over their head. The man looked up at Caroline and smiled, his cheeks pink.

"They did a good job," he said. "Don't you think?"

"Who?" Caroline asked.

"Everyone, wouldn't you say? They're all playing their parts perfectly. Everyone is doing exactly what they're supposed to do."

Caroline tried to swallow. Her mouth was too dry.

"Even you," the man said. "You've done a good job, too. Not bad for an amateur, anyway."

"What?"

The man's smile broadened. Caroline's brain flipped him upside down, and she recoiled at the white grapes of his eyes in their black sucking holes. He wasn't in his fake police uniform, but she recognized him all the same.

Caroline felt herself borne aloft, carried by a wave of people, all forward momentum to the open door. Her feet touched down on the threshold just as a man in a black windbreaker stepped in front of her, barring the way.

"Private club," the bouncer said. "Members only."

"Since when?" she demanded. "I was just here a few nights ago. Last night."

"Well, you're not getting in now."

Caroline stared at the bouncer's pink calves under his denim shorts and the black joystick of his holstered gun. Bodies swelled around them, then the crush abated as more people were admitted into the club. Through the open door, Caroline could see the circular bed made up with pink-and-purple satin sheets positioned in front of the bar. A few girls—but not *the* girls—were jumping on the bed. Through their scissoring legs Caroline thought she could see Adam sitting on a pink pillow, frowning at his phone. Then the girls collapsed in a heap, and he disappeared under the pile of their bodies. He was gone. He had never been there. It had to be almost nine by now. He had to be getting on a ferry soon. The door swung closed.

"Look," Caroline said to the bouncer. "You need to let me in. I'm trying to find my son, and I think the girls who took him are in there. Here—I'll even show you who they are and what they look like, you can see for yourself—"

Her camera was already on. She flipped it to play mode, expecting the LCD screen to light up with the photographs she'd taken inside the yacht club, but instead she saw images from days ago—bright sun, Gabriel on a beach blanket looking up at her with slack mouth and blank eyes.

"Hold on," said Caroline. "Just a second."

She wound the wheel forward. The days flew by in a blur of baby flesh, blue water and sky, and amber light, ending with a few shots of the previous night's performance at the amphitheater before starting over again with the first pictures Caroline had taken after they'd arrived on the island—Saturday morning, her husband and child asleep in their dark and disordered room. Caroline wound the wheel forward and back, but it was no use.

All the pictures from inside the yacht club were gone.

She came to the last photograph on the card—the white-blond girl who was Gilgamesh, keening over her dead friend as she promised to begin the search for everlasting life.

Caroline took one step back, just enough to allow the pajama-clad crowd to swallow her up. No one seemed to notice when she walked away.

SHE FOUND HERSELF AT THE AMPHITHEATER. SHE had expected it would be deserted, so she was surprised to see all the stage lights were still on, though the benches were empty, the audience gone. Oona Vita sat on a cream leather upholstered armchair at center stage, wearing a galaxy-print dressing gown and holding a book. The child actors were in their pajamas as well; they surrounded Oona, some kneeling, some sitting cross-legged, some lying with their heads in each other's laps, all listening to the story being read aloud.

"'And so, though the little girl knew deep down in her little human heart that the answer to the mystery lay elsewhere, she knew that she still had to go through everything that had been commanded. Yes, she would have to make the descent down the sixty-two cellar steps, endure the long walk through the darkness, and find the secret meeting place of the forgotten ghosts that had succeeded in fleeing their machines. Once there, she would have to find the door to the other side, wherever it was.'"

A child's hand shot up. Oona nodded in its direction.
"Yes?"

"My grandma has *two* refrigerators in her cellar."

"How interesting, my dear."

"And a *lot* of wine."

"Wonderful."

"Mine has *three*," shouted another child.

"We have a whole gym!"

"My, my."

"And Daddy's office!"

"How very nice of you to share."

When Caroline came forward out of the gloaming, Oona and the children did not seem surprised to see her. Caroline remembered the children's unwavering composure on the cove when she'd come upon their rehearsal. She stood there, hesitant with fear, before she finally gathered the strength to break the silence, her voice harsh and quavering on the night air.

"Can you help me?"

No one answered. Their eyes glowed pale and murky. They were no longer the children on the cove—they had become the doe and her fawns, watchful and still.

"I need your help," Caroline said. "I've lost my baby, and I don't think I can trust anyone else."

She took a breath.

"Not even my friends."

Saying it out loud, finally, she knew that it was true. They had deleted her photos. They had been leading her on this whole time.

"I'm just hoping that you know something about what's going on," she said. "Can you tell me what's happening here? On the island? Who is really in control? I thought it was some kind of cult, but now I don't know."

Oona laughed then, a deep and throaty chuckle. She laid her crossed her hands on her breasts, as if to hold herself together.

"Oh, honey." She sighed.

She turned to the children, who had become human again,

fidgeting and rocking on their bottoms as the spell of story time was broken and their attention began to wander.

"What do you think?" Oona asked them. "Should I tell her!"

"Yes!" the children cheered. "Yes, yes!"

Oona beamed.

"The thing is," she said, turning back to Caroline, "they're part of the cosmic hunt. Or at least they think they are."

"Who is?" asked Caroline.

Oona laughed again.

"They all are," she said. "Everyone who comes here, whether they know it or not at first. Eventually they find out, and then they embrace it. Even the youngest among them."

Caroline shook her head.

"I don't get it."

"Still?"

Caroline held out her hands, as if their emptiness explained something.

"It's about purity, right?" Caroline asked. "Purity of bloodlines? That's why they don't want any outsiders. That's why they perform their rituals, to scare everyone else away. That's why they took my son."

"They'd like you to think that." Oona sighed. "But it's not the whole story."

"Then what is?" Caroline asked. "What is the whole story?"

Before Oona could say more, the children began to call out over each other, fighting to be heard.

"If you want to be an angel and go to heaven—"

"You have to run to the horizon."

"Why explore the stars—"

"When you can leap and become them?"

Caroline saw the walls of the spaceship house again, ink leaching into wood that was rotting from within. She pushed against the walls in her mind and they began to give way.

"I'll tell you what *I* don't get," said Oona. "The earth is almost dead."

"The coral are skeletons!" a child cried.

"The polar bears are all gone!" shrieked another.

"No chance of spending eternity here at home," said Oona.

Their words were both familiar and not, half-remembered ramblings that Caroline hadn't fully grasped when she'd first heard them. She closed her eyes, trying to make sense of it all. But when she opened them again she still felt just as lost as before.

"We won't be much help to you," said Oona. She gestured at the children. "It's too late for them. And it was too late for me a long time ago."

"But why?"

"You have to see for yourself. In the other place."

"What other place?"

Oona pointed offstage, toward the camp cabins huddled in the darkness.

"Go and see," she said.

Terror seized Caroline. The thought of Gabriel in one of those cabins—no, she couldn't.

"What am I going to see?" she asked.

Oona wouldn't answer. She turned the pages of the book in her lap, singing to herself.

The children took Caroline by the hands and led her away. When they reached the door of the far cabin they left her, blowing kisses and waving goodbye.

The door opened easily. A few crickets whimpered in alarm as Caroline entered; she breathed in salt and mothballs. The cabin was empty except for an unmade child's cot, the bare mattress stained with blooms of varying shades of brown.

There was a deck of cards on the cot. Caroline knew even before she had them in her hands that they would be the same deck of Fortunes that she'd seen everywhere. Now, holding the cards, she saw for the first time the inscriptions scrolling around their edges: *Love flows to me. Life flows to me.* The back of each had a different picture, pieces of a whole. Some kind of puzzle.

When she laid the cards out face down on the floor they formed a map. Caroline recognized the long arm of the island in the water reaching for something beyond its grasp, the black maze of Haven like a chain around its wrist. The spaceship house was trapped somewhere in that maze, at the water's edge. The only other marking on the map was a black rectangular box—a town a couple miles to the east, on the other side of wilderness.

The town that had been burned.

OUTSIDE, THE WOMAN AND HER YOUNG DAUGHTER WERE waiting for Caroline. They'd spread a quilt on the ground and were lying down on it, apparently stargazing. Caroline was not surprised to see them as she emerged from the cabin, the Fortunes cards still in her hand. The woman and her daughter made room for Caroline on the quilt, and she lay down with them, clutching the cards to her chest, the way she'd once clutched her morning solitude, like a gift.

"I'm sorry about earlier," the woman said. "On the beach."

"That's all right," said Caroline, magnanimous.

"There were too many people," the woman explained. "If they had seen me speaking to you, they would have known exactly what I was telling you, which would have endangered us both."

"I understand."

The woman's daughter got to her feet and began to circle the quilt, spinning with her arms outstretched and murmuring under her breath, lost to some deeper purpose. Her footsteps thundered in Caroline's ears and heart.

"She's my second," said the woman.

"Oh," said Caroline. "I didn't know."

"They at least replace them. They give you exactly what you want. More, even."

Before Caroline could respond, the woman reached over and snatched the cards out of her hands. Caroline sat up, her vision black with alarm.

"I need those," she said, blinking back the darkness. "Please."

"You saw the way. You don't need them anymore. There's only one path."

"Mama."

The girl tugged the log of her mother's arm with both small hands, rolling the flesh back and forth.

"Mama, watch."

"Watch?"

"Watch! Watch!"

"No honey, it's not time to watch right now."

The woman sat up, swept dark hair out of dark eyes. All at once, she looked much older. Haggard. Though her own features had once flickered in and out of that face, Caroline saw now that she and the woman looked nothing alike. She didn't understand how she ever could have seen it any other way.

"Try not to think about it," the woman said, as if reading her thoughts. "Don't try to compare. It's the thief of joy, you know?"

Caroline nodded.

"Go to the place on the map," the woman said. "You know what it is, don't you?"

"I think so," said Caroline, unsure. "It's the other town, isn't it? The one that Haven burned down?"

"Yes."

"But why do I need to go there?"

"I can't tell you anything else," said the woman. "You'll see when you arrive."

She reached out and scratched Caroline under the chin.

"Don't let them see you."

CHAPTER 12

After leaving the woman and her daughter, Caroline followed the boardwalk into the telescoping tunnel of trees, away from the town, deeper into the dark maw of the night. Once she left the last houses behind, the boardwalk dead-ended into sandy dirt. A few steps farther on, she found herself at the edge of the wilderness, standing before a splintered sign that had been erased by the elements, but that she recognized as the marker for the national park. A single, incongruous streetlight with an orange bulb marked the beginning of a narrow path—the one path—that led through the woods.

Caroline walked for a long time, listening to her breath, the liquid stirring of the leaves, the crack and pop of dead branches beneath her feet. She had begun to doubt she would ever make it to the other side, when suddenly the dense trees fell away, and she found herself out in the open. A vast ocean of beach grass yawned before her, an endless prairie of interior dunes. She could see the remnants of the town up ahead—charred ribs of wood like mountain peaks, all that remained of the burnt houses.

The tall reeds shivered in anticipation and delight, parting at the touch of her hands, feet, and knees to let her through. The crickets in the grass fell silent as she drew near. Once she had passed they resumed their insistent chirping. The only other sound she could hear was the whir and hush of the soft breeze on the soft grass.

The place was a degraded recollection. She remembered the wheat fields beyond her family's farmhouse, the acres of land that used to belong to them, before it was bought out for pennies from beneath their feet. Another vast, soft ocean. Wheat shuddering in rolling swells with each gust of wind. At fifteen years old, she stalked the fields with her 35mm-film camera, looking for things to photograph after her mother had shooed her away from making portraits in her father's sickroom.

One late autumn afternoon she'd come upon a dead dog. Someone's shepherd, a working dog gone missing. Its belly had been ripped open, its entrails half eaten by some other animal. Flies crawled over the muck of guts and matted fur, shimmering wings blinking like eyes. Caroline stood above the corpse, pressing the shutter again and again, trembling with excitement.

When she approached the farmhouse, her mother was waiting for her on the porch, coatless, hugging herself in the cold. The mountain lion had been shot in a field nearby just a week before. Caroline slowed down before she could be seen and waited until her mother's shoulders were shaking with sobs before she came running out of the grass, the exhales of her laughter ghosting before her in the early dark.

"YOU BLAME YOURSELF TOO MUCH."

The tips of the tall grass were golden, lit by the fattened sun on its descent to the surface of the river. They held gloved hands, walking bundled in overcoats on the curve of the pedestrian path along the waterfront downtown.

It was the week before Adam started working at Corridor, and even though everything seemed to be going well, Caroline couldn't help but worry that it was all about to be taken away from them again. She'd picked a fight over brunch for no reason and had ruined one of the last lazy afternoons they'd have for a long time. Hours later, she was still tearful, still self-flagellating.

"You blame yourself too much," said Adam, "when the reality is, in the vast majority of situations, you have no control."

"That surprises me, coming from you."

"Well, it shouldn't," he said. "The universe doesn't care. Misfortune dispassionately aligns. Look at my life. Look how much I've fucked up. Look at my family—"

"What's wrong with them?"

"No one ever did as well as they should have, and no one was ever as happy as they should have been, and after all that it was just cancer and loneliness and death. Things just seemed to happen for no reason, and for the longest time I let that thwart me. Only once I accepted that I had no control was I actually free to succeed.

"I mean, how many times have I done this? How many times have I started over? And yet, here I am. Even now, I'm still getting up. There's a necessary numbness, and that numbness gives you confidence. Nothing can stop you, and everything can stop you. So the only thing you can do is keep throwing yourself forward."

Caroline followed his gaze out over the water to the sea wall, the stone and steel barrel of a wave that would never crash down.

"It's simple," Adam went on. "Ultimately, everyone is faced with the same question. Do you accept the terrain? Or do you spend your life fighting against it?"

"You fight?"

Adam shook his head. He shot her a grin that was a grimace.

"It's counterintuitive, but—"

"What?"

"Acceptance is the only way. If you fight, you'll only slip backwards."

Caroline squinted at him. The sun was in her face, blinding her. She raised her hand to shade her brow, trying to see him more clearly.

CAROLINE BLINKED. SHE HADN'T IMAGINED OR REMEMBERED it, the sudden light in her eyes. It was still night, the sun still well below the horizon of the island, but as she drew closer to the blackened ruins of the abandoned town, she saw the light again. Before her in the tall grass lay the cracked egg of a geodesic dome. The building had partly collapsed, but was still standing, a pantheon in the wild. The beam of a flashlight moved through each window, catching on thin fangs of shattered glass, signaling.

Inside, Caroline saw that the dome had been—and maybe still was—a place of ritual. The interior was dominated by the crater of a conversation pit, the white leather of the seat cushions ripped and stained, the space lit by several camping lanterns. In each corner of the pit sat several cairns of rocks, driftwood, and broken glass. There were patches of char along the baseboards, where small fires had once been lit.

There was writing on the walls, of course. Writing and drawings. There were old symbols that she couldn't see because they had been scratched out, replaced with new icons that were more uniformly geometric, more like the kind of logos you might see on a water bottle, backpack, or article of high-performance clothing. And there at the center of it all, painted in black onto the floor, was a baby's head, screaming with an open mouth at the center of a jagged six-pointed star, encased in the boundaries of a half-open door.

"You made it."

Caroline stumbled backward, shocked by the hand on her shoulder and the warm breath in her ear. She recognized the voice. It was Jane.

Caroline whirled to face her, and Jane took Caroline's hands in hers.

"Sit with me," Jane said.

She led Caroline to the center of the conversation pit and motioned for her to sit down, setting the flashlight like a lamp between them. Caroline saw that one of the cairns nearby was built out of half-full liquor bottles and cellophane-packaged snack cakes. Jane took a white bottle of Malibu from the pile and held it out to Caroline, who shook her head. She'd had enough of drinking what other people gave her.

"I don't want any."

"It's not going to hurt you. I found it here, in one of the cabinets. No one has touched it. It's safe."

"No."

"Suit yourself," said Jane. She dismantled the rest of the pile, spreading out the selection of treats: fluffy golden batons, dark pucks with lace zippers of frosting down their centers, pink globes furred with white coconut.

"I found these in the cabinets, too. Full of preservatives. Still good."

She tried to give one of the cakes to Caroline, but Caroline drew her hands away, as if she'd burned them.

"Come on," said Jane. "Aren't you hungry?"

"No," she lied.

"You need to eat, Caroline."

Jane's eyes were black, completely dilated. Whatever she was on, it was not the usual drug. She was skittish, vibrating with energy.

Caroline let her body begin to sag. She was so tired.

"What is all this?"

Jane ignored the question.

"I'm glad you're here now," said Jane. "Now you can see."

Caroline stiffened again, wary.

"See what?"

Then Caroline saw that next to the bottles of alcohol and plastic pillows of snack cakes there was a large portfolio folder. Jane began to pull the folder apart, extracting ever-smaller, more slender folders from within and dumping the contents of these folders onto the floor, until the two of them were sitting in a nest of worn composition books, yellow legal pads, and all kinds of paper—documents finely striped with text, high-contrast black-and-white xeroxes, small pearlescent rectangles.

"Why do you have all of this?" Caroline asked.

"The same reason you take your photos," said Jane. "To see what's going on."

Jane sorted the material into piles, inscrutable in their organization.

"Everything in analog," Jane said. "Can't trust the cloud. Can't trust any digital space, really. Things get hacked, surveilled. Deleted.

"And if I'm being honest with you, I can't trust my own memories, either. I've been holding on to this for so long, I know it's made me crazy. Paranoid. When you start checking your own therapist's office for recording devices, you know you've truly lost it."

Jane kept sorting the papers, smiling oddly. She was not well, that much was certain. Why should Caroline trust her?

"Did you delete my photos?" she asked, lifting her camera.

"*They* deleted your photos. So you already know that you can't trust them. You can't trust anyone at Corridor. Not even your husband."

Caroline almost laughed. Not trust Adam?

"But Gabriel is his child, too," she said. "He would never—"

"Don't say he would never. You have no idea what they're capable of."

Caroline felt ill. She looked at her hands, which were trembling.

"I don't understand."

"I'll explain. You know HEOL, Humane End of Life?"

"Yes. Sort of."

"Right," said Jane. "Most people, if they know about it, try not to think about it. Too upsetting. But I've had to think about it a lot, ever since it became a huge part of my job.

"Everyone thought it was just going to be for people with terminal illnesses who didn't want to linger—you know, people who were in unendurable *physical* pain. But overnight we were getting pressure to counsel clients to choose euthanasia because they were struggling with their mental health, or because they were about to lose their housing. People who were considered unproductive members of society, a tax on a system with ever-scarcer resources. There were whispers about organ harvesting, but I really thought it was as simple as the powerful wanting to kill the poor."

Jane took a swig from the Malibu bottle before continuing.

"I had one client, a twenty-year-old girl. She'd had a hard life, but she'd worked really hard to get clean, and things were starting to turn around for her. Then her ex-boyfriend overdosed, and she was so depressed that she started using again. She got kicked out of her apartment and lost her job. We tried to get her into treatment facilities for months, but there was no space anywhere. Every week she would visit our office, and every week it was bad news. But those HEOL applications were right at the front desk, a big fat stack of them. One day she took one and submitted it. She got approved for death in less than a week.

"The day after her euthanization, I called in sick and just lay in bed crying all day. I felt like I had failed her—actually, it was more than that. I felt responsible for her death. That's what I kept saying over and over, that I had killed her. Perry was trying to comfort me, and that's when he let it slip. What he knew."

Jane took another long drink and swallowed hard.

"He was sitting on the bed next to me," she continued. "He kept running his hand up and down my arm, as if he were trying to smooth me out. He asked me to look at him. Then he told me I should stop crying, because the truth was that HEOL had been a Corridor initiative from the very beginning. Not only had Corridor secretly funded the original lawsuit—they'd hand-selected and manipulated those poor plaintiffs, essentially manufacturing the case out of thin air. And if that weren't enough, they bought or blackmailed more than half of Congress to make sure the legislation passed. Perry told me all of this, and he told me there was nothing anyone could do to stand against it, and because of that it was pointless for me to blame myself because nothing I had done or could do would have mattered. He told me that I had to let it go, and that all we could do was keep moving forward."

Caroline winced, remembering Perry's hand on her own arm, just above her elbow.

"I remember I just kind of lay there," said Jane. "I was so stunned, I couldn't even argue with him, even though what he was saying went against everything I believed in. I wish I'd said something instead of doing what I did next."

"Which was?"

"Exactly what he said—I tried to let it go, and we moved forward together," said Jane. "At least, we *seemed* to move forward, from the outside. We made a few changes, of course. We decided to open our marriage—I mean, we'd talked about it in the past, so it wasn't totally out of the blue. But things had been feeling so heavy lately, and we couldn't seem to give each other what we needed. It seemed like a way to just live a little bit, you know? Even though it created even more distance.

"But even though I tried, I found that I couldn't let it go. What happened to my client, what I had found out about the link between Corridor and HEOL—it had broken me in a way that I couldn't fix.

"I had to do something. I told myself I just had to wait. Wait, and pay attention. I was good at compiling case files for my clients. I decided I'd make a case file on *this*, and it would be my best one. When I had enough evidence, I would take it to the press. At that point, I had rationalized it all to myself. I convinced myself that Perry had been brainwashed. By exposing Corridor and the fact that they were the dark money and driving force behind HEOL, I thought I would get Perry back, and everything would be like it used to be. But that's not what happened."

Jane took a deep breath.

"By then we'd already been trying to get pregnant for over a year. We started getting testing done, and everything seemed fine on Perry's end. The doctors kept saying the problem was with me—they're surprisingly direct about that kind of thing, once they run all their little tests and have the evidence they need—but no one could figure out exactly what was wrong with me, and no one could fix it.

"I did thirteen egg retrievals. Surgery under anesthesia once a month, for over a year. Weeks of swallowing pills, and getting plasma infusions and stem cell therapy, and dialing up the human growth stimulation on my primordium implant, and injecting myself with the highest dosage of every drug imaginable, and then they'd knock me out and go in with a needle and try to extract whatever eggs they'd managed to grow inside me.

"I was so distressed in my daily life that I actually started to look forward to being put under. They'd lower the lights and project a galaxy of stars on the ceiling, and I'd take a few deep breaths, and then I'd be gone. I would always wake up vomiting and have to spend the next two days in bed, but even that was kind of nice—not having to do anything, having Perry there to take care of me, pretending the outside world didn't exist."

"God," said Caroline.

"Finally, we had what we thought were enough embryos, even though they were poor quality. We weren't completely hopeless, even though I wouldn't say that things were great between us." Jane pressed the bottle against her stomach.

"It had gotten really hard for me to be around babies, people with children. Even just walking around our neighborhood on the weekends was excruciating for me. And Perry didn't get it. He told me that my bitterness was 'antisocial' and 'unbecoming,' that I needed to snap out of it before I alienated everyone in my life.

"I almost left him then, but I couldn't. I couldn't leave my embryos behind, even if they were half Perry. I was so desperate for a child, any child. I knew this was my only chance.

"And then I had eight miscarriages. Eight. They'd place the embryo in me, I'd see it on the screen, and it would even implant and hold on for a few weeks, but eventually it would die. My own body kept killing my babies."

Caroline tried and failed to think of something to say. Jane didn't wait.

"After the eighth miscarriage I had some retained tissue, and they had to suction everything out. Then I hemorrhaged, and that was the end. I don't even remember it. I woke up at home a week later and went into the kitchen and there was Perry, and he looked *happy*.

"He kissed me and told me that things were about to change, and that soon we would be able to have our own children, that there was another way. And not only that—our children would be special. They would be the first inheritors of the new world. He said it was within our power. That because of our sacrifices, we would be taken care of.

"I didn't know exactly what he meant, but I thought I knew. He was an insider, and if I stayed with him, I would have access to all the cutting-edge benefits that Corridor could offer. I knew Anima was starting to do uterus transplants pretty regularly, and I'd heard they were working on other interventions with artificial wombs. I thought I just had to wait a little longer, and then I'd have my child. And I told myself that once I had a child, I could face anything. That I would figure out the rest of it then, even if it meant leaving Perry. So again, I stayed, and I told myself it was only temporary.

"I didn't realize what it would take. What Corridor really was. When Perry talked about our sacrifices, I thought he meant the ones we'd already made."

Jane wiped away tears. Caroline stared at the spread of images on the floor and was startled to see a photo of her and Adam leaving the hospital with Gabriel buckled into the car seat; a selfie she'd taken in the bathtub a month before her due date, her bump rising out of the water like a breaching whale; more of the charcoal sketches that were actually ultrasound images, just like the ones she'd found at the house. But these images were larger, and they showed the progression from coiled larva to the perfect moonlit profile of a face, Caroline's last name printed in careful white text at the top of each image, unmistakable. She couldn't breathe. Jane kept talking.

"I tried to focus on my work, to keep going with building the file, but I messed up. It was just too hard. I stopped going to therapy, I was blacking out from drinking and self-medicating all the time. I just couldn't deal, I—I couldn't stay sober. If I had, then—"

"Then what?"

"We might have been able to save him."

Caroline brought her hands to her face. First over her eyes, then over her ears, then over her mouth. They were silent for a long moment, staring at the spread of evidence as the ponderous mass of belief settled in Caroline's gut. She picked up one of the prints and saw that it was a picture she had never seen before. She was in the NICU, hunched over the aquarium tank that held their baby, her hands reaching through the portholes to feel his fragile skin, her eyes red and raw. Adam had taken the photo, angling the phone overhead to get a complete family portrait—his face was half cut off, but there was enough of him there in the frame to see that he was trying to smile.

It couldn't be true.

It couldn't be true.

Caroline crushed the photograph against her mouth.

"This is only the beginning for these people," said Jane. "They think they're all going to upload their consciousnesses to the cloud and live forever in their robot bodies. It used to be good enough to molest children; that was the twisted sign of being more powerful than God, of nothing being off-limits to you once you reached a certain echelon of influence. Now anything short of getting what you want for all of eternity isn't enough. And they'll kill anyone to get it—genocide of the poor, the ill, the inconvenient, you name it. Then it's off to space for the ones who have the means to survive."

Jane closed her eyes and took another sip. "But why would you want to live forever if it means floating in a great big cold dark nothing? I never understood it. I still don't."

Caroline moaned again. "But I didn't, I would never—"

"I know," Jane said.

"This isn't what I signed up for."

"It *is* what you signed up for," Jane said. "You just didn't know it. I mean, I'm not sure that any of us did. It's a good life, for the most part. Why look too closely, even when we know deep down that there's something wrong?"

"But I didn't know," Caroline insisted, even as the epiphanies kept rushing in, assaulting her.

"Okay, sure," said Jane. "Sure. Let's say that's true. You didn't know. You didn't know what you were agreeing to when Adam took the job. And you didn't know what would happen when you decided to come to the island. But you must know by now."

Did she? What did she know? What had she ignored? How much had she deceived herself? The questions were too huge and unwieldy, too awful to answer.

"There's not much to be done now," Jane said, as if Caroline had asked her what they should do. "But we can go back to the house and face them together. Confront them. Let them see what we know."

Caroline stared at her, mind still reeling. She thought of the white spaceship, the glass walls, the people waiting inside. She shook her head. It had to be the island cult with their infant sacrifices and blood rituals. That was the only reasonable explanation. Not Corridor, and certainly not Adam. She straightened up, suddenly sure.

"No, we have to get off the island."

"Caroline—"

"We have to go get real help. The real police, the FBI, someone who can—"

"There are no *real* police," said Jane. It was the slow, deliberately patient voice she must have used with her clients, before her own life had come apart. "There is no one who will help us. Everything is under their control."

"That can't be true."

"I'm sorry, Caroline."

Caroline got to her feet, kicking over the flashlight that had stood between them, sending it spinning across the floor. Jane raised her head, but she was looking past Caroline—perhaps at the wreckage of the dome, perhaps at something invisible beyond even that. In the flare of light Caroline could see that Jane's eyes were gray again, her pupils no longer dilated, their surfaces glossy with tears.

"You go back there if you want," said Caroline. "I'm getting off of this island."

Before Jane could stop her, she walked away from the paper evidence, away from the painted effigy of the baby's head in the box, out of the trap of the conversation pit, and through the hole in the wall that passed for an open door.

CAROLINE GOT LOST IN THE WOODS. SHE WANdered through the wilderness, her hands flung out to skim the spindly tree trunks on either side of her whenever she stumbled on a buried root. Her dead phone banged against her belly. She no longer had her camera—she must have left it in the dome, with Jane. Caroline commanded herself to calm down and breathe.

More degraded recollections. Caroline was walking through different woods, and she was wearing new caramel leather hiking boots that she'd bought specifically for the trip, because it was their first time going to the cabin upstate. Peak foliage, according to the most accurate apps, the leaves all shades of blood and gold, though it was still warm for late fall.

Adam was walking beside her, and he was fooling around,

pretending that she was stumbling and about to fall at every step, making a show of being ready to catch her.

It would still be a long time before the baby felt real to him. The top-of-the-line, multipiece *Transformers*-style stroller system blocking their vestibule wouldn't trigger it, nor would the weekend spent emptying the small room they had once used as an office, now to become a nursery.

It was only at thirty weeks, when the first set of newborn clothes arrived in the mail—organic cotton in tasteful neutrals, booties and rompers and burp cloths—that Adam had blanched, laughingly uttering an expletive as Caroline laid out the pieces on their bed.

"What?" Caroline asked, grinning as she held up a tiny ivory bodysuit. "Why this, and not everything else?"

"Because that's the shape he'll be," said Adam, opening his arms to enfold her. "It's too real."

They had only walked to the nearby river instead of doing the full hike with the others, because she was just out of the first trimester and already her blood pressure was cause for concern.

They were starting to tell people.

Back at the cabin, Adam made a fire and Caroline made some tea from the unlabeled bags in the mason jar that Taryn had brought up from the city. Then she fell asleep on one of the living room couches. She was always tired in those days, always falling asleep. She half awoke when the others came back from the woods, but then she kept slipping back into sleep and into dreams. In one of her dreams, she saw the others were sitting in a circle around the hearth, naked. Adam was also naked, but he was standing in the far corner of the dim room with his back to her, firelight smeared across his shoulder blades.

In the dream, Caroline was awake, but she couldn't move. At the center of the circle of naked people there was a card game in progress, and at the center of the card game there was a cup of dark liquid, swirls of blood and gold glowing before the flames. Nori cowered next to Caroline, nudging her arm with her nose, whimpering as the firelight quivered in her black eyes. A rectangle had been drawn on the floor, its dark and heavy borders encasing a jagged six-point star, a crude rendering of a half-open door.

IT COULDN'T BE TRUE.
　It couldn't be true.
　Was it true?

CAROLINE FOUND THE SPLINTERED LIP OF A BOARDWALK jutting out of the sand, the start of the road back to town. She walked for a while longer before the path split into tributaries, different routes snaking away into the trees. She chose one on instinct and it brought her through a maze of tall reeds to the bayfront, dead-ending at an isolated dock. A thick spray of moths fluttered beneath a single lamppost, and under the lamppost stood a man dressed all in black.

He was motionless, his back to Caroline. She felt cold all over, infused by a terror that rooted her to the spot. Slowly, slowly, the man turned and looked directly at her.

For a long moment, neither moved. Then Caroline stepped forward and joined the man on the dock.

As she came closer, she could see him more clearly, but there wasn't much to register. He was of average height and build, with the kind of face that was utterly forgettable. So forgettable that it had to be purposeful.

"I've been looking for you," said Caroline. "We all have."

She felt ridiculous, as if she were reciting lines in some kind of surrealist play or piece of performance art, the kind of production you'd see in a raw space on Canal Street. Then again, she felt as though she had passed into the surreal a long time ago. The man did not answer, and turned away from her to look at the horizon.

"Who are you?" Caroline asked.

The man said nothing. He kept staring out over the black water, the lights of the mainland too far away to see. Caroline had the sudden urge to push him into the bay.

"Tell me what happened to my baby," she demanded. "What you did to him."

Finally the man sighed.

"Fuck it," he mumbled to himself. "What the hell."

He turned and met Caroline's eyes. His were a washed-out gray, almost colorless.

"I didn't do anything to your baby."

"But you—you were there, you—"

"You have the wrong guy."

He reached into his back pocket and pulled out a crushed pack of cigarettes and a lighter. He lit a cigarette for himself, then offered one to Caroline, but she shook her head. He took a long drag and then let out his breath, the stream of smoke like a comet's tail, pale against the night.

"I was hired to come to this island," he said. "Asked to do certain things."

"What things?"

"Go into your house that night. Leave the cup of piss on the ramp. Be careless with my campsite, skulk around looking suspicious. I don't know why they wanted me to do those things, but that was what they asked for."

"They? Who are they? Who hired you?"

"I don't know that, either. Someone paid someone to pay someone else to hire me. That's how these people do things. Like Russian nesting dolls or something, you know? Shell inside shell inside shell. Meet in an anonymous hotel room in midtown, sign an anonymous contract with the names blacked out, get the routing number and log-in information for an anonymous bank account. I'm only telling you this because they're screwing me out of the last installment of my fee. Should have known better. It's always the same with these people."

"Which people?"

The man shrugged. A ferry was approaching, windows blazing, the dark hull of the boat moving leisurely toward the shore. Adam had said the last boat to Haven left the mainland at nine, but it had to be much later than that now. Maybe he'd gotten the schedule wrong. Maybe he was already at the house, waiting for Caroline.

"You really don't know who hired you?" she pressed the stranger. "And you don't know what happened to my baby?"

"I'm sorry," the man said. "I really don't know. All I did was the job I was paid to do. And now I'm going."

A teenager in cargo shorts and a ferry T-shirt stood at the railing on the upper deck, lit by a single red bulb. When the ferry was almost to the dock he threw a noose, which caught on one of the wooden pilings.

"Line's on!"

There was no one else on the boat. The metal door of the ferry swung open, the hinges groaning in impatience. The man nodded to Caroline, then strode forward and stepped onto the boat.

There was a part of Caroline that knew she should get on the boat, get off the island. It was what she had told Jane she was going to do. Maybe if she followed this man, she could somehow convince him to tell her more.

But another part of her knew that she had to stay. What this man had told her—the circumstances of his employment, the blacked-out contract, the shell inside the shell inside the shell—it all added up to something she could no longer ignore.

And if she left the island now, she knew she would never find Gabriel. She would never see him again, would never know what had happened to him.

The man disappeared into the hull, and the door slowly swung shut behind him. Caroline watched the boat cleave itself from the dock and turn back toward the mainland. It made for the horizon, trailing foam, leaving her behind.

SHE WALKED FOR ANOTHER HOUR BEFORE SHE FInally reached the town. On the promenade outside the yacht club there was still a crowd of people, even though it was now very late at night. The fake police bouncer in the black windbreaker was still there, his bulk perched atop a tall stool with impossibly skinny legs. But when Caroline approached, her feet dragging with exhaustion, he simply grinned at her and pushed the door open with one open palm, tilting his head to beckon her inside.

She passed through the bar and went out onto the deck overhanging the bay. The lights in the pool were on. Three heads bobbed at its center, dark in the brilliant water.

"Caro!"

The girls rose out of the water like wraiths, T-shirts streaming. They wrapped towels around their torsos. Caroline sat down on a nearby chaise. She couldn't believe it was really them, even though she had also somehow known they would be there.

Now that she'd found the girls, she didn't know what to do. She opened her mouth and closed it again several times as the girls surrounded her, the bleached brunette and black-haired redhead sitting on either side of her, the rust-dyed blonde kneeling before her. They smiled at her, expectant.

"I've been looking for you," Caroline said finally.

She didn't know what else to say. The girls pouted, as if she had hurt their feelings.

"Didn't you ask around?"

"Yes," Caroline deadpanned. She couldn't believe she was having this conversation. "I did."

"Oh. Well, you must not have asked the right people."

Caroline could say nothing. She was so tired, more tired than she had ever been.

"We're sorry about it," said the blonde. "We really are."

"Sorry about what?"

"That we had to take Gabey."

They were smiling again, horrible smiles that turned into laughter, their open mouths like gaping wounds. Caroline felt a shock of adrenaline. Words were like clumps of wet sand in her throat—she couldn't get them out fast enough.

"Where is he? What did you do with him?"

"*We* didn't do anything," explained the redhead. "All we did was take him."

"We're just the delivery girls!" said the blonde.

"Don't shoot the messengers!" said the redhead.

"That was our job this time," said the girl with black hair. "Everyone out here has their role, you know."

"It's why we play Fortunes."

"To decide who does what."

Before Caroline could respond, the heads were whispering to each other, nudging at each other's arms with their elbows.

"Show her!"

"You show her!"

The redhead handed Caroline a phone, the upper-right corner of the screen shattered into lace. A video was already playing, muted or without sound.

"Here. We saved it for you."

"We thought you would want to see."

"See what?" Caroline asked, trying to control her voice. "What would I want to see?"

"Just watch!"

Caroline looked at the screen in her hand. A pendant swung back and forth before a man's face; a woman's hands kneaded a naked back mottled with hives; masked faces peered at a wizened fetus hooked up to a spiderweb of tubes; a small figure that could have been a child sat on a stool with a bag over their head. A dying baby shark writhed against an open sky; children in animal costumes formed a misshapen circle. Six sets of fingertips trembled around a glass of dark liquid; one pair of hands shot forward to grasp it, a gold band glinting on the ring finger of the left hand. Bodies from the neck down all dressed in white, dancing. And then, just for an instant, before the screen went black and the pendant began its metronomic swing again, Caroline thought she saw Gabriel. Just his face—peaceful, asleep. Just for an instant. She gasped. The three heads grinned at Caroline, their teeth glowing in the dark.

"Isn't it good?"

Caroline rubbed her finger back and forth along the slivered panorama on the bottom of the screen, manipulating each cross section of a second to try to find her son's image once more. Her touch made the hands release the glass, made the hives vanish into unblemished flesh, but it never showed Gabriel's face again. She couldn't find him.

"What is this?" Caroline asked. "What am I looking at?"

The girls peered at her, tilting their heads to one side. Caroline recognized the look on their faces—the incredulity of omniscient youth, confronted by an adult who didn't understand the obvious.

"You don't know?"

"No."

"Oh, Caro—"

"We *always* make a video."

"A new one every time."

"They don't let us post any of them on our feed, but they keep all of them. That's how important the videos are."

"That's all we did, really!"

"We made the video, and we took Gabey and gave him to the people that needed him."

"What people?" begged Caroline. "Who has him?"

The girls looked at her again, their faces masks of puzzled wonderment.

"*Your* people," they said together.

Caroline gagged. She tasted metal and bile.

"Do you need a drink?"

Caroline shook her head.

"Of course she needs a drink."

"After what she's been through."

"No," said Caroline. "I don't want a drink."

"Aw, Caro."

"Come inside with us anyway."

"Come on."

"You have to."

Too weak to do anything else, Caroline let the girls lead her inside the packed yacht club. The pajama party was still going on. Somehow there were four empty stools at the end of the mirrored bar; Caroline and the girls sat down, the crowd quickly closing in around them, absorbing them into the organism of the room. No one seemed to care that the girls were still soaking wet under their towel wraps, or that puddles were forming beneath them. A man sat on the stool to their right, refilling his wineglass from an open bottle of pink Sancerre. Caroline saw that the man was the grocery store manager—his meaty shoulders slumped, his web of purple scars peeking out from the unbuttoned neck of his pajama shirt. When he noticed Caroline staring at him, he nodded at her companionably, then went back to his drinking.

"Four Dirty Shirleys, please!"

The drinks came, deep sanguine and clotted with cherries. The girls knocked their cups together, the plastic denting without a sound.

Caroline refused to drink. She looked into the mirror in front of her. Her face was unrecognizable again, a pale and poorly molded death mask. She looked up into the rafters, through the net of fairy lights, into what she saw was another mirror overhead.

In her psychiatrist's office, there was a small round mirror on the wall, hung at a height so that when you were lying on the couch for your session and looking straight at it, you saw nothing of your own reflection, just the wall behind you. Only when you sat up and shifted could you see yourself, what the mirror really had to show you.

She had asked her psychiatrist about it once.

"What's the deal with the mirror?"

Her psychiatrist wrote something on her pad. There was a long silence.

"I mean," said Caroline, "what's that supposed to be about?"

Another long silence. Caroline decided that she wouldn't speak again until she got an answer. She closed her eyes and waited, until finally she heard the wet click of her doctor's swallow, the soft pop of her stuck lips parting.

"What do *you* think it's about, Caroline?"

But the mirror hanging over Caroline now was not a mirror. As her vision resolved, she could see that it was a television tuned to a three-camera sitcom. Or maybe it was one of the old-style reality shows about finding love, before everything became compilations of viral road rage brawls and customer service meltdowns. Two couples and their single friend in a candlelit living room, talking. After a moment she realized that she recognized the actors.

She hadn't known that any of their friends had ever been on television. Taryn, she could almost believe—she could see Taryn on a reality show, pretending to compete for an engagement ring while building her personal brand. But the others, no, they would have never. Noa and Wynn would have looked down on it as beneath them—let the great unwashed masses entertain *them*, not the other way around. Blaise likewise would care too much about how it looked—he didn't want to be seen as just a himbo. And Perry just wouldn't.

And yet there they were on the screen. How strange, to see them all together like this. They were smart people, private people—they would never have sought exposure like this.

This fantasy lasted only half a minute before Caroline understood what she was seeing. The television on the ceiling was connected to the full-length dark mirror of the television in the living room, and it was showing everything that was happening in the house. She watched as the sitcom morphed into something terrible, a different kind of show—the men were shirtless, and the women slapped them hard across their faces; they all formed a circle, holding hands; there was a flash of light in the center of the room, illuminating the dark red streaks on the white couches and the things that had been drawn on them. It was all there, all connected in the dense forest of surveillance—deeply rooted, all-seeing, everything kept for when it was needed. Caroline stared up in horror as the voices of the girls and the drunks around her grew louder, more boisterous.

"She sees now."

"She does! I can't believe she didn't before."

"How could she have known?"

"How could she *not* have known?"

Laughter.

"Never mind, never mind."

Pure adrenaline flooded her again as Caroline lunged to her right and grabbed the grocery manager's bottle of wine by the neck. The girls stared at her.

"Caro?"

"Are you all right?"

Caroline didn't answer them. She left the yacht club and stalked off into the night, toward the single lamppost that stood sentry at the edge of the promenade. Caroline smashed the base of the bottle against the pole, then lifted her dazzling, dripping weapon so that it caught the streetlight. The shattered points of glass gleamed in a way that was almost audible, like the sound of crystals cascading in a video game.

She headed toward the house, the broken bottle gripped in her fist.

CHAPTER 13

All the lights inside had been turned off, the glass doors and windows dark screens once more. Caroline leaned against one of the stilts holding up the house, hidden in its shadow, still holding the broken bottle.

Jane should be back by now. Caroline hoped that she was nearby, and that she was ready to fight.

She would need all the help she could get.

Nori ambled out of the darkness, wagging her tail. She nudged Caroline's hand with her wet snout, asking to be petted.

"Shhh," Caroline whispered.

Nori drew back and looked up at Caroline, head cocked. Then she sneezed and pawed at the ground in front of her, grunting and huffing.

"What?" asked Caroline. "What is it?"

She was afraid that the dog would start barking, but when she bent to try to soothe her, Nori jumped up and ran behind her, ramming her velvet head against the backs of her knees.

She was trying to herd her.

"Okay," Caroline whispered. "Okay. I'll follow you."

They set off. Nori kept circling back to make sure Caroline was still there, leading her away from the house and to the far end of the cove.

They were almost at the fence of reeds when Caroline saw,

from a distance, a small mound of something that was not sand. Something solid that did not move.

She stopped. She didn't want to get any closer to whatever it was, at least not yet.

Caroline squinted at the thing in the sand for a long time, until the moon emerged from behind the clouds. In its glow she could see more clearly.

She turned away and began to walk in the opposite direction, as far away as she could get from where the dog had tried to lead her. She took out her drowned phone to see if it had somehow come back to life, but it was still dead. Exhausted, delirious, she began to hum to herself, a lullaby she used to sing to Gabriel.

It felt like a dream, singing to herself on the moonlit cove. The doe and her fawns appeared at the water's edge. Nori approached them and they did not run away.

Caroline continued toward the water, to where the animals were. That felt safe—she could get to the water without getting near the thing in the sand. It would be a good test, going to the water. If her feet got wet, it would mean she wasn't dreaming. If the water was warm, it would mean she wasn't dreaming.

She reached the shore. They were talking, the dog, the doe, and the fawns, speaking without moving their mouths. Caroline found that she was only half surprised that she could understand what they were saying.

They were all meant to be there together, skirting the border of revelation.

"You see," said Nori. "They have to prove what they believe."

"Indifference to the body," said the doe. "Indifference to the human form."

"Because what happens in this world isn't what matters," said the fawns.

"And the purest expression of what they believe is to destroy the most innocent."

"All for the greater good, of course."

"Yes. All for the greater good."

They didn't seem to believe what they were saying. The fawns were crying now, nuzzling their faces into their mother's flank. Their mother was crying, too. Nori was bawling, as if she herself were human, or had been, once.

"You've tried so hard, but you'll never see your son again."

Caroline's feet were wet. The water was blood, thick and warm, like the milk draining out of her aching breasts. She knew she was not dreaming.

And she knew that it was all Corridor. Adam's friends, the island and its people, Adam himself—everyone was under the juggernaut of its power. It was a cult of eternal life, of getting everything you want forever, no matter what had to be offered. Sacrificed.

There was nothing left to protect her. She shivered, defenseless. There was nothing left for her to do but see what was waiting for her behind the half-open door.

"I'll never see my son again," she said to Nori, whose eyes were black and wet in her black face. Nori could only whimper in response. Then the dog trotted up the shore to the thing in the sand and began to lick it all over.

Caroline walked out of the water and over to the dog and the severed head cradled between its paws. There was black blood around the ragged stump of the neck, black blood thick around a wound between the open gray eyes. The dog's tongue darted in and out of its mouth, all over the eyes and cheeks and lips, pink then black, pink then black. Caroline dropped the broken bottle. She gently took Jane's head away from the dog and into her hands. With her thumb she wiped away the blood from Jane's forehead to see the shape of the half-open door carved into it before it filled up with blood and darkness again. The black box of her camera rested in the sand, the marker of the grave.

Caroline looked up. The looming shadows of people were growing closer. They were calling her name.

She ran, stumbling through the sand and up the long ramp, panting, the dog's damp muzzle close at her sand-crusted heels. She had lost the broken bottle. The sliding glass door was open, the house waiting for her to enter. She slammed the door shut behind her and threw the bolt to lock it. The others had reached the deck; they stopped and stood silent and motionless amid the outdoor furniture. Caroline leaned her forehead against the glass, gasping for breath. She stared out at the unmoving shadows; they stared back.

A hand touched her shoulder.

"Babe."

CHAPTER 14

Caroline shrieked. She sprang away from Adam, blocking him with crossed arms as he came toward her and tried to embrace her.

"Caro, it's me! It's me!"

He placed his hands on either side of her face, holding her head where he wanted it. Caroline slapped him away.

"Don't fucking touch me!"

"Caro, just let me—"

"No!"

Caroline looked around the dark living room, searching for something else that she could use as a weapon, but everything seemed to be clean and in order. A blanket had been thrown over the television. The images on the television in the yacht club must not have been real after all—that, or she had simply imagined the evidence of ritual. She looked out the glass doors. Perry, Wynn, Blaise, Noa, and Taryn were still standing on the deck, looking in at them. Caroline turned away, fearful. She faced her husband, who also looked afraid.

Maybe Adam could help her, Caroline thought desperately. Maybe he would have all the answers, the way he always did. She wanted to believe it.

"It's not safe here, Adam."

"Babe—"

"I know what happened," she said, her words coming in a rush. "What's happening. It's not Mosaic, or the military, or the island cult, or any of the other stuff you said. It's Corridor. They're in control of everything, here on the island and probably everywhere else. I don't know what they're trying to do—but I know they're the ones who took Gabriel."

She stopped abruptly. Adam was looking at her, and she saw that she had been mistaken—he wasn't afraid. He was looking at her with an expression she recognized, one she had hoped to never see again. It was his face from the long summer on the cliff, the other time in their life together when he had resigned himself to forces that he believed were insurmountable, beyond his control.

"What is it?" she asked.

He tried to smile at her, his mouth twitching at one corner before going slack again.

"Adam, what?"

"It's okay, babe," he said. "You don't need to do that."

She backed away from him.

"I don't need to do what?"

"You don't need to tell me."

He tried to smile again. She could see that the effort pained him, that it sent a wave of nausea through him.

"Here," he said, motioning to the nearest couch. "Let's sit down."

He turned on a lamp, muted gold leaping up the walls at the touch of his hand, the light exposing the ashes at the center of the room, the dried blood drawings of half-open doors on the couches and the floor—Corridor logos, all of them. Caroline began to shake. She shook her head, hugging herself.

"No," she said. "I'm not going to sit down."

"Please, Caroline."

"What the fuck did they do to Jane?"

"Shh. I won't let anything happen to you. I won't let anyone hurt you."

Adam reached for her hands and caressed them.

"Look," she whispered. "Just look around us."

"I don't need to look. I know."

He sat down on the couch, but wouldn't let go of her hands, which he continued to rub, kneading her palms and the nubs of her knuckles.

"I didn't agree to it," he said. "And I didn't know what they were planning."

He drew in a shuddering breath.

"I mean yeah, there had been other—other things. I probably should have known more than I did. Known better, I mean. But I swear it never occurred to me that—I mean, I just thought it wasn't serious, the stuff they talked about. It couldn't—it couldn't be real. Even some of the stuff I did—I didn't think—"

He paused, gathering himself.

"Look, everything I said to you after he first disappeared was true. Everything. I swear. It wasn't until I spoke to the others alone that I understood what was already in motion. What I had been called upon to do."

He swallowed hard.

"And once they told me what was going on, it was too late. Even then, there was a part of me that thought I could fix things, that I could somehow make it all stop—but—but—"

She had ignored the signs. She had wanted so badly to believe that Corridor had chosen Adam for his brilliance, his talents. She had refused to see why they had really chosen him—because they knew they could capitalize upon his vulnerability, his desperation.

"Where were you?" she asked.

He shook his head again.

"I can't tell you."

"Adam!"

"Just—just know that I was warned to stay away from you. I had to stay away. Or else they would hurt you, too."

He trailed off, unwilling or unable to say any more. Caroline stared at him. She couldn't breathe.

"But what—" she croaked. "What did they *do* to him?"

They looked at each other. Adam was very pale; his hands

holding hers were cold and heavy, dead machinery. They looked at each other for a long time.

"Do you really want me to say?" Adam whispered finally. "Don't you know already?"

"No."

"You do."

She did. She didn't want to. She cried out.

"You said—you said it was *infrastructure*, Adam."

"It is."

"How?"

Still holding her hands, he began to sob. With each deep breath in he let out a long cry, as if he were vomiting, expelling something out of his body. Caroline wrenched her hands from his grip. Her body moved toward the television, as if drawn by magnetic force. She pulled it from the wall and threw it to the floor, black glass shattering over her feet.

"Where is he?"

"Babe—"

"Where is he? Where is he?"

She fell upon her husband, striking at his face and neck and shoulders with her fists, her knees clamped around his waist. They toppled to the floor.

"Gabriel. Where is Gabriel? What did they do to him? Gabriel! Gabriel! Gabriel!"

She screamed her son's name until it became a mush of sound in her mouth, her throat raw. She was out of breath, weakening. Adam seized her by the wrists.

"I know," he said. "I know."

He tried folding her into his arms, tried to get her to lie down with him. She scrambled away from him and stood panting, steadying herself against the glass door. Without looking, she knew the others were still outside, just behind her, watching. Adam lay on the floor on a bed of broken glass. His eyes were filled with tears.

"He was so fragile," he said. "So frail. How could you bring something so helpless into the world and not do whatever you can to protect it?"

"But you didn't protect him. You let them—"

"No," he said, cutting her off. "It was too late for Gabriel. But it's not too late for the other children we'll have."

"No," said Caroline. "No more children. Not with you."

He ignored her and went on talking.

"Look. Right now, we're like people out of time. Think of the monkeys on the plains. The ones who used tools first were the weird ones, and then everyone caught on. We're living at the tail end of the period where ethics and morality have primacy, and we're entering the age where science and logic will be most important. This is where the world is going."

"That has nothing to do with us!"

"But it does!" Adam shouted, his voice cracking. "Of course it does! That's what's so hard about it, Caroline. Understanding the stakes, even when that understanding brings you despair."

"Adam—"

"And I know on some level you understand it, too. You always have. You know that greatness—no, fuck greatness, that *truth*—requires some ugliness. Some loss of yourself, to ascend to where you're meant to go."

He sat up and lifted his head to look her in the eye.

"And if you're going to be a god, you have to make an offering. You have to sacrifice."

The word hung between them, draining the air from the room. Caroline brought her fists to her eyes and wailed.

"But why? Why did they need him?"

"They needed him to extend human life."

"I don't understand."

"It's like stem cells," Adam explained. "They've found that something really special happens at this stage of development, right when they stop being newborns—something in the cells that only exists in the brains of babies this age. They needed to harvest it. *Harness* it, I mean.

"And they needed the genetic material from two high-IQ, healthy people with no fertility issues, to ensure best quality and outcomes. I mean—this isn't the kind of biomatter you can just get on the black market. It wouldn't work."

He was in engineer mode now, trying to teach her. Caroline clenched her jaw, trying to keep her teeth from chattering. She couldn't stop shaking. She didn't know how much longer she'd be able to stay standing.

"So you're saying that because of Gabriel, there will be eternal life?"

Adam shook his head.

"Not *eternal* life," he clarified. "Extended life. And even that, we don't know for sure yet."

He paused.

"Everything is still in the research and development phase. But the technology is coming soon, I promise.

"This island—it's much more than just a summer retreat for tech people. Corridor made a deal with the original Haven families. They could keep living here, and they could keep their rituals—in fact, Corridor *encouraged* the rituals, to maintain a sense of danger, keep the masses out. In exchange the company was given free rein to turn the town into a laboratory for the future. So much has been tested and pioneered out here. New implants, new limbs, new child-enhancing methods and practices. All sorts of incredible stuff. But even with all of that, they've—I mean, *we've*—never been able to achieve anything like this until now. It's all for the greater good. And it will all be because of us. You and me. And Gabriel."

Caroline turned away from him. Their friends had settled onto the deck furniture, lounging on the chaises and chairs. If she listened carefully, she could hear their murmured conversation. It was dawn now, and light was beginning to come into the sky. Soon it would be a new day.

"I need you to know that I didn't want this, Caroline. Not at first. The fact is, this—this horrible thing is just something that happened to us."

He paused again, then spoke in a voice she didn't recognize. "All we can do now is move forward."

She turned back to look at him. She could tell he was close to breaking down again, but he tried to smile. His mouth stretched itself grotesquely, his teeth pink with the sheen of blood.

"We'll have everything we'll ever need, for life," he said.

"We already had what we needed."

"Your mom, too," he said. "Think of your mom. We can move her to New York, take care of her for real now."

"Don't say that," Caroline said. She saw her mother sagging to the floor of the bank, saw her weeping in her cell. "You don't mean that."

"I do. I promise. She'll be here to see our children grow up. And they'll be set for life."

"No."

"Did you hear me? We'll have more."

"I said no, Adam!"

"More children, Caroline. Just like Gabriel! We'll get him back."

"I'm not doing any of your VR bullshit."

"Not VR. I mean we'll actually get him back, for real."

"That's impossible! You can't just replace our son!"

"It's true, Caroline. Trust me." His voice was gentle. "Everyone is replaceable. And I will make it all up to you, I promise."

She was dizzy. She felt herself falling backward into blackness. She lay on a quilt, looking up at the distant stars. She heard again what the woman had told her.

They at least replace them. They give you exactly what you want. More, even.

She was so tired.

She lay down and let her body go. She couldn't even feel her breasts anymore, couldn't tell if she was still in pain, if she was leaking the milk meant for her child. Adam crawled over to her and curled himself around her, fitting his bent knees behind hers. She had nothing left to offer but her silence, her stillness. Adam kept talking.

"I know this has been awful, but I promise you'll see him again."

...

"I can't even begin to tell you what we're capable of now. What we'll be able to do."

...

"Honestly, babe. It's incredible."

...

"Trust me. In the end you won't want it any other way. *We* won't want it any other way. I promise."

...

"Caroline."

...

"Babe."

...

"Look at me."

...

"Please."

...

...

...

"There. There you are."

...

"I love you so much."

CHAPTER 15

Caroline lay on her back on the beach. She was brutally hungover, her lungs like raisins, her vision hazy and pulsing with nausea. She had come to the beach because the only thing she felt up to doing was lying down. Being a lizard, bleaching her thoughts in the sun.

Behind her was their house, with its floor-to-ceiling windows that looked out onto the sand and the changing colors of the waves and sky. Her mother was in the kitchen, preparing lunch. Adam had been working in the city all week, but he'd be out on the last boat that evening. They would meet him at the ferry dock, and he would bounce off the boat, cutting through the crowd to clobber them with kisses.

Caroline's head throbbed in anticipation. Somewhere nearby, someone was screaming. She shut her eyes to shut them out.

IN THE END, THE PROCESS WAS BOTH BETTER AND WORSE than Caroline had imagined. Adam handled all the tasks that were impossible for her. He gave her all the injections, and he collected all the required materials: the pacifier, the knitted cap lined with fine strands of hair, the flakes of skin that dusted the fitted dinosaur sheet in the crib. He took care of Caroline as she got sicker and weaker, until the injections had done their work.

The facility was a few hours north of the city, a campus of white cottages scattered like teeth amid rolling green hills. As they wheeled Caroline into the operating room, she repeated the mantra she'd been holding on to for months, the promise that Adam had made to her and that she had made to herself. *We'll get him back*, she told herself. *We'll get him back.*

She turned her head to the side to watch the doctor spear her with the trocar, the gold-plated awl sinking into her flesh. The doctor chuckled.

"Usually people look away for that part," he said.

Caroline didn't answer. There were stars on the ceiling. She inhaled and felt the drugs seep up her arm and spread over her collarbone, settling in her heart as the stars faded from view.

They stayed in one of the cottages for the next three days, until it was time to implant. At the seven-week scan they discovered the embryo had split, two gray smudges bobbing in the darkness. Adam tightened his grip on Caroline's hand.

The pregnancy was easy, the full-term birth even easier. The boys were perfectly healthy, perfect copies of one another. Fair-haired, like Caroline. Of course they would need vitality infusions for the rest of their lives, but the technology had advanced a lot since Caroline's days caring for the Geller children. The same treatment was only needed once a month, and recovery took less than a day.

Sometimes, when Caroline looked at the babies lying with their heads close together, these new iterations of her son, his exact DNA, she would feel a mild wave of nausea. Disgust. Sometimes, when she wanted to dig her fingers deeper into the wound, she would hide in the bathroom, take out her phone, and watch the video of the ferry ride over to the island. She would press her fingertip to the screen, time turning forward and back at her will, the way she'd once wanted to search for the man in black, the intruder on the surveillance feed. Forward and back, forward and back. The lost hat still on her head, the lost baby still in her arms. Still there, even when it was already too late.

Don't compare, someone had told her once. Comparison is the thief of joy.

When the twins turned one, an occasion celebrated with identical white-buttercream Funfetti cakes smashed by identical pairs of fists, she deleted the file.

"They don't look like him at all," she said to Adam once. He'd looked up from his laptop and blinked at her in bafflement, as if he had never seen her before.

"What?"

She wanted to scream. She almost did. Tears sprang to her eyes and she closed them, trying to hold herself together.

"Babe, I didn't hear you," said Adam. "What did you say?"

She opened her eyes and looked at her husband. He peered back at her, his eyes soft and searching. Lost. She decided he must really not have heard her. Somewhere, buried under all the layers of dedication to his work and love for their twins, everything that kept him moving forward every day, she knew he still suffered like she did.

He had to.

Caroline crossed the room and draped her arms over his shoulders.

"Nothing," she murmured into the back of his neck. "Never mind."

It was too painful to talk about Gabriel, so they didn't. By the time the twins were three and running wild in the apartment—seemingly impervious to injury, even as they bashed into furniture and fell face-first to the hardwood floors—her eldest son's name had become something unpronounceable and foreign, an utterance from a prayer whose function and meaning had been lost to the passage of time.

An unknown word, a combination of sounds, like any other.

A shadow fell over her face and she opened her eyes. Perry knelt beside her beach towel, looming over her with his one-year-old daughter in his arms. Caroline closed her eyes again.

"Adam says we should come over for drinks after we put Viva to bed."

Caroline didn't answer. She pressed her palms into the burning sand and the heat sent shivers up her body.

"We'll have the monitor. And Sasha can always go back to our house if she wakes up."

As if responding to her mother's name, Perry's daughter let out an animal howl. Even with her eyes closed, Caroline could sense her wriggling in his grasp, trying to break free.

"No!" Viva cried. "No!"

Perry waited another moment, still trying to subdue his child, still waiting for Caroline to respond. Then he got to his feet and walked away.

When she knew that he was gone, Caroline sat up to watch the twins playing in the surf. They were tall for their age, the tallest boys in their second-grade class. They would grow up to be taller than their father. They had found long, severed arms of driftwood in the dunes and were fencing, lunging and feinting, jabbing the sabers of wood into the soft hollows beneath their ribs. Caroline watched as the swordplay deteriorated into even more savage violence. Her boys raised their sticks and beat each other about the head, shrieking with delight.

She lay down again and closed her eyes. She lay very still, surrendering to the heat of the sun, and listened to the screams of her children.

ACKNOWLEDGMENTS

THANK YOU TO:

Julia Kenny, for your enduring trust and steadfast advocacy.

Allie Merola, for sharing the vision and knowing what was needed. Camille LeBlanc, for your insight and tireless efforts in bringing us over the finish line.

Sonia Gadre, for the insider knowledge; Elizabeth Yaffe, for the gorgeous and perfect cover; Sabrina Bowers, for the brilliant page design; Chelsea Cohen and the copyediting and production team; Emily Fishman, Raven Ross, and everyone else at Penguin.

Ren Khodzhayev and CJ Gineros, for the early feedback and encouragement.

Sophia Louis, for teaching me everything about the newborn stage and for taking care of my newborn so that I could finish revising this book.

Sara J. Winston, for the seed of the story and for modeling how to be an artist and mother.

My parents, for making every dream possible.

Edwin, for your unsparing editorial critiques, your unwavering support, your integrity, and your love.

And Ramona—for being you and for being here.

ALSO AVAILABLE

A Good Man
A Novel

Thomas Martin was a devoted family man who had all the trappings of an enviable life: a beautiful wife and daughter, a home on Long Island's north shore, a job at a prestigious advertising firm. But what happens when Thomas's fragile ego is rocked? After committing a horrific deed, Thomas grapples with his sense of self. Maybe if he tells his version of the story, he might uncover how and why things unraveled so horribly.

PENGUIN BOOKS

Ready to find your next great read? Let us help. Visit prh.com/nextread